SOMEONE TO KISS MY SCARS

Brooke Skipstone

FOREWORD FROM THE AUTHOR

This book contains scenes of sexual abuse, self-mutilation, and suicide. It should not be read by teens who wish to be shielded from such harsh realities their peers may be enduring alone. Nor by anyone who desires to remain in the dark despite being in a position to shine light. However, those who suffer in private or wish to help those who do—please read this story and share its contents.

I live in a state where adults suffer three times the national average of rape and where children suffer six times the national average. Fifty percent of women in Alaska experience sexual violence during their lifetime, either from intimate partners or others or both. Yet most of their stories remain conveniently hidden behind graphs and spreadsheets.

Across this country one in four girls and one in six boys will be sexually abused before they turn eighteen years old. That's a lot of teens suffering from a "hidden" problem to remain on the fringes of public consciousness, but there it looms—statistics without a human face or scream.

Twenty-five percent of girls (much higher in some states) and about ten percent of boys self harm, numbers which continue to increase. Many of our youth are cutting and burning themselves, yet this activity remains not only a secret, but also continues to carry the label, for some, of a disgusting, perverse aberration which shouldn't be discussed lest it infect more teens.

Why should stories about the teens experiencing these problems be diluted and palatable, full of allusions to events but not the events themselves? If they slapped us in the face and demanded our attention, perhaps more awareness would lead to more outcry and thus more prevention.

Are these topics inappropriate for teens? This is an ironic question since teens are very often the ones having to deal with the abuse. As characters in this book state,

"How would normal people react if all these stories were published and read?"

"They'd think they're . . . too dark. Even adults wouldn't want to read them. Too much sex and violence."

"Tell that to the kids in these stories. One reason this stuff keeps happening is because it's kept secret . . . . We hide our problems from everyone so the normal people can live in their fantasy worlds."

Many parts of this book are difficult to read and were very difficult to write. But there is much truth in these pages, some profoundly ugly and some beautiful in its resilience. As one character says, "I have to believe I can still love and be loved. We can't stay broken forever."

And they shouldn't be unknown forever. People need to feel the pain of others.

CHAPTER ONE

Hunter's fingers typed furiously across his keyboard as his vision of two teenage boys having sex in a store dressing room invaded his mind, compelling him to watch.

After they'd finished, Parker stood up in a panic, trying to find his clothes among the tangled pile on the floor. "I have to go," he gasped. "I need to leave."

The other boy smiled as he sat naked on the bench. "It's OK, Parker." He stood up and found the two pairs of pants Parker had brought in with him crumpled on the bench. "You want to take these?"

"No." Parker frantically pulled up his underwear and shoved his feet into his pants. His heart raced as he desperately tried to breathe.

The boy held his shirt out for him. "Here. Stick your arm in."

Parker looked at the smiling boy, his eyes lingering on the boy's lips before forcing himself to look at the shirt being held out in front of him. The boy helped Parker fasten the buttons, but when his fingers wandered around the shirt below his waist, Parker broke away and sat on the bench to put on his socks and shoes. He tried to avert his gaze as the boy slipped on his underwear and pants. His cheeks felt on fire, and he blinked his eyes to keep tears from trickling down them. He looked at the floor and shook his head, but despite his guilt and shame he couldn't stop thinking about the orgasm he'd just had a few minutes ago. He was sure someone had heard his whimpers and groans. How couldn't they?

Parker stood, checked himself in the mirror, and started toward the door. The boy moved in front of him.

"Hey, that was fun. Thanks."

Parker's chest heaved as tears moistened his eyes. "Please don't tell anyone."

"Just between you and me." He straightened Parker's collar. "Maybe we'll see each other again sometime."

Parker bolted from the room then tried to walk slowly and calmly out of the store while he was sure everyone watched him leave.

This was the seventh vision Hunter had been forced to watch today. About two months ago, they appeared in his mind, playing and replaying in his head until he typed them out completely. Only then would they leave him alone until the next one started.

He would hear the pounding first, like a ball hurled repeatedly against a wall, then see himself stumbling or running down a hallway inside a house past a closed door. A bedroom? The wall at the end of the hall always disappeared just as he stepped through it. The story then played like a movie in his head, this time in a department store dressing room.

Hunter thought he had seen that hallway and door before, but he couldn't place them.

He stared at the screen as he scrolled back to the top of the story—several pages of text. He typed the time and date—April 5th, 2:15 am—then added a title: *Sexual Encounter. Store Dressing Room.* After he sent it to his printer, he raked his fingers through his wet, tangled blonde hair. His shirt felt glued to his back. After every vision his skin flooded with sweat. He rubbed his neck, trying to relax, but his brain raced, and his eyes burned. He knew he wouldn't be able to sleep.

So many of the stories he had written shocked him. He'd seen naked teens and adults crying, grunting, screaming, moaning in pleasure and pain. At times he could hardly see the computer screen through his tears. Watching those two boys, knowing that one had been torn between lust and shame, while the other fully enjoyed the hunt and consummation, aroused conflicting feelings, most of which Hunter didn't understand. How could he see such visions? How could his seventeen-year-old mind create these stories when he had no experience with any of these activities?

Unless he'd forgotten.

He'd been trying to remember his past before moving to Alaska. Where had he lived? Who were his friends?

What had his dead mother and brother looked like?

But no memories came.

He leaned over his desk, hanging his head between his shoulders. He couldn't remember the last time he'd slept for more than a few hours at a time. Somehow, he had to find a way to block the visions from entering his mind.

He'd told his father about his trouble sleeping and being bothered by . . . what? Daydreams? Fantasies?

His father had given him a bottle of melatonin pills. Hunter had taken two at eleven and slept for maybe an hour before the pounding started again. He needed something stronger tonight, so he climbed onto a chair and pushed up one of the ceiling panels above his bed to find the small thermos of whiskey he'd hidden.

His high school English teacher had wanted everyone to find an object at home with special memories for an assignment the next day. Until then, the fact that he had nothing from his past had merely irritated him. But now with the all the stories going through his mind, all the trauma he had witnessed, he realized how much he didn't know. His past was like an empty room.

Before his father came home from work, he searched through his father's bedroom, looking for any reminder of his past—a photo, a document, a keepsake—anything. While rummaging through his closet, he found a full-length mirror on the back of the door. Hunter stared at himself for a few seconds then ripped off his long-sleeved t-shirt, revealing a network of scars across his chest and down his arms. He saw them every morning after his shower in his bathroom mirror, but they never grabbed his attention, just remnants of a bike crash on a gravel road—the story his father had told him. But now that story didn't satisfy. The lines were straight, many in rows. How could falling on gravel cause them? Maybe from the spokes of his wheels? But spokes were inches apart, and these lines were much closer together.

Wider welts marred his wrists. What had caused these? How much pain had he felt? How could he not remember?

He searched the room for an hour, being careful to return everything to its place. All he found was a Mount Rainier knife in a sheath, a small piece of whale baleen, and a book of matches from a hotel in Deadhorse, Alaska. None meant anything to him. He hid them under his mattress.

He also found a bottle of Jameson whiskey his father had stashed inside a boot in his closet. Hunter filled his thermos and added water to the bottle to hide his theft.

Hunter sat at his kitchen table, drumming his fingers, waiting for his father to come home. His insides churned with impatience. He had to get some answers!

As soon as the front door opened, Hunter stood and peppered his father with questions. "Why are there no family pictures in the house? Isn't there an old toy from my childhood somewhere? Why don't I remember the first sixteen years of my life?"

His father pursed his lips and set a bag on the table with Styrofoam containers of chicken he'd bought from the cafeteria at the nearby Air Force Base where he worked as a mechanic. Joe was about Hunter's height, still trim and fit, with pale skin hidden inside a garage all day rather than exposed to the bright sun of April.

"Why are you suddenly interested in the past?" Joe went to the sink and washed his hands.

Hunter's head hurt, and for a second he thought he would see another vision. "I've been writing stories . . . "

"You've always written stories."

"These are different. They invade my brain. I have no control over them. Sometimes they have people I know—like students at school I see every day. Other times they don't. But before I actually see the story, I'm in a hallway and I see a bedroom door. It has panels—five, I think—and a silver handle, not a doorknob. It's always closed. Then at the end of the hallway is a wall. The stories always start when the wall disappears."

"Disappears?"

"Yeah, like it fades away. I want to know what our house looked like, the one we lived in before . . . before the accident."

Joe slowly shook his head. "It was just a house, Hunter. It looked like a thousand other houses." He turned back toward the sink, slinging the towel onto his shoulder.

"Why won't you tell me?" Hunter shouted to his back. "Could I be seeing our old hallway? Did our old house have doors with handles?"

"Maybe. I'm really not sure."

"Why won't you help me?"

Joe grabbed the towel and slapped it onto the counter. "Because I don't want to remember anything about that house!" He turned around. "Nothing." His eyes narrowed, glaring at Hunter. "And you shouldn't either."

Hunter felt tears on his cheeks as he stood before his father's angry face. It revealed no sympathy, no caring. Hunter couldn't remember his father hugging him, even touching him.

Joe's breathing calmed a little. "For your own sake, don't try to remember. Leave the past alone." He set two large containers, packaged utensils, and a small cup of gravy on the table. "We should eat this before it gets cold." He pulled out a chair and sat down.

"My English teacher wants the class to find an object with special meaning to us. We're doing a writing exercise tomorrow."

"All that stuff got burned in the fire at the storage unit."

"Why was all our stuff in a storage unit?"

"Because we were moving but hadn't found a house yet."

"What about on your phone? Don't you have pictures on your phone?"

"Like I've told you a hundred times already, I lost my phone, and for some reason the backup failed. So my new one started with nothing—no photos, no contacts. It was a pain in the ass."

Once again, Hunter noticed that his father was not upset about this loss. He always gave this answer with no emotion, except exasperation at being asked.

Hunter rubbed his eyes and collapsed into the other chair. He thought about his mother and little brother who had died in a car wreck on an icy road. When? Some years ago. He wasn't sure. "I can't remember anything from when they were alive." His chest felt hollow. "I can't even remember their names."

His father looked at him for several seconds.

"Can't you tell me?" Hunter watched his father's lips quiver. "You won't tell me their names?"

Joe sighed as he poked at his food. "Savannah. And Frankie."

Hunter expected he'd feel something upon hearing their names, but the words simply passed through him. "That's it?"

"I'm sorry, Hunter." He lifted his eyes to meet his son's. "There's nothing else I can say." He averted his gaze.

They ate in silence.

That had happened eight hours ago.

Since then Hunter had Googled her name, looking for images, social media references, anything. Pictures of girls and women appeared on his screen, but none looked familiar.

Now Hunter lay back on his bed and took a few sips of whiskey, thinking it would be difficult to swallow, but amazingly it went down smoothly. He wondered why since he'd never drunk alcohol before. At least he didn't remember doing so. He drank another sip and felt the warm buzz creeping up his neck as his brain numbed.

He sat up, sipped, and gazed outside. A full moon lit the snow around his house in the Alaskan woods like it was daytime. He walked to the window and opened it, allowing the cold air to rush in, numbing his face and chest. He looked at the thermometer outside his window, nailed to a birch tree— ten degrees.

He could've walked through the trees without a flashlight it was so bright. And he wondered if he walked far enough out into the woods, the visions wouldn't bother him anymore. Maybe he would fall asleep in the snow and never wake up. He honestly thought about trying but felt too tired to climb out the window.

He had no idea why the visions started two months ago, but since then he hadn't touched his fantasy folder full of stories and drawings about the world of Marian he'd been creating. Hunter had always been a daydreamer and a writer. The school counselor had suggested he might be fantasy prone because for the first five months at the Clear Creek School, he'd frequently tuned out of class to write yet another story about the Tremarians, the group trying to eliminate pain and misery from their planet.

The original stories were the only things he still had from his past and only because he'd kept them hidden. He'd never shown them to his father. He didn't remember why. Did he ever show them to his mother? When had he started writing them?

He couldn't remember.

He'd almost left them under the mattress at the only house he remembered in Washington, the last one before they moved. Something clicked in his mind just before he left his room to get into their truck to drive to Alaska. He'd lifted the mattress, removed the stories, and shoved them into his suitcase. After they'd moved into their latest house, Hunter assembled the stories into one folder, which was now in a hole behind a small whiteboard he had nailed up above his desk.

But those stories were ones he *chose* to work on. These latest ones invaded his brain like dreams at night, forcing him to watch and experience.

He looked at the whiteboard. When had he started writing those stories? Possibly before his mother and little brother—Savannah and Frankie, he now knew—had died. He hadn't read the early stories since . . . when? He had no idea. Maybe he should reread them all. Maybe he could find clues about . . . something.

He plugged in his phone and noticed a text from Jazz. *I've got something cool to show you tomorrow morning! Try to get here early—for once!* Jasmine was his only real friend at school. She had liked his Marian stories, but he hadn't shown her any since the visions started. Jazz was a genius. She could read the stories and probably figure out what might have been happening in his life when he wrote them. But first he'd have to tell her about the visions, something he'd avoided because she might think less of him. What would she think about the story he'd just finished?

He took another sip of whiskey and felt the comfort of drowsiness envelop him. Before he crashed, he replaced the thermos in the ceiling then pulled his latest story from the printer, intending to pin it to his wall where dozens of others hung. But blessed sleep came suddenly, and he fell onto his bed, the pages of *Sexual Encounter* drifting to the floor.

CHAPTER TWO

T he next morning, Joe found his son sprawled sideways on the bed, oblivious to the alarm clock ringing on his desk. For a few seconds, he watched Hunter's chest to make sure he was breathing, a habit he'd forged years ago when he worried what he would find coming into his room each morning—his son curled into a ball in the corner, or bleeding from a fresh wound, or staring blankly at the ceiling.

"Wake up, Hunter! You can't be late to school every day!" Joe silenced the clock then pushed on the bed. "You want some coffee?"

Hunter wiped his eyes and pushed his hair out of his face. "Yeah."

Joe left the room to pour a cup of coffee. When he returned, Hunter had already turned on the shower in the bathroom. Joe noticed some papers on the floor, two with heel indentations. He picked them up and found the first page with the title: *Sexual Encounter. Store Dressing Room.*

Sexual encounter? His heart skipped a few beats. What was Hunter writing about?

Joe started reading.

A teenage boy carrying two pairs of pants over his arm walked along the row of closed dressing rooms until he found a door ajar. He pushed it open and saw another boy about his age standing in his underwear. His skin was pale with just a whisper of hair across his chest. The boy with the pants stared at the other boy's abs and the trail of hair that led down from his navel into his underwear. He noticed the bulge, then pushed his eyes back to the boy's face. The boy in his underwear licked his lips, catching the perusal with a flicker of amusement.

A glimpse of a memory flashed in Joe's mind.

The boy with the pants blinked, snapping out of his trance and turned away. "Sorry," he said as he backed out of the room.

"Hey, no problem. I was just getting ready to leave. What's your name?"

"Um, Parker."

"Cool name."

The boy shot a big smile at Parker. He had a nice smile, and Parker liked the way it made the corners of his eyes crinkle, deepening the blue of his irises. "You can use the room."

"The door was open. I thought no one was inside." He could feel his pulse pounding in his throat.

"You can close it now so no one else comes in." He laughed. "Might get crowded."

"You sure you're through?"

The boy walked toward him. "Hey, I like those pants." He took both pairs from Parker. "I was actually going to try this pair on but forgot to carry them back. Do you mind? We're about the same size."

Parker hesitated. He should leave now. Giving him the pants kept him in the dressing room. He had to force himself to keep his eyes above the boy's waist. He licked his lips and swallowed. "No. Go ahead." The boy took the khakis and gave Parker the jeans.

"Great. Hey, don't let me stop you from trying on that pair."

The boy slid the pants up each leg while Parker watched him. The boy smiled back at him. "Try on yours. Bet those will look good on you."

Parker felt pressure against his zipper. His bulge would be obvious when he moved the jeans to try them on.

Beads of sweat had gathered on Joe's forehead. He listened to make sure the shower was still on then read the next lines.

Parker kicked off his shoes, took a deep breath, then undid his buckle. He looked at the boy to see if he was watching him, but he was posing in front of the mirror. Parker turned slightly away, dropped his pants, then tried to get them off his feet quickly, but he stumbled. He cursed under his breath and reached down to pull his pants off one leg, hopping around. Then he pulled off the other. Parker quickly picked up the new pants and held them to his waist, hiding the stiffness beneath.

"I might like those better," said the boy as he turned toward Parker and pulled down his pants. Parker's eyes were frozen as he saw the boy's underwear slip down his hips.

Parker dropped his pants to the floor.

Joe's heart pounded in his chest. *How?* he thought. *How could he know this?* Joe reached for the corner of the first page as if to turn it, but hesitated. Many years ago he had walked in on a kid named Parker in a dressing room. He thought he had shoved that memory into a vault, never to be opened. He honestly thought he had forgotten the incident.

But now it lived again.

Joe started to flip back the first page and read the rest, but heard footsteps in the hallway.

"Dad? What's wrong?" asked Hunter as he entered the room in boxers carrying a long-sleeved t-shirt in his hand. "You look like you're about to faint."

Joe took a deep breath and cleared his throat, feeling his own erection growing in his pants. He worried Hunter would notice, so he shook the papers in front of him. "Where'd you get this story?"

"It just came to me. Just like all the others." Hunter frowned. "Did you read it?"

Joe swallowed, trying to get some moisture into his throat. "Yeah. Part of it." He tried to think of something to say. "Seems like I read something like this before." He tossed the papers onto the desk. "You better hurry. You're going to be late for school."

Joe tried to glimpse the scars on his son's arms and chest as Hunter slipped on his t-shirt. He didn't see anything fresh, just the rows of pale welts, some thicker than others. Every few days he checked Hunter's room for knives. Joe didn't want his son cutting himself again, not only because of the wails and blood from Hunter, but also the guilt cutting through Joe's conscience. This was one of the main reasons Joe had sought drastic treatment for Hunter a year ago.

Afterward, Joe had been able to fill his son's head with any story he wanted. Hunter's scars came from a biking accident. His mother and brother were killed in a wreck on an icy road.

Only recently had Hunter asked questions and been more skeptical of Joe's answers.

Hunter turned to grab his shirt off a hook in the wall. While Hunter worked the buttons and put on his jeans, Joe wandered around the room looking at all the papers.

"So many! How late have you been staying up?"

"Haven't slept much lately."

Joe turned to look at his son and noticed the dark skin under his bloodshot eyes. "The melatonin doesn't help?"

Hunter shook his head. "Seems like as soon as I write one down, another one pushes in. I thought you were going to take me to a doctor."

"No. I never said that," he said while rubbing the muscles in his chest. "It was just the school nurse who suggested that. What does she know?"

"She's a nurse. So why don't we go?"

Joe had already taken Hunter to dozens of psychologists and psychiatrists. Only the last one had done any good. "There's no point. What's a doctor going to do? Give you a shot to fix your overactive imagination?"

Hunter looked to the floor.

Joe turned back to the wall full of papers. "Do you have to write down every one of them?"

Hunter sat on the bed. "Like I've told you before, if I don't, the same story keeps playing in my brain. I can't get to sleep or think about anything else." He pulled on his socks and stomped his feet into his boots. "You said you read that story before?"

Joe felt cool sweat collecting in his armpits. He knew his face had lost color because he felt nauseous. He kept his back to Hunter, pretending to examine the stories on the wall. "Maybe. Coulda been a TV show. I don't know." He scratched his bristly face as he moved to another set of papers. "Kind of an inappropriate topic, don't you think?" His eyes flashed at Hunter then back to the papers. "How can you know about such things?"

"Dad, I don't know anything about most of my stories. At least, I didn't. That story was pretty mild compared to the others. I just describe what I see in my head."

"Well, if this story were a movie, I wouldn't let you watch it."

"I wouldn't want to watch it, but I have no choice, same as the others. Two boys having sex. Boy and girl. Two girls. Brother and sister."

Joe gasped. "Are you in any of them?"

"No. I see it . . . and feel it." His shoulders slumped. "It's not like I want to. Sometimes it's pretty hard to watch."

Joe picked up the *Sexual Encounter* papers. "Was it hard to watch this one?"

"It was better than watching a rape or child abuse. At least neither boy forced the other. I felt bad for Parker. He felt excited and ashamed. I'm pretty sure that was his first gay experience."

Yes, it was, thought Joe.

"Watching two boys having sex doesn't repulse you?" Joe peered intensely at his son, looking for any signs of disgust.

"Watching anyone have sex embarrasses me, but I've seen so much in the past two months, I'm not shocked anymore. Why? Does gay sex repulse *you?*"

His eyes widened. "Not my preference." He tried to chuckle and even wink. "Guess I'm old school."

At his son's age, Joe played every sport, raced cars on weekends, and kept two or three girls interested in him. Many times in the past Joe had thought of his son as a Mama's Boy and couldn't help feeling disappointed in him. But he knew now Hunter wasn't to blame.

Joe wondered how disappointed his son would be in him if he ever knew the truth about Joe's past.

Most of the time, Joe thought he was living with a stranger, never sure what to talk about, so they hardly said anything to each other.

Until Joe read this story. He probed some more to assure himself his son hadn't remembered anything about the wreck four years ago. "Maybe I saw this story on one of those HBO movies. Probably fell asleep and you had to turn off the TV. I'll probably think of it later."

"Let me know if you do."

"Sure. You better go."

Hunter grabbed his keys off his desk and turned to leave.

"Where do you get the names?" Joe said with a quivering voice.

Hunter stopped in the doorway, looked at his father, then shrugged his shoulders. "I don't know. They're the ones people use in the story."

"Only one of the boys in this story had a name. Why didn't the other one?"

Hunter shook his head. "For some reason the name didn't come to me or wasn't mentioned in the story. Happens sometimes. Gotta go." Hunter ran out of the house. Joe heard the truck engine rumble to life then move farther away.

Joe looked at the pages in his hands and realized he couldn't remember what happened next, other than the obvious. But the details were missing. Maybe he should put the story down and walk away.

But he couldn't. He had felt excited as he read, a feeling he hadn't experienced in years—an urgency, a need he couldn't stop thinking about. He had forgotten what lust felt like.

He pulled out his phone and punched in the number of his supervisor at work. "Hey, Matt," he made himself cough. "This is Joe. I've been up all night puking. Think I need to stay home today. I don't know if I caught a bug or ate something, but I know you and the guys don't want this." He listened. "OK. I'll call you later today." He ended the call.

Before he turned the page, he looked at all the stories on the wall.

Would he find himself in any of the others?

Then a larger worry slammed into his gut.

Had Hunter written about his mother?

CHAPTER THREE

The wind flung Hunter's tangled blond hair across his mouth, hiding the hairs barely growing across his lip and chin. He still saw the look of horror on his father's face when he walked into his room. *Why did he seem scared?* Hunter decided he would talk to his father about it this evening.

He always felt his father was hiding something from him. Was there really a fire? Did he really lose his phone?

He noticed rabbits lined up on the shoulder every fifty yards or so along the gravel road that undulated through a forest of black spruce and naked aspen. It was early April in the Alaskan Interior, and humps of snow lingered among the trees, slowly revealing the death of the past few months. The already blinding sun flashed like a strobe light through the trees as Hunter picked up speed. He felt sluggish and so sleepy. For a few seconds, he phased out in the blinking sunlight. He almost heard a beat in the background—**Da**dadada**Da**dadada**Da**dadada—then just before his truck missed the curve on the road, he jerked his wheel to the left, his right tires kicking up gravel from the shoulder.

He breathed again as his truck stopped fishtailing. He couldn't see the sun flashes any longer. This stretch of road had hundreds of alders and willows bent over like cat claws reaching for the pavement. The snow had weighed them down for months, and only now were they beginning to straighten up as the weather warmed.

Spring here did not burst forth with colorful life. It dripped from the melting dirty road snow and swelled into tiny buds at the top of willows, popping into fuzzy catkins barely visible from the ground.

Hunter had driven this road to school for the past eight months after he and his father had moved from a small town in Washington. His dad had said he wanted a change of scenery and found a mechanic's job at a remote Air Force Base near Clear Creek.

Hunter was happy to leave. There was nothing keeping him there—no friends, no memories.

They'd arrived in late July and found a house a week later—isolated, off the highway, about ten miles from the nearest school at Clear Creek.

He'd met Jasmine Williams during new student orientation in mid-August.

Jazz had chosen him to mentor, she said, because they had the same last name. She devoured fantasy and sci-fi novels and showed immediate interest in Hunter's stories about the Tremarians. No one had ever read them, as far as he knew. He remembered her first comments as they entered the gym during the Open House before school started.

"Everyone is genderless in this story?" Jazz asked. She wore a dark red, floral housedress she said she bought at a garage sale, cinched at the waist (not much of a waist) with a wide leather belt and silver buckle. Her bell-bottom jeans emerged from under the dress and covered the high-top leather uppers of her combat boots.

"Yeah," he shrugged. "Sex causes every problem in the world."

They moved to the top row in the bleachers past students, parents, and alumni and sat down next to each other.

"*Every* problem?" Jazz frowned. "I would argue against that premise, but continue."

"Tremarians eliminated gender bias in their culture and gradually modified their bodies until their genitals became vestigial, like the appendix. You know, kinda shriveled and useless. Or at least the Tremarian's considered themselves evolved beyond their use."

She looked at Hunter with arched brows and a slight smile. "I know what vestigial means. So how do they reproduce? And more importantly, how do they have sex, or did they eliminate that, too?"

"No sex," he said.

"Are you kidding me? What creatures would willingly eliminate orgasms?"

Hunter's mouth dropped open, his face warming. "Because their leaders recognized that deriving pleasure from sex would perpetuate the abuse of women."

"Only women?"

"Sometimes males . . ."

Hunter!

He turned around, hearing someone call his name, but saw no one in the gym paying him any attention. Odd.

He turned back to Jazz, who wore a quizzical expression and said, "Sorry."

"Let's look at this from a purely scientific standpoint," said Jazz, "since I'm an aspiring scientist. I just read an article claiming that 40 percent to 60 percent of women do not have orgasms during sex with men, while men have it 98 percent of the time. Of course, because we live in such a male-dominated, conservative society, which prohibits real sex education in the schools, why would guys ever learn anything useful about a woman's needs? The article also claimed that 20 percent or more of women do not have an orgasm their entire lives. So at least in your Tremarian world, that disparity doesn't exist." She chuckled slightly. "Though I think both sides attaining 98 percent would be preferable to both at zero, don't you think? At least in the real world."

He found himself just staring at her. Jazz was so smart and seemed able to talk about anything.

She stared into his eyes. "Do you think it's OK for only half of women to enjoy sex while nearly all of men do? Is that fair?"

"No. Both should be the same, but on Marian—"

"I think you have an interesting premise, and I would love to read more of your stories, but I'm glad I don't live on Marian. I hope that my future lover will care about how I feel at least as much as he cares about himself."

"I hope so, too."

Her smiled beamed. "What a nice thing to say. Thank you, Hunter."

She leaned against him briefly, sending a flash of warmth up his arm.

Music blared out of the speakers hanging in the rafters as seven cheerleaders ran onto the shiny wooden floor, shaking pompoms as they screamed, "Go Grizzlies!"

"Oh, my God!" Jazz scoffed. "These girls are serious athletes. They play volleyball and basketball, yet they become silly cheerleaders for boys' games. How many guys do the same for the girls' games? Hmmm? Take a guess."

"None?"

"Bingo! The least the boys should do is lead cheers for the girls' games. Don't you think?"

Hunter smiled at the mental image of the guys' basketball team in cheerleader outfits pumping up the crowd. "Yes, I do. At least 98 percent of the time."

"Give me five!" She held up her hand, and he slapped it.

He liked talking to her. He never knew when she would make him laugh. He couldn't remember a time when he had talked to a girl. "It's fun talking to you."

"Thank you. You're pretty cool yourself." She smiled at him and took off her large, round red glasses.

Hunter was struck by the beautiful almond shape of her bottle-green eyes and the thick long lashes that framed them.

"You have pretty eyes," he blurted out.

"I know." She put her glasses back on. "These glasses accentuate my best feature, or what I consider my best feature. Everything else about me is nonstandard and subject to jokes by the cheerleaders and their friends who are all standards. Meaning they don't have too many freckles or zits, their bodies indent significantly above their hips, and their BMI is in the normal or below normal range. None of which, I am sure you noticed, applies to me."

He studied her. She was a large girl, tall with a pronounced bosom, yet her hands were small for her size. Her lips, though, were luscious and painted hot pink.

She removed her glasses and then put them back on. "Which way do you like better? On?" She put them on. "Or off?" She took them off.

"Either way. I like their color. But there's such a size difference!"

"I know. I'm farsighted. Like seriously."

"I really didn't notice. You look fine to me."

"Well, thank you. You look fine to me, too. However, all those girls down there are going to think you're more than just fine and wonder why you're talking to me instead of them. Drew and Molly have boyfriends, but Tatiana is available."

Hunter glanced back at the floor where the cheerleaders were hopping around and cartwheeling to their chants. They all looked about the same, though two were shorter than the others. "I don't know them. Besides, I don't think I'm the kind to initiate conversations with strangers."

"You don't *think* you are? Why wouldn't you know?"

"Because I haven't been around my peers very much. I've been homeschooled."

"Until now?"

"Yeah."

"Why?"

"I'm not sure. Just what my dad told me."

"He *told* you?"

He looked at her, thinking he might say, *Yeah, because I don't remember,* but caught himself. The odd look she gave him told him he should pretend he didn't hear her.

The music stopped, and the cheerleaders ran and cartwheeled back to the bleachers. "Where are your parents?"

Hunter lifted his arm and pointed to Joe. "My dad's sitting over there. He's wearing the green baseball cap."

"And your mother?"

He looked at her, wondering if he should say anything other than *She's gone.* But she seemed so friendly, and he had no one else to talk to.

He took a deep breath. "My mother and little brother died in a car wreck on an icy road four years ago."

Her mouth fell open. "I'm sorry. That must have been tough."

Now what would he say? Make up some story about how tough that time was, when he had no memory of it? He thought she would see through his lies and wonder why he had no feelings. He'd be a jerk in her eyes.

"I don't remember anything about it."

"Seriously?"

"Seriously. Like a big hole in my life. Actually, everything before moving to Alaska seems to have disappeared."

"Trauma can cause memory loss. People with PTSD either can't stop thinking about the bad event or can't remember it. Maybe it's better not to remember."

"What if you couldn't remember most of your life?"

"Sometimes I think that would be a good thing." They locked eyes until Jazz lowered her gaze to her feet with a heavy sigh. "There are a lot of things I wish I didn't remember."

"I'm sorry."

She looked up at him and smiled. "Thanks."

The new principal at Clear Creek School, Mr. Blake Bentley, then stepped out onto the basketball court to loud applause. He was a tall man in his late thirties, wearing jeans and a Grizzlies t-shirt.

He raised his microphone. "As most of you know, I graduated from this school twenty years ago. I spent too many years Outside going to college and starting my family, but I am so glad to finally come home."

Hunter whispered, "What does he mean by outside?"

"Alaskan for Lower 48."

Hunter shook his head.

Jazz smiled. "You know, the states *outside* of Alaska."

Blake continued. "I hope we get crowds this big and noisy at all our home games!"

"We would if you were still playing," one of the old-timers hollered, causing the crowd to laugh.

"I don't think I can keep up with our current varsity players. I'd like you all to come cheer, not laugh."

Mrs. Christian, the President of the Parents' Association, stood. "I still remember that half-court shot you made to win the game!"

Several shouted, "So do I." Many clapped.

Blake then smiled. "I think your memory is a little off. I made a half-court shot to tie the game at halftime, then missed the same shot at the end of the game. We lost by two points."

"You won the game!" shouted Mrs. Christian. "We all remember it."

Many shouted in agreement.

"Well, I sure like it better that way!" He'd walked to the jump circle. "Where was I when I shot it? Over here?"

"A little behind the line."

"More to your right."

Blake moved at their direction until Mrs. Christian stood again. "That's the spot! Right where you're standing!" She led the applause and cheers.

"OK!" shouted Blake. "At each home game during halftime we're going to have a contest. Two dollars to enter. Whoever makes the first shot from this spot will get half the pot. The rest will go to the sports program."

Most stood and shouted their approval.

"How interesting," Jazz said. "He remembers the event as his failure, and they remember it as the best thing he ever did. How can people remember things so differently?"

"At least he remembers something."

"He'd like to remember it differently, though. I wish I couldn't remember some things, and you wish you could. You would think memories wouldn't be so complicated. Things either happened or they didn't. Right?"

"Or they get lost and disappear. How do we make memories anyway? And where are they kept?"

Jazz's face lit up and turned red. "That's it!"

"What is?"

"That's going to be my science project! I'll do something with memory—how they're formed. Where they're stored. Thanks, Hunter."

He furrowed his brows. "What did I do?"

"You gave me the brilliant idea." She held out her hand. "Friends?"

Hunter smiled and shook her hand. "Yeah. Friends."

"That's a beautiful smile, Hunter. You should use it more often." She smiled back at him, pushing her cheeks into her glasses.

"I like your smile, too."

"Cool."

A basketball bounced across the road, jerking Hunter back to the present. He slammed on the brakes and felt his stomach lurch into his chest. Where would a ball come from? He looked for someone walking along the shoulder but saw no one as his truck rolled slowly down the road. A house appeared through the trees to his right. He saw an old basketball goal stuck above the garage attached to the wall.

A big truck coming toward him in the opposite lane blared its horn as it plowed into the ball, popping it. The sound scared him, and he twisted his wheel, taking his truck over the shoulder toward the driveway leading back to the house.

For some reason the ball seemed important to him, but he had no idea why. He kept trying to remember a connection . . .

His hands twisted around the steering wheel as he stared blankly in front of his truck. Sometimes he thought he was going crazy. He felt he couldn't control his brain or his thoughts. At any moment people would do things and say things inside his head. Was that ball real or not? How could a real ball just bounce across the road on its own?

After looking one more time at the house, he pulled back onto the highway and soon turned on to the road toward his school.

Some things he had no trouble remembering, while with others he drew blanks. Yesterday in English class, Ms. Tucker had asked them to remember a special place from their childhood then describe it using all five senses. He'd tried and tried to think of a place, but no image formed in his mind, so he'd made something up. She'd also asked them to describe the face of a friend at school without looking around the classroom. He'd described Jazz's face easily but couldn't recall a friend he'd had before meeting her. Then she'd assigned the significant object, and everything he'd found yesterday afternoon meant nothing to him.

Except his folder. But all he could describe were the stories it contained, not why they were important or when he started them or why the war was over gender rather than something else.

His chest felt hollow as an overwhelming fatigue chilled his body. He saw the upcoming curve approaching, and a thrill of awareness shot through him as he pressed the accelerator, sending his truck faster toward the trees bordering the road. *I can just keep going straight and end this now.* He felt no fear, just a numbness as his eyes lost focus.

Why couldn't he be normal? He pressed harder on the pedal. Why couldn't he remember anything in his past? Why did he have to witness so much pain? Why was his brain assaulted by other people's stories when he could remember nothing of his own?

He felt hypnotized by the roar of the engine and the increasingly larger trees heading toward him. He closed his eyes and imagined he was flying.

His phone buzzed. He flinched but kept driving. It buzzed again. He shook his head, realized he might not make the curve, and felt his stomach lurch into his chest as he braked hard and turned the wheel.

He slowed down and looked at his phone showing a message from Jazz. *Where are you?*

He then recalled what Jazz had told him months ago. "There are a lot of things I wish I didn't remember."

He'd never asked her what those things were. Why hadn't he? Because he was so consumed with his own problems he couldn't make room for anyone else's. How selfish was that?

She cared about him, was always happy to see him. Would she keep smiling after he was gone?

He turned into the curve and headed toward school. He needed to be a better friend to her.

CHAPTER FOUR

Jazz waited for Hunter inside the front doors of the K - 12 school, home to 150 students from the small town of Clear Creek and ten miles in either direction on the nearby highway. Her big boots stomped on the metal grating just inside the door as she paced, wondering what was keeping him. Her flatworms had regenerated their heads and tails and still remembered what she had taught them prior to decapitation. Memory can exist outside the brain! How cool was that? She couldn't wait to tell him.

"Girl, you need to get to class," said Patty, the secretary, in her loud, thick drawl. She was a large woman with a big smile, born in Texas, who lined her eyes in dark blue, wore big hoop earrings and gaudy silver necklaces. Today she wore jeans, boots, and a bright yellow top with white fringe and turquoise pieces sewn into the fabric. She loved the kids, and most loved her back, including Jazz.

"I need to show something to Hunter. It's so cool!"

"Mr. Roberts approved you being out of his class?"

"He knows. He said it was OK."

She had advanced to the state science fair a month ago and now wanted desperately to go to the international fair next year, her last chance before graduation. Maybe she could win a scholarship or some money for college.

Mr. Roberts, her science teacher, had given her a corner of the school lab to run her experiments even through the summer. She'd been hired as extra maintenance help at the school, so she would have access to the building through August.

Jazz straightened up and put her hands on the glass door as she saw his truck roll into the parking lot.

Jazz watched Hunter park his truck and run toward the front door. As usual he looked flustered and a little clumsy when he ran, but God was he cute! She loved his long, floppy hair, his thick eyebrows over his dark brown eyes. And his mouth was gorgeous—so full and soft. He was the only guy in school who didn't think she was weird for loving science and who smiled at her like he meant it. He was her only real friend. Before he came in August, the only people who cared about her were the teachers and Patty.

Just as he reached for the entry bell, Jazz pushed the front door open.

"Hey, Hunter!" She knew from the heat she felt in her cheeks she was blushing behind her big smile.

"Hey, Jazz. Sorry I'm late. I know you wanted me here early."

"It's OK. I have something to show you." She grabbed his arm.

"I've got to get to class," he said, panting.

"Patty said she'd give you a pass. C'mon!" Jazz pulled him down the hallway.

"I said no such thing!" yelled Patty as the two kids ran past her.

"You know you will!" shouted Jazz over her shoulder.

Jazz dragged him down the hall to the science wing, opened the lab door, and walked to the far side of the room near the fume hood and a short lab table against the wall—her domain. One of the florescent tubes flickered on the ceiling. She looked up and shook her head. "That won't do. Can't have another variable in here. I'll talk to Mr. Roberts later to have this fixed."

She carefully removed a cover from a small shelving unit to reveal a series of petri dishes containing small brown worms. "Ta da!" said Jazz.

Each dish lay inside colored tape strips, labeled with names and dates. A clipboard with the color-code key hung from a hook.

Hunter bent closer. "Worms? Did you make them?" He wrinkled his nose.

"Kinda. I trained them with food and bright lights until they remembered what to do in different environments to find their food. So if those memories were stored in their brain, which is similar to ours, you would think that if their heads were amputated, the new regenerated brain wouldn't remember their training. But they did!" She threw out her hands in excitement.

"Yeah?"

"Yeah! As a group they didn't do quite as well as the trained, uncut controls, which were not decapitated, but the ones that regrew their heads did as well as those which regrew their tails. And both groups of regenerated worms found their food faster than an untrained group. "

"Meaning what?"

"Meaning memory is not confined to their brains!" She lifted up onto her toes and felt warmth radiating throughout her body. "If it were, the ones that grew new brains wouldn't remember the training. Don't you see? So many people think memories are stored in the brain, but they may be stored in other parts of the body or outside it."

"At least in worms. What about in humans?"

"Could be the same. I haven't figured out an experiment for them yet." She moved closer and straightened the collar on his shirt. "But I'm looking for volunteers to help me." She touched his nose with her finger. "How about you?"

"Sure. Unless you plan to chop something off me."

She moved closer, enjoying the tease, locking her eyes onto his. "First, I train you, then I chop." She picked up a ruler off a table next to her and slapped it into her hand. "Do you respond better to punishment or reward?" She walked toward him, shaking the ruler. "I used bright lights and raw liver on the worms."

He backed away, chuckling. "So which one of those is the reward?"

"The liver, obviously. But for you . . ." She thought of so many things she wouldn't dare say to him. "How about fresh chocolate chip cookies after school? I could come by your place."

"Cool. I'd like that."

He was so much fun. "When are you going to show me more stories about the Tremarians? I haven't read any for a while."

A pained look crossed his face. "I had to start writing something else."

"You *had* to? Why?"

"I'll explain later. How about when you bring the cookies?"

"OK." She noticed his frown and felt a chill. "Are you all right?"

"Sure. Well, not really."

"What's wrong?" She almost reached out for his hand, but pulled back and clasped her hands against her chest.

"I realized this morning I never asked you about the things you didn't want to remember. When we first talked. In the gym months ago. I told you I wanted to remember my past, and you said there were things you wanted to forget. What are they? And I'm sorry for not asking you before now."

She felt her eyes widen and her heart race. *How could you remember that?* "So many things, Hunter, but none of them involve you."

His shoulders slumped.

Jazz felt a rush of fear. Had she offended him? "What made you think of that now? I mean, I love that you care enough to ask, but what brought that up?"

Hunter bit his lip and frowned. "I haven't had much sleep. I tried to find something from my past in my dad's room, but the few things I found meant nothing to me. And I think he's lying to me about . . . why we came here." His chin quivered.

She moved closer to him, unable this time to resist, and reached for his hands. He tensed, causing her to pause. "Do you mind?"

"No."

She held both of his hands and felt them quivering within her own. "I'm your friend, Hunter. Something's going on with you, and I want to help." She looked into his brown eyes and saw them twitch. "Why don't you come to my house for lunch today? I've got some leftover spaghetti and meatballs."

He looked at their hands touching and smiled slightly. "That would be great. I forgot to bring anything to eat today. Lucky this school allows us to go home for lunch."

"Good." She squeezed his hands then let them go. "You better get to class."

"Yeah, thanks." He turned to leave and opened the door then looked back. "So what's the brain for if not to store memories?"

"It's a receiver and transmitter, like a TV set. A signal comes in, and a movie memory plays in your head."

His eyes widened as he just stared at her with his mouth open.

"Are you OK?"

"Yeah. Gotta go." He left the room.

She thought he would be excited or awed about her conclusion, but he seemed terrified. Why did he *have* to write something else? Something was going on inside Hunter's head. She'd sensed it since they first met. He said he couldn't remember his past, yet he often seemed haunted.

She knew what nightmares the past could bring.

CHAPTER FIVE

Hunter trotted down the hall toward Patty's office. He had to get a pass, but he couldn't stop thinking about Jazz's words—*a movie memory plays in your head.* That's exactly what he was experiencing. But these weren't his memories. Whose were they?

"Slow down, Hunter," shouted Patty as he burst through her doorway.

"I'm sorry. Jazz was showing me her worms. She's discovered something amazing."

"Well, come back later and tell me about it." She handed him a paper. "You know that girl likes you, don't you?"

Hunter's eyes moved from the pass to Patty's eyes. "As a friend. We're just good friends."

Patty chuckled. "God, how can guys be so clueless? More than a friend, Hunter. Take my word for it. Now get!"

He stared at Patty as he backed out of the office. *She likes me?* He remembered how warm her hands felt just a few moments ago. And the tingling up his arms.

Not paying attention, he backed into the nurse outside the office. "Oh, sorry, Ms. Green." She was so small and wiry, he wondered how she remained standing after he plowed into her.

"That's OK, Hunter." She straightened her glasses. "Has your dad said anything to you about making an appointment to see a doctor?"

"Yeah." He had to get to class and didn't want her calling his father again. "He said he'd look into it."

She gave him her crooked smile. "Make sure that he does."

He nodded then ran toward Ms. Tucker's room, hearing Patty cackling behind him. He stopped at the door and took a few deep breaths, hoping the room wasn't entirely quiet when he walked in. He opened the door and saw everyone staring at computer screens, working on their descriptions.

Except for Eric who was leering at Ms. Tucker as she walked around the room. He seemed in a trance with his mouth open.

Hunter walked quietly to Ms. Tucker and gave her the note. She was a new teacher, having taken over for Ms. Hartland who had to take care of her sick parents in Wisconsin. All the boys thought Tucker was hot and looked like a high school student. And her soft, breathy voice was the subject of many imitations and comments outside her classroom.

"Did you find your special object last night?" she whispered with a smile.

"Yeah."

"OK, you know what to do."

As he walked to his desk in the rear corner, he saw Eric's whole body turned sideways in his chair, ogling Tucker's butt.

"Eric? Do you have a question?" asked Tucker with her brows raised and arms folded around her chest.

Eric snapped out of his reverie. "No."

"Then why aren't you working?" He continued to stare until she moved her hand in a circle, indicating for him to turn back around. She walked back to her desk.

After Hunter sat down, Eric turned to him and sneered. "Must have had a hot date last night, eh, Hunter? Male or female? Or was it Jazz?"

The others around them snickered. Most days he didn't acknowledge Hunter's existence, but when he was late, Eric usually said something to him.

Hunter smirked, undeterred. "Sorry, Eric. I don't kiss and tell. And Jazz is very much a female."

"Oh ho!" said Lanny sitting on the other side of Hunter. "Got you there, big guy," as he laughed.

"Boys," said Ms. Tucker in a throaty whisper. "You have an assignment."

Eric glared at Hunter who flipped open his computer then gazed outside. He'd decided to make up a story about the Mount Rainier knife. He and his dad had gone there many times, just father and son, camping and hiking. *Fat chance,* he thought. Or maybe they did. How would he know any differently?

Without warning the pounding started. *Dammit!* He needed to do this assignment. When the stories first started coming to him, there was one or two a day and rarely during school. Now they happened all the time. His grades had plummeted.

He closed his eyes and tried to see Mount Rainier in his head. Instead he saw himself walking down the same hallway past the door on the right. Then he stopped. He could hear something from behind the door. Laughter? It faded away. He continued down the hall, through the wall until he was outside a log duplex two blocks from the school. Eric walked from behind the house, sneaking through some willows. He looked both ways along the street then went to the door and knocked.

Ms. Tucker opened the door wearing sweatpants and a tank top. "Hey, Eric. Thanks for coming by."

Eric noticed her makeup and the strong scent of vanilla. For him? he wondered. Probably. He gave her his special smile. "You said you needed help."

"Come in." She held the door open for him, so he had to walk close to her to get inside. "Sorry the place is such a mess." Her voice sounded extra breathy

to Eric. "I thought you could help me move things around. The movers just plopped everything down before I had a chance to say where to put it."

"No problem." Eric saw boxes everywhere, some opened, some still sealed. This place had always been a dump, dark and dingy.

"You seem to be the strongest boy in school." She winked.

He nodded. "Maybe." As Eric walked around the room, he removed his jacket, revealing a cutoff nylon t-shirt. He tightened his arms muscles as he draped his jacket over a chair. "I've been here lots of times. Lots of people have rented this place." He stretched his arms above his head, revealing most of his torso. He noticed where her eyes roamed. "The price is good."

She wrinkled her nose. "Kind of musty smelling, though."

He moved closer. "The vanilla scent is doing a good job of hiding it."

"You like it?" She held out her hand.

"Is that from you?" He leaned closer to sniff her arm. "Mmmm. Smells real good." He moved to her neck. "It's even stronger up here." He could feel the heat radiating from her skin. "I wonder if it tastes as good as it smells." He had to fight his urge to kiss her neck.

She laughed and stepped away. "It's a new body wash I just bought. I love it. I told you after school today I'd give you twenty dollars for helping me."

Eric saw her eyes linger on his abs. "I didn't come over for the money," he said. "How old are you anyway?"

"Twenty-two."

He watched her red lips pucker twice. "How old again?"

"Twenty-two."

"Sure is fun to watch you say that. How old?" If she said it again, he was going to kiss her.

She bit her lip and smiled. "How about yourself?"

"Eighteen. You don't look old enough to be a teacher. I mean, your body does, but your face looks much younger."

"Is that supposed to be a compliment or a complaint?" She bent over to pick up a small box. He could see her large, honey breasts hanging from her chest

"Just an observation. Mmm. Like your top."

Her eyes met his before she rose and saw the direction of his gaze. She placed her hand on the top of her shirt and tilted her head.

"Thank you." She stood up and flicked her hair back behind her shoulder. "I started college at seventeen, graduated when I was twenty-one and was a substitute in Anchorage until I got this job."

"You must be smart as well as pretty."

She smiled. "Thank you, again."

He moved within inches of her. "If you weren't my teacher, I'd ask you out on a date."

She blushed. "If you weren't my student, I'd accept."

They smiled at each other.

Eric's gaze moved slowly downward, then up again. "Well, right now I'm just a friend helping you out, not your student. And I think we can be good friends, when we're not in school."

She sat on the sofa. "We're not in school now." She patted the cushion, and he sat next to her. She grasped his knee, pulling his leg against hers then moved her fingers around in circles.

"We are definitely not in school." He smirked at her touch.

"Maybe tomorrow you'll be bragging to your buddies how you spent all afternoon helping your cute teacher."

"I didn't say anything about you being cute."

She lifted her brows and folded her arms across her chest. "You don't think I'm cute?"

"Better than cute. But with those baggy sweats you got on, it's kinda hard to tell how pretty you really are."

She stood up. "I don't normally wear these in the house." She pulled the sweats off slowly to reveal tight, spandex shorts. "I like to be casual when I can." She put her hand on her hip. "So, cute, or not?"

He stood up and moved closer to her, aching to hold her. "I think you're the hottest girl in town."

"Really?" she purred. She touched the bottom of his t-shirt and ran her fingers around the edges.

He put his hands on her hips and pulled her against him. "Maybe I should start in the bedroom, and then work out from there."

She lifted her face up to his and barely touched her lips to his. "I think there is something you can help me with in there."

Eric wet his lips. "What's your first name?"

"Vanessa."

"Vanessa." He kissed her. "I like that."

She took his hand and pulled him down the hall.

"How are you doing, Hunter?" asked Ms. Tucker as she headed toward him.

Hunter's heart pounded. He hadn't noticed her near him. He quickly saved the document, then emailed it to himself.

"You've been typing up a storm. Can I see what you have?" She bent over to look at his computer screen.

Hunter tried to speak, but all he could do was gasp.

He grabbed the screen with his hands then swallowed. "I'm not finished yet." He began to pull the lid down.

She put her thumb on the top of the screen and lifted it up. "That's OK. Good writing is never finished."

Hunter wanted to run out of the room, but she'd knelt on his left side where he would exit the desk. He tried to glance at Ms. Tucker without turning his head. Surely she would hear his heart throbbing! He closed his eyes and tried to think of something else, but all he could see was Vanessa and Eric undressing each other in her bedroom no matter how hard he tried to block them out or focus on Ms. Tucker next to him.

He looked at Eric who had put on earphones, bobbing his head to the music.

"Where did you get this story, Hunter?" Her voice quivered.

He looked at her, noticing the swollen vein on her forehead. Her face was red, and her eyes were moist. She looked scared.

"Just popped into my head. Has been happening to me a lot lately."

"This just popped into your head?" Her whisper was sharp. "Seriously? Do you think I'm stupid?" She lowered her voice and put her mouth close to his ear. "Did Eric say anything to you?"

"Eric and I don't really talk."

"Why did you use these names?"

"I just write what I see and hear."

"This didn't happen, Hunter. I don't know where you got this story." She flashed an angry look toward Eric. "But it did not happen."

"It's just a story, Ms. Tucker," he tried to reassure her.

He saw Vanessa and Eric kissing each other on the bed. His heart throbbed in his throat. "I don't know where they come from."

He heard them moan. He could feel sweat dripping inside his shirt.

Was it all imagined? Were the dreams more than they appeared? What if they were real? Did Eric and Ms. Tucker really . . . ?

Her eyes narrowed. "You've written others?"

He swallowed and nodded his head. "Yes."

"Like this?" Her eyes flashed wide open.

"Not about . . . someone else with your name."

Her whisper sounded angrier as her mouth approached his ear again.

"My name is not Vanessa. Where'd you get that?"

"That's what you said . . . what Ms. Tucker said . . . in the story . . . "

"Have you shown these to anybody?"

He thought about his father, but technically Hunter had not shown him the story. "No."

That seemed to calm her anger. She straightened up and looked around the room. "Keep working everyone." She put her hands on her legs and bent over until her eyes were level with his. "Would you do me a favor and not show this one to anyone else? Please?"

Her scooped neck dress hung down, revealing her breasts barely contained in a pink bra. How could she not know what he could see? He moved his eyes up to hers.

She smiled. "Please?"

"Sure." He pushed his computer lid down and stared at his desk.

"Would you mind deleting that story? Hunter, please look at me."

He lifted his eyes. She tried to smile, but her lips trembled.

"Would you delete it? Please?"

In his mind he saw Eric and Vanessa squirming against each other. Vanessa gasped.

The bell rang.

He flinched. "OK, but I have to go."

"Promise?"

"I promise."

"Thank you." She stood up. "Listen everyone. Send what you have to my dropbox before you leave school today."

Hunter moved away from her quickly and joined the crowd exiting the room. Lonny leaned over to him and said, "She gave you a long look at her boobs. How'd you manage that? Man, you're sweating like a horse!" He walked away laughing.

When he stepped through the door, Hunter looked back and saw Ms. Tucker talking to Eric by her desk. His hands were up, and he shook his head. Tucker flung her arm toward her door, pointing her finger. Eric moved away.

In Hunter's mind, she lay on her back while Eric pressed against her, stroking her face, grinding himself against her while she moaned.

The scene seemed so real.

How was that possible?

CHAPTER SIX

When he saw Eric leaving the room, Hunter turned around and walked toward the commons area, bumping into a couple of students and apologizing as he went along.

"Hey, Hunter!" shouted Jazz from the seating area called the Pit. It was a round step-down from the commons floor outside the main office with curved seating along the sides.

"Come here." She smiled at him, patting the bench. In his mind he saw Vanessa patting the sofa. He shook his head.

Just as Hunter lifted his foot to step down, he felt someone crash into his side, his stomach lurching as he fell, sprawling onto the floor of the Pit. A sharp pain flared in his knee. For a second he thought he would puke.

He heard Eric's voice from behind him. "Hey, sorry man. Guess I wasn't looking." Then he laughed.

"What the hell!" shouted Jazz. "Hunter, are you OK?"

He saw her boots near his face.

"You piece of crap, Eric!" Her boots raced away from him.

As Hunter tried to sit up, he heard a stomp.

"Hey! Damn you, bitch!" shouted Eric.

Hunter turned around and saw Eric lifting his foot in pain. Jazz's hands were clenched into fists, ready to slug him. She was going to take on Eric? For him? How amazing was that? How could Jazz be so tough?

Mr. Bentley came out of his office. "That's enough! Both of you come with me." Bentley turned around, stomping the floor all the way to his office, followed by Eric and Jazz.

Hunter picked up his computer and walked gingerly up the step, stopping to rub his knee, before moving toward the office. He wanted to explain what happened to Bentley so Jazz wouldn't get into trouble, but Bentley's door closed just as Hunter got to Patty's desk.

"Where are you going?" asked Patty.

He tried to control his breathing. "I need to speak to Mr. Bentley."

Patty's face stretched into a big smile. "Told you that girl liked you. Lucky she didn't break Eric's foot. Go on in." She lifted her phone, punched a button, and said something just as Hunter knocked on Bentley's door.

"Come in," said Bentley.

Hunter opened the door.

"Are you OK?" asked Jazz.

"Yeah. Thanks." Hunter looked at Eric. "What's your problem?"

Eric started to say something, but caught himself. "It was an accident. Just wasn't looking where I was going."

"That's BS," snarled Jazz. "I saw you walk right into him," seemingly ready to stomp his foot again.

"Jazz," said Bentley, leaning forward on his desk, "even if you saw that, you know that attacking Eric is not the appropriate response. Yes or no?"

Jazz's eyes squinted as her face flushed red. "Hunter could have broken his neck!"

Bentley slapped his desk. "Yes or no?"

She glared at Eric. "Yes."

Bentley smiled. "Good. What should you have done?"

Jazz stood. "Kicked him in the nuts!"

Eric leapt out of his chair with fists clenched. "Just try it, you fat, ugly bitch!"

Bentley shot up. "Sit down, Eric!"

Jazz moved toward Eric just as Hunter slipped in between them, facing Jazz. He placed his hands on her shoulders.

"It's OK, Jazz." Hunter said. "I love that you want to defend me, but he's not worth you getting hurt or in trouble."

Jazz stopped glaring at Eric and looked into Hunter's eyes.

"OK?" asked Hunter, realizing how long his hands had lingered on her shoulders. He flinched and lifted his hands to jerk them back.

She nodded and grabbed his wrists just before he pulled them away. "OK."

His stomach clenched. Why had he touched her? He felt beads of sweat pop out on his forehead.

"Eric, you and Jazz meet here after school for twenty minutes of detention," said Bentley.

Eric groaned. "I've got practice!"

"Twenty minutes. If there is any more arguing or threats from either one of you for the rest of the day, you will be suspended. Is that clear?"

"Yes," said Eric.

"Jazz?" called Bentley.

She lifted Hunter's hands off her shoulders and squeezed them before letting go. "Yes."

"OK. I need to speak to Hunter for a minute. Eric, go to your next class."

Eric mumbled something, jerked his chair to the side and left the room.

"Jazz."

"Yeah. OK," she griped, then softly to Hunter, "Talk to me after class?"

"Sure."

She smiled at Hunter one more time then left the room. He could still feel her touch on his hands as he stared at the door.

"Sit down, Hunter," said Bentley.

Hunter turned around and sat in her chair.

"What were you writing in Ms. Tucker's class?"

Hunter's heartbeat raced as his skin tingled. *How could he know?* He stared at Bentley.

"All school computers have monitoring software so I can see what's on your screen anytime I click on your name. The district wants me to do this occasionally to make sure our students are focused on their classroom activity and not using their computers inappropriately. I checked out a few of the students' screens in Ms. Tucker's room last period before I saw yours. I was very disturbed by what you were writing."

Hunter felt his throat tighten. "I already talked to Ms. Tucker." He tried to swallow. "I've had these stories run through my head lately. I don't know where they come from."

"And you happened to write a story about Eric and Ms. Tucker?" Bentley squinted his eyes.

"Yes, sir. It just came to me."

"A story like that could be very damaging to him and Ms. Tucker. Do you have any reason to believe this even happened?"

"No! The story just popped into my head. I made it up."

"What were you supposed to be doing?"

Hunter hung his head. "Writing a description of a significant object."

"I see. You are to delete the story now and send Ms. Tucker a note of apology and your description before you leave school today."

"Sure. OK."

"Will you delete the story now?"

"Sure." *I don't want anything to do with it.* He opened his computer and dragged the file into the trash.

"Empty the trash, please."

Hunter did.

"You will not speak about this story to anyone. Is that understood?"

"Yes, sir."

"Ms. Tucker doesn't need rumors spreading about her and students. You need to go to class."

Hunter stood up.

"Ask Patty for a pass."

"Yes, sir."

He left the office and stopped by Patty's desk.

"I need a pass." His mind whirled. If the sex between Tucker and Eric weren't real, then where did he get the story? How could he make it up?

He noticed Anthony, a fifth-grader, sniveling in a corner chair. Hunter raised his eyebrows at Patty, who whispered, "Classmates teasing him about that fire last summer."

She gave him a pass.

"Jazz sure looked happy when she came out of that office," Patty teased. "I asked her why. She said, 'He likes me.' Did you tell her that?" Patty leaned back in her chair, her eyes twinkling in mirth.

Jazz thinks I like her? Do I?

"No, but I stopped her from kicking Eric in the nuts."

"And?"

"I held her shoulders. Then she held my hands." He remembered the fear he felt when he realized he had touched her, but it had felt so natural to reach for her. Why? He couldn't remember anyone touching him before Jazz.

Patty smiled from ear to ear. "You two are so cute together."

He left the office and headed toward history until he saw Ms. Tucker walking toward him, holding a stack of papers. *What will she say now?*

"Ms. Tucker, I deleted that story. I'm sorry I wrote it."

She studied his face. "I don't know what kind of game you and Eric are playing. He denied saying anything to you."

"He didn't. He pushed me into the Pit after class. We're not friends."

She folded her arms and tightened her lips against her teeth. "For your information, he came to my house this weekend to help move boxes and furniture. Ms. Fenster was also helping me. She would've slapped Eric and called the police if he'd done anything like you describe in that story. Evidently, Eric has quite the imagination. Or maybe, you do."

"I can't explain it, Ms. Tucker. I'm sorry. I didn't know he went to your house this weekend."

She raised her brows and shook her head. She didn't believe anything he'd said.

"Do you still want me in your room after school?"

"No, but if I hear anything about this story again, I will take you to Mr. Bentley."

"He already knows."

"What?" Her nostrils flared.

"He was monitoring my screen when I wrote it. He made me delete it."

One hand grabbed her throat. "Oh, my god! He knows?"

"He didn't believe the story. I promise."

She gritted her teeth and left.

Hunter's stomach fluttered as he backed down the hallway, watching her stomp toward the copy room. How was he ever going to get square with her?

He turned around, walked to the classroom door, and opened it. The room was dark, and everyone was watching a video. Hunter waved his pass so Mr. Flynn could see it. He nodded and gestured toward an empty seat. As he walked to it, Eric grabbed his arm and pulled him down so Hunter's face was level with his own.

"Don't mess with me, Hunter," he growled.

"Not trying to, but answer this one question."

"What?"

"Was Fenster at Tucker's when you went over this weekend?"

"Yeah. Who told you? Stay out of my business, Hunter."

"Guys!" shouted Mr. Flynn. "Pipe down."

"Sorry." Hunter sat down. "What are we doing?" he asked Lonny next to him.

"Taking notes for a quiz on this video."

Hunter flipped up his computer lid and looked at the images moving on the SMART Board. Something about the Alaska Constitution. As he watched it, he realized his visions weren't like movies in his head. He was actually there. He saw everything in three dimensions, and he could smell odors like the vanilla on Tucker's neck.

He opened the story of Eric and Vanessa he'd emailed to himself and looked it over. Maybe both of them were lying. But they both claimed Fenster was there. So confusing.

The pounding started. *Shit! Not again.*

He focused on the video, trying to concentrate, but the thumping grew louder and louder. He saw himself walking down the hall and stopping at the door. He listened but heard nothing. He reached out his hand toward the silver door handle then saw the wall fade away at the end of the hall where he saw a boy sitting on the porch of a small house, throwing pebbles into the yard. Hunter turned from the door and walked toward the boy.

Mosquitoes buzzed around the boy's face as he sat sweating on the front porch of his house off the Parks Highway in early June. The sun beat on his back as he swatted bugs away from his ears. The boy rose and knocked on the front door.

A man's voice shouted from inside the house. "Stay outside!"

"I'm bored! I want to watch TV!"

The boy heard rapid steps approaching from inside, so he ran down the steps into the yard. A man in boxers opened the door and glared at the boy.

"Anthony, I've been away for a week and want some time to talk to your mother, so you need to find something to do out here."

"For how long?"

"About thirty minutes."

"Why can't I watch TV while you talk to her?"

"Anthony, I already told you what you need to do. Get the ashes out of that burn barrel, shovel them into the wheelbarrow, water them down, then take them out past the trees."

"Gordon, I'm ready. Come and get me!" Anthony's mother called from inside the house.

Anthony saw a big grin stretch across his father's face as he looked back toward the door. "On my way, Ariel." Then he barked at his son, "Get to work!"

"Yes, sir."

Gordon almost skipped back into the house and shut the door behind him.

Anthony dragged himself to the burn barrel out in the yard. He stopped two feet from the barrel and turned to the side, breathing slowly and deeply. Suddenly he lifted his knee, turned toward the barrel as his foot shot out in a side kick while he yelled, "Kiai!"

The barrel tipped over with a thud. He got the shovel, dropped down on his knees and stuck it into the barrel to scoop out ashes, which he then dropped into the wheelbarrow. Clouds of ash and perhaps some smoke drifted above the pile. He walked back to the house, grabbed the end of the hose, and pulled it to the wheelbarrow. About ten feet away, however, the hose tangled and wouldn't stretch any farther. He turned on the water and tried to squirt a stream into the barrow. After a few minutes of mostly missing the ash pile, he tossed the hose down and strode out to the barrow, which he lifted and wheeled toward the trees. Right at the edge of the yard, near a pile of lawnmower clippings, he dumped the wheelbarrow over. After shaking it empty, he started pushing it back toward the house.

He didn't see the fire until he pushed the wheelbarrow alongside the porch and turned around. The clippings were in flames! He grabbed his hair and pulled, stifling a scream. What should he do?

He picked up the hose and started to run toward the trees when the hose locked up, causing him to roll onto the ground. He scrambled back to the tangle and tried pulling lengths of hose through loops and out of others.

The fire had spread to a couple of trees as a gust of wind blew by him.

His nostrils flared as he screamed, "Dad! Dad!"

He grabbed the wheelbarrow, pushed it to the hose and filled it halfway, all the time looking at the spreading fire. Then he ran with the barrow across the yard. By that time the flames were dancing above his head. He tried to get closer, but the heat burned him, so he shoved the barrow as hard as he could then ran backward. When the wheelbarrow turned over spilling water into the grass several feet from the flames, he raced back to the house, screaming. "Dad! Dad!"

He banged on the door then tried to open it, but his father had locked it from inside. Gasping for air, he banged harder as he screamed. He collapsed to his knees as he banged on the front window.

Finally the door opened. "What the hell do you want?" his father screamed, leaning halfway out the door.

Anthony pointed at the fire.

"Damnation!" Gordon ran out onto the porch in his boxers then ran back inside. After a minute, he ran back out with pants on, trying to put on his shoes. He yelled back inside, "Call the fire department! We have a fire!"

Gordon ran to the hose, cursed at the tangle, frantically pulled and pushed *the nozzle until he could pull it to the edge of the yard. He shot water as far as he could, but the flames had already moved north, spreading quickly in the wind through dry grass toward another clump of trees.*

He dropped the hose and ran to his son. "I told you to fill the wheelbarrow with water before you dumped the ashes!"

"I couldn't get the tangle out!"

"Then you shouldn't have dumped the ashes, you moron!" He grabbed his son's waistband and spanked his bottom several times. The boy collapsed on the grass, crying. Gordon sat on his heels and grabbed his head.

"Gordon! What happened?" yelled Ariel from the porch, wearing only Gordon's shirt.

"Your son started a fire!" He grabbed Anthony's shirt and dragged his crying son roughly back to the porch where he flung him at his wife. "Put him in his room and don't let him out. And get your clothes on!"

Anthony clung to his mother, crying, one eye peeking at his dad who ran to the garage, pulled out a fire extinguisher and a shovel, then ran toward the fire as sirens blared down the road.

"Hunter! Hunter!" his teacher yelled from the front of the room.

Hunter blinked and saw everyone in class bending over their desks.

"Here, Dude," said Corey sitting to his right, holding out a sheet of paper. "Take it."

Hunter took the paper from Corey's hand and looked toward his teacher.

"You have fifteen minutes to take this quiz. You can use the notes you took."

Hunter stared at the paper and realized he had missed the entire video. Before he started making up answers, he sent his latest story and the one about Eric and Tucker to Jazz with the subject line "Do not open yet." He needed her help to figure this out, but how would he explain either one? She'd think he was crazy. He had to talk to her.

As he wrote random answers to each question, he remembered last summer driving down from Fairbanks for the first time, heading toward their new home. A large fire had spread along both sides of the highway for about twelve miles up to the edge of Nenana. Firefighters were still knocking down isolated flames near the road as they drove by. He remembered following the blackened area, noting its twists and turns until it stopped near a house—the same house he saw in his story. A sudden coldness hit his core.

This happened.

If it did, then how could the other one not have?

CHAPTER SEVEN

Joe wondered if Hunter would know whether a story or two on his wall were missing. The two he held in his hands had to disappear.

He had thought seriously about burning them all, just like he had burned all the family photos and mementos several years ago. Except this time, Hunter still had the files on his computer.

Doctors had warned him about the impact of triggers on memory. They had told him whatever progress Hunter had made dealing with his PTSD could disappear quickly if he saw a photo of his mother or brother. Who knew what item would hold special meaning for him. Better to burn everything than leave some small thing, which could set off the screaming and depression and self-mutilation again.

The story in his left hand described the dressing room incident, which he had shoved deep into his past, blanketed with shame and confusion and fear. For weeks afterward, he had worried that someone would have heard them, but nothing happened. He'd made extra efforts to say something sexual about girls in front of his friends, even boasting he'd had sex with one or two. In locker room showers, he'd kept his gaze well above the waist, refusing to participate in pulling towels off of freshmen or making jokes about penis size.

He'd never admit to others or to himself the excitement he'd felt with Parker. He rationalized the event as enticing because it was illicit.

The story in his right hand described another incident, one he'd totally forgotten until he read it.

During a basketball trip when his team slept in the home school's library, something else had happened. A teammate slept on a cot near where Joe lay on the floor on top of his sleeping bag. He thought he was having a sexual dream about a girl when he woke up to find Sam's hand hanging off the cot holding his erection. Joe tried not to move, though his heart was racing. He kept staring at the hand as he panted for breath. He watched for any signs that Sam was awake then turned his head around to see if anyone else watched them. All was silent and still except for the throbbing below his waist. He tried to pull himself away from Sam's hand, only to hear the boy mumble something in his sleep and grip tighter. Joe tried to think of something else so his erection would disappear, but he couldn't. He tried to deny his excitement, but couldn't.

Then he was sure he felt Sam's hand move. And again. Joe looked around once more, then reached down to Sam's hand and slowly pulled it off of him. Joe quickly got up and quietly exited the library, heading for the bathroom. He locked himself inside a stall and tried to slow his breathing.

A moment later he heard the bathroom door open and footsteps until he saw bare feet under his stall door. It was Sam.

"Hey, Joe. You OK? You need some help?"

All of this plus what happened afterward was in the story his son had written, this time using Joe's name. The story was dated a month ago. Joe could remember nothing in Hunter's behavior during the past few weeks that suggested he suspected his father was the kid in this story.

A homosexual. Something he tried desperately to hide from his father and himself. His dad would have killed him if he'd suspected.

He kept denying what he was for years, even marrying and having kids, but he never felt the same excitement as he had with Parker and Sam. Or with another man in Fairbanks four years ago.

He'd lost interest in pretending to enjoy sex with his wife when he began working at Prudhoe Bay. On one trip home, his plane was diverted to Fairbanks due to a volcano south of Anchorage erupting ash. During the day he spent waiting for another connection home, he visited a bar and met Stanley, an off-duty detective. Joe spent the night at Stanley's house. On subsequent trips, he made sure to spend at least one day in Fairbanks going to and coming from Prudhoe.

He wasn't sure if Savannah had started drinking before or after that change. She had accused him of having an affair with a woman, of course. When a private detective told her about Stanley, she'd threatened to tell his boys. She'd called him a "fag"—as if she were able to judge him.

He had called her much worse and threatened to call the police.

Where was Hunter getting these stories? How could he know about these events?

Something bad was happening to Hunter. No normal kid would be forced to write these stories day after day, watching the most intimate details of other people's lives. After reading thirty of them that morning, Joe couldn't believe Hunter hadn't gone crazy. Stories of pain and abuse and disappointment, but still, none of them coming close to the horror of Hunter's own experience, which had caused all of this.

And they were all probably as true as those about Joe.

His son was seeing other people's memories! Not just everyday events. No, these were painful, traumatic, or joyful in their illicitness.

In many ways, so similar to Hunter's own experiences.

Why had Hunter seen those particular memories from Joe's past?

What if he'd seen others?

Hunter's memories were erased, but Joe's weren't. He trembled at the prospect of Hunter learning more about him and about Stanley in Fairbanks. Or what really happened that last day when Savannah and Frankie died.

How was this possible?

He had to call Dr. Ru.

Joe had gone to that doctor as a last resort, knowing his methods were unorthodox, even dangerous. But Hunter had spent over three years screaming or in a fog or trying to kill himself, so what else could Joe do? He wasn't foolish enough to believe his son was cured or wouldn't have future problems, but having his head invaded by foreign memories wasn't on anyone's list of possibilities.

At least not Joe's.

After his final session with Hunter, Ru had said to contact him if his son showed signs of regaining his memories. "How would I know?" Joe had asked. Ru had replied that Hunter might become violent or depressed. Joe had seen no sign of either, but Ru had added, "or other unusual behavior." As Joe recalled the conversation, he realized Ru clearly expected Hunter to change in some way. But seeing the memories of other people? Surely not.

Joe had hidden his old phone in a broken boot sole taped to the leather uppers. He'd retrieved it and left it charging for the past twenty minutes. He opened his contacts, found Ru's personal number, and called from the kitchen.

The phone rang several times before going to voicemail.

"Please leave a message."

Joe cleared his throat. "Hello, Dr. Ru, this is Joe Williams. You treated my son, Hunter, a year ago to eliminate his memories of the deaths of his mother and brother. I need to speak to you about some unusual behavior Hunter has displayed during the past two months—"

The line clicked, and Ru's voice cut in. "Hello? Mr. Williams? This is Dr. Ru."

Joe heard Ru's distinctive Asian accent, lyrical and kind.

"Oh, hello," replied Joe, "I—"

"I'm going to call you back on another line. Please disconnect and answer the next call."

"OK." Joe disconnected then took a quick peek out the windows.

His phone rang, displaying an unknown number. *Why did he have to call back on another number?* He accepted the call.

"Hello? Dr. Ru?"

"Yes, Joe. How can I help you?"

"Should I use this number to contact you in the future?"

"Yes. Please. What is Hunter doing that concerns you?"

Joe sat down at the table and told him about Hunter's stories, but did not reveal the content of the two from Joe's youth.

"Have you heard of anything like this?" asked Joe.

Ru paused. "A few patients have experienced their old memories and did not recognize them as theirs. Another boy complained to his parents that he heard voices, but I haven't spoken directly to him to know any specifics. How do you know these are real memories and not just fantasies?"

He pinched his nose between his eyes. "Because two of them are about me. All the details are correct."

"Can you verify any of the other stories?"

"No. Not entirely, but a few seem to be from people he's met before, some friends of mine. I haven't read all of them yet. I'm worried that he'll remember his mother and her death through my memories, even though his are gone."

"Has he said anything to indicate any memories have returned?"

"Yes. He said he sees a hallway and a door with a handle before his visions start. He asked me if our old house had handles on the doors. They did. But that's all he's mentioned. Dr. Ru, how can Hunter see my memories?"

Ru paused before answering. "Maybe I should see Hunter. Do you still live in Washington?"

"No. We moved last summer."

"Where are you living now?"

For some reason, Joe hesitated. "Far enough away that returning to see you would be very inconvenient."

"I see. This sounds very serious, Joe. Have you told anyone else about these stories?"

"No."

"Does Hunter know these stories are real memories?"

"I don't think so. We haven't talked about them. He knows I read one of the stories, but not any of the others."

"Have you noticed anything in common among the stories? Is there anything to connect them to each other?"

Joe felt his face flush with heat. "Yeah. A lot of sex, most of it hidden or inappropriate."

"Give me an example, please."

"Incest, homosexuality, assault. Things like that."

"I see. Maybe they are connected to aspects of his original memories."

Joe thought about the story events and saw similarities to Hunter's past situation. He stood up and gazed out the window. "Now that you mention that, I can see connections."

"I cannot explain why he would see other people's actual memories, but it is possible that Hunter's old memories are coming back to him. Is there any possibility that I can speak to him?"

Joe hesitated. Hunter had no memory of Ru or his treatment.

"Wouldn't that be a little awkward since Hunter doesn't remember you?"

"You could tell him that you asked a psychiatrist to talk to him about his stories. He doesn't have to know my connection to his past. I believe talking to me would help Hunter."

Joe was hoping for another option, one that wouldn't accidentally trigger Hunter's memories.

"Is there anything else we can do?"

Ru paused.

"There is . . . another possibility."

Joe thought he sounded unsure.

"You could try resetting the chip in his brain."

Joe gasped. "He has a chip? Did you mention this to me before?"

Again, Ru paused. "I'm sure I did. The chip does nothing now, but it can be activated."

"What would that do?"

"Reset his memories to what they were when he left my office."

"So basically no memories."

"Or something close to that."

Joe remembered how Hunter was after the treatment. He knew Joe and some basic facts about himself, but otherwise he was like a teenage baby. "How would I do it?"

"I can email you instructions. Is your old email address still good?"

"Yes."

"I will send instructions in a few minutes."

"Would this require us to see another doctor?"

"No. You can do it yourself. I purposely made the procedure simple to perform, yet unlikely to happen by accident."

"Is there any danger in doing the reset? Could all his memories return if I do this?"

"Resetting the chip would not be dangerous to Hunter, and there's no reason why his memories would return afterward."

"OK."

"Joe, if in fact Hunter can see the memories of other people, that would be of great interest to scientists. And possibly government officials. You can imagine how such an ability could be exploited."

"Meaning what, exactly?"

"Meaning it might be better for Hunter if this ability were kept secret."

Joe paused. On the one hand, this ability would make Hunter's life more complicated and even dangerous. On the other hand, it could also be worth a lot of money. "What would you do if you had a patient with Hunter's ability?"

"My first priority, as always, is to ensure the safety and well-being of my patients. Subsequent to that, I would try to discover the factors that affect which memories he sees, such as proximity to the person, type of memory, and so forth. And ultimately whether he could learn to control memory acquisition and whether others could learn the technique. But all that is probably not in Hunter's best interest. Is he bothered by these memories?"

"Yes. He can't sleep. They seem to be happening more frequently. He's also been more determined to get information about his past."

"You will have to decide what is best for him, Joe. Perhaps the reset is worth pursuing. How was he before the memories started?"

"He seemed to be all right. Still spent a lot of time writing on his computer, but he wasn't so desperate. He was definitely better than he is now."

"On which computer does he write these stories?"

"It's the school's property. Each student is issued one during the year."

"Perhaps it would be better if he used his own computer to ensure that these stories aren't seen by others. For Hunter's sake. What do you think would happen if Hunter's stories became public? Especially if others recognized their own memories like you did."

Joe's mind filled with trooper car lights flashing outside his house and angry people banging on his door. *What's the penalty for hacking memories,* he wondered? "I understand. I'll get him another computer."

"I will send the instructions shortly. Please call me if you need anything else."

"Thanks, Dr. Ru. I appreciate your help." He disconnected.

Joe stared ahead, seeing nothing in particular. He reached vaguely for a chair to sit in and almost fell on the floor when he missed the seat. What should he do?

If he did nothing, the chances that Hunter would see more of Joe's memories increased, as did the chance that others would discover Hunter's abilities.

If he reset the chip, things might go back to normal, whatever that was in Hunter's life, or they might not. Maybe all of his old memories would return. Ru seemed unsure of the results.

His phone dinged. Joe opened Ru's email:

Hunter's chip can be reset by a specific sound. Since music, especially one particular song, played such a large role in Hunter's relationship with his mother, I programmed the chip to reset when it senses the opening riff of that song played backwards repeatedly. A speaker placed above his right ear against the skull while the backwards riff plays will prompt the reset. Make sure he hears only the riff backwards.

Joe knew the song—"Whole Lotta Love" by Led Zeppelin. One common interest he had shared with Savannah was Zeppelin and classic rock. Frankie and Hunter must have heard the *Mothership* album a thousand times. Now Hunter never listened to music. He had no songs on his phone or computer. Joe had never heard him play the radio in the car.

He understood why.

Joe's hairs on his neck tingled as he realized that Ru had acted suspiciously. Why did Ru email the instructions rather than tell him during the call? And why did he not name the song?

Because he's worried about being discovered? By whom? Who would be interested in the song title?

Could someone be monitoring his phone or Ru's? Who would care?

And why had Ru called back on another number? And the chip. Joe would've remembered Ru telling him about an implant into his son's brain. So Ru was lying. Why?

Maybe he should buy another phone, as well as a computer. He should drive to Fairbanks. Now.

He still had stories to read, so he hurriedly removed all the papers from Hunter's wall and put them in a box, which then went into his truck. He would text Hunter later to explain.

And say what?

His son was not ready for the truth about his mother's death.

He never would be.

After another five minutes, he pulled out of his driveway. He had a little over an hour of driving to Fairbanks to figure out what he and Hunter were going to do.

CHAPTER EIGHT

Jazz waited outside the classroom as Hunter walked out, his face focused on the floor, not looking where he was going. Her heart fluttered as she reached out for his arm. "Hunter? Are you OK?"

He stopped, lifted his head, and smiled at her, but it didn't touch his eyes. "I just failed a quiz. I sent you two stories."

"I know, but you said not to open them. What's going on?" His shoulders slumped as he leaned against the wall. She so wanted to give him a hug, but they had never really touched. Sometimes she thought he would reach out to her, but he held back, like he was scared.

He pushed himself from the wall. "Let's walk down to the gym. Just for a minute."

They walked side-by-side, forcing others to move out of their way. The lobby outside the gym was empty.

Hunter clutched his computer to his chest and sighed heavily. "I keep having visions flash through my mind at all hours of the day. I write them down and when I'm home, I print them out. The two I sent you were from classes this morning, one about Eric and Ms. Tucker. The other is about how the fire started on the Parks Highway south of Nenana."

"Yeah, the father blamed his son for starting it."

"There's more to the story. I saw it happen. In my head, Jazz." His eyes opened wide. "The stories run through my head like a movie, just like you said this morning."

Jazz saw his bloodshot eyes as he blinked too rapidly. She ached for him. "Since when?"

"About two months ago. One night I had just finished another Tremarian story, and I heard a sound. Like a pounding. Then I saw a hallway and a door, and then the story started. It kept looping in my brain over and over until I decided to write it down. Once I finished, I stopped seeing the story. But here's another thing that's really strange. I wrote a story in English today about Eric and Ms. Tucker having sex at her house this weekend."

"Having sex?"

"Yeah. I saw the entire thing. Just when I was describing how they ran back to the bedroom, Tucker came by my desk to see how I was doing. She read the story and got upset. She didn't want anyone else to read it. She got angry with Eric after class, which was why he pushed me into the Pit. They both claimed nothing had happened between them. But I saw them, Jazz, as clearly as I saw Anthony start the fire. Why would my head make up a story about Tucker and Eric screwing each other?"

Jazz saw the confusion and pain in his face and noticed the vein pulsing in his neck. She reached for his hand.

"How can one be real and the other not be?" asked Hunter. "Do you know how Anthony started the fire?"

"Supposedly, he tossed some burning coals into the trees."

"OK. I never knew that, but that's exactly what I saw in the story. His father forced him to stay outside while he and his wife had sex inside. He told Anthony to dump the coals from the burn barrel into the woods to keep him occupied so he wouldn't come into the house."

"Really? The father told everyone that Anthony did it on his own."

"Not in the story I saw." He shifted his feet and tried to swallow. He looked desperate, almost crazed.

Her chest hurt with worry about him. "Hey, we'll figure this out." She pushed some hair out of his face and tried to smile.

"Do you believe me?"

"Of course, I do!" Did she? This sounded crazy. But he had always listened to her when she needed to talk, had always smiled when he saw her. She would not fail him now. "I'm worried about you."

"*I'm* worried about me."

His eyes twitched and his breathing quickened.

"This morning I was going to drive into the trees. I couldn't stand it anymore. Then my phone buzzed with your message."

"Hunter!" she gasped then wrapped her arms around him. "No, no, no. You will not do anything like that."

"I need help. I need someone to talk to." He crushed her against him.

Jazz felt a rush of panic but also a flood of warmth feeling him hug her. When was the last time anyone had hugged her out of sympathy? She couldn't remember. Tears ran down her cheeks as her stomach twisted. Hunter was her only friend, and he could have died this morning! She couldn't lose him.

"Hunter, I will help you. We can talk at my house during lunch. Just one more class period to get through. OK?" She leaned back from him and held his face in her hands. "OK?"

"OK. Thanks." He wiped her cheek with one hand. "And then you can tell me what you want to forget."

Jazz smiled. "Deal. And promise me you won't drive toward any trees or do anything else like that. I couldn't stand you being hurt."

"We'll go in your car. You drive."

She hugged him hard again. The bell rang. "We need to get to math." She grabbed his hand. "C'mon."

They ran down the hallway until they got to Ms. Fenster's door. Jazz squeezed his hand then let go, opened the door, and walked inside, trying to ignore Fenster's scowl. Hunter followed right behind

There weren't two empty seats next to each other, so Jazz sat in the back row while Hunter sat in the row in front of her and to the side.

* * * * * *

Hunter still saw Jazz's face in front of his, tears on her cheeks, but smiling. Adrenaline streamed throughout his body. She would help him.

He tried to focus on Fenster's lesson but couldn't. Scenes ran through his mind. The fire, Tucker's reaction after reading his story, the basketball on the road, his dad's face that morning.

He felt a paper wad hit his neck. He turned around and saw Jazz with her computer lid up, gesturing for him to do the same. He opened his computer, noticing the red dot on his Mail icon.

An email from Jazz: *Can I open the files now?*

Yes, he replied. At least now, Jazz knew the context for the stories. Still, he felt he was baring himself in front of her. Would she understand that he didn't make up the stories, and that they had appeared to him?

He then looked through the two documents he had sent her, wondering how she would react. He was halfway through Anthony's story when the thumping started. He grabbed his head. The sound was much louder and more frequent than earlier. It seemed like two different sounds playing together at different speeds.

"Hunter! Pay attention!" yelled Fenster.

"Yes, ma'am." He tried to watch Fenster draw numbers on her SMART Board and copy them on his computer.

Then he saw himself walk down the hall and stop at the door.

"What's wrong with you?" a woman shouted. "I waited two weeks for this? I can't take this anymore!"

He heard a door slam from inside. Then silence.

He walked down the hall into a gravel driveway outside a house in the woods. The moon was almost full, lighting up the scraggly primrose and dandelions around the edges of the gravel. He started typing.

Jazz rubbed the shoulders of a tired, haggard woman slumped at the kitchen table while the faint sound of a shower could be heard in the background. She wore a faded nightgown. A smear of blue eye-shadow highlighted her blood-shot eyes; the red on her lips caked in the corners of her mouth, which occasionally puckered around a straw to drink from a tall glass next to her. Her hair lay in tangles on her head. One of her cheeks was bruised.

"Jazz, you should be a masseuse. That feels so good."

"Lean over, Mom." Her mother bent forward as Jazz kneaded her muscles slowly, forcing groans from her mother's lips. Jazz massaged her scalp then dragged her fingernails down her back a few times. "Feel better now?"

"Mmmm." She poured a little more Coke into her glass and sipped again. "Want some?" She lifted the glass toward Jazz.

"Yes." She sipped and grimaced. "Lots of vodka in there, Mom." Way too much!

"I know. My hand was shaking so much when I poured in the vodka that more came out than I wanted."

Jazz rolled her eyes, took another sip, and put the glass on the table. Jazz knew why her mom drank, but when she got too drunk, she let him do anything to her.

The sound of the shower stopped. They both looked up toward a door just down the hall from the kitchen.

"You going to be OK?" asked Jazz.

"Sure, honey."

"Don't take any shit tonight."

Her mother lit a cigarette, blew the smoke above her head, and sipped some more of her drink. Jazz wrinkled her nose, waved the smoke away, then kissed her mom's head. "I'll be close by." Jazz walked out of the room and sat on the sofa in the living room, listening.

Soon she heard a door open and knew that Leon would be emerging from the bathroom. Jazz thought him disgusting—covered in hair and tats, his head shaved, a silver chain necklace hanging on his bloated, sagging chest. Yet he thought he was God's gift to women. Why did her mother latch onto these worthless assholes?

"Already drunk, aren't you?" he sneered. "Claire, you're really something to come home to. Couldn't you fix yourself up a little bit? Do something with your hair? Wear something pretty? Act like you care about me at all?" He slapped the table.

All her senses sparking, Jazz sat up straighter on the sofa and reached for her pack next to her.

"How much have you drunk today?" Jazz heard his footsteps. "That's almost pure vodka. And you've been drinking that all day, haven't you?"

Jazz heard her mother yelp and gritted her teeth. C'mon, Mom, don't take it!

"Haven't you? You used to be pretty. You used to be fun to be with. Now you're just a fat, ugly drunk. I don't even want to come home to you."

"Then don't," she mumbled softly.

Jazz smiled a little then braced for his response. She knew what he would do.

"You want that?" Leon yelled. "You want me to leave. Is that it?" Her mother yelped again. "Answer me!"

"No, Leon, I can't wait for you to come home every night. Don't know what I'd do without you." She chuckled.

Jazz unzipped her pack as she heard him slap her face, then the crash of a glass hitting the floor. Jazz stood, baring her teeth, her muscles tensing.

"You need to clean that up," Leon growled.

"You did it." Claire's voice quavered. "Why should I clean it up?"

"Because you made me do it. Now clean it up!"

Jazz heard her mother scream and stumble. Jazz reached into her pack. She heard a chair scrape across the floor. C'mon, Mom! Fight back.

"I wish I'd never met you, bitch! You've ruined my life! You and that ugly daughter of yours. Now clean up that mess!"

Jazz heard what sounded like the table being pushed across the floor then her mother's scream.

Her blood boiling, Jazz yanked a pistol from her pack.

Her mother screamed. "Aah! Please! Stop! I'll clean it up."

"Hurry up, bitch!"

Jazz burst into the kitchen holding the gun in front of her with two hands. Leon had lifted a chair above his head, ready to bring it down on her mother crying on the floor.

"Get out!" Jazz snarled at Leon as she pointed the gun at his face, moving slowly toward him. "I told you to get out!"

"Jazz, don't," Claire pleaded.

"He will not hurt you again. Ever." She pulled back the hammer and planted her feet wide apart. "I will shoot you."

Leon smiled and tilted his head. "What d'ya know? Jazz got herself a gun." He laughed. "But I don't think you'll shoot it."

He took a step forward. Jazz smiled and pulled the trigger, sending a bullet past the side of his head, thudding into the wall.

Leon flinched and turned sideways. "Shit, girl!"

Narrowing her eyes, Jazz calmed her breathing and made sure he would not doubt her intentions. "The next one goes into your face. Now get out!"

Claire pulled herself off the floor. "Get out, Leon!"

"I don't have any clothes on!"

Jazz pulled the hammer back. She so wanted to fire again. Her pulse pounded in her ears.

Claire walked quickly into the bathroom and came out with his jeans, shirt, and shoes. "Here." She dropped them on the floor.

"Get dressed and leave," said Jazz. "I won't say it again."

She kept the gun pointed at his face as he scrambled to put on his jeans and shirt.

"I've got things here that belong to me!" he yelled as he pulled on his shoes.

"We'll make arrangements with the trooper to be here when you get your things," said Jazz. "Other than that time, you will never come back here. If I ever see you around my momma, I will shoot your ass. Got it?"

"You crazy bitches deserve each other. Hope you enjoy living with your drunk-ass mother."

Jazz jerked the gun toward the door. "Out!"

He bolted out of the house, jumped into his truck, and left.

Claire collapsed onto Jazz crying.

"It's OK, Mom. He's gone." Jazz's hands trembled. She led her mother to a seat and helped her sit down. "He won't hit you anymore," she said through a thick throat. Her legs wobbled as she tried to slow her breathing.

"Thank you, Jazz. I'm so sorry. So sorry." She put her head onto the table, crying in spasms while Jazz rubbed her head.

Hunter gasped. "No!" He coughed then choked.

"Gross!" someone yelled.

He turned around to look at Jazz, tears forming in his eyes.

"Hunter? What's wrong?" asked Jazz. Her face was ashen.

He coughed again, then turned around and stood. "I'm going to be sick."

"Then get to the bathroom. Don't you dare puke in here!" shouted Fenster.

He grabbed his computer and bolted out of the room. Stumbling down the hall, coughing and crying, he made it to the bathroom where he found an open stall. He dropped to the floor, his computer scraping across the tile, then he heaved into the toilet. His body jerked as he cried, his face vibrating on his arms flung across the toilet lid.

He spat and tried to deepen his breaths. After another minute he pulled himself up to sit on the toilet seat, holding his head in his hands.

Calming down, he tore off toilet paper and blew his nose. Then pulled off some more to wipe his face. He reached for his computer on the floor and put it on his lap.

He opened the lid and started typing the rest of the dream out. He had to get it out.

Jazz helped her mother stand and led her back into her room at the end of the hall. She pulled back the covers and helped Claire lay down then kissed her cheek as her mother cried herself to sleep.

Jazz walked back into the kitchen and pulled a glass and vodka bottle out of the cabinet. Once again they'd be short on cash. Her brain felt numb. She poured two inches of liquor into the glass, added ice, and sat at the table, staring out the window. What would they do now? Her mother would sleep, and Jazz would drink herself to oblivion. She felt so empty, so alone. Tears spilled over her lashes as she tried to think of her grandparents.

The scene faded in his mind, but Jazz's face lingered, as if in a tiny spotlight gradually blurring to darkness. Hunter had never seen her look so sad. She was always happy, always smiling when he saw her. Now he had some idea what memories she wanted to forget.

Sweat ran down his neck. He grabbed more paper and pushed it across his forehead.

"Hunter?" Jazz yelled from outside the bathroom.

"Yeah! I'm in here." He saved the file and closed the lid.

The door burst open. "Where are you?"

Hunter stood up and opened the stall door. "You can't be in here."

"Says who?" She ran to him and hugged him. "Are you OK?" She pulled her hands from his back. "You're sopping wet."

"Yeah. Always happens once the vision fades. Sorry."

"I don't mind." She hugged him again. "C'mon. We need to get out of here." Holding his hand, she pulled him toward the door exiting the building.

CHAPTER NINE

unter sat in the front seat of Jazz's old Ford Ranger, clutching his computer to his chest as Jazz pulled out of the school parking lot. Was Jazz's story real? Had she threatened Leon with a gun, even fired at him? What a horrible life she'd had to endure with her mother and Leon. And the drinking. Did Jazz drink?

He couldn't get the last image of Jazz out of his head, sitting at a table with a glass of vodka, with such a look of fatigue and defeat. How could she endure that home life and be so happy and caring at school?

Jazz was his best friend, but they hadn't talked about home issues. He'd never mentioned the silence between him and his father. She'd never talked about her mother or Leon. Science, world events, school gossip, and his Tremarian stories filled up their time. Now he realized that was all a façade. The real stuff was much darker.

But how did he know any of what he saw was real?

Every story he'd seen today was about someone he'd been physically close to. Two of the three stories were tragic, while the other seemed almost too perfect. Both Eric and Vanessa were willing players in the seduction, no hesitation or doubts, yet a teacher and a student had steamy sex. There was no conflict, unlike in the story his dad had read.

Why?

He had to figure out whether the stories were real events or not.

"Why are you so quiet, Hunter?" Jazz asked as she slowed for one of only five stop signs in town and looked at him. Her brow wrinkled as her mouth tightened.

"Just trying to figure things out." He returned her gaze. "Can I ask you a personal question?"

"Sure."

"How long did Leon live with you and your mother?"

Jazz's jaw dropped. "Much too long. How do you know about him?"

"He was in the last story I wrote. Along with your mother."

They locked eyes with each other for a few seconds until Jazz turned hers toward the road as she crossed the intersection.

"Hunter, this is too weird."

"Ya think?"

"You had three visions this morning?"

"Yeah."

"Is that normal?"

"No. Never been that many before lunch. I don't see how I can pass my classes if this keeps happening."

"Was I in the story?"

"Yes, very much so."

"Did I have all my clothes on?" She looked over at him and winked.

"Yes. Why'd you ask?"

"After reading about Eric and Vanessa, I wondered. Maybe you'd fantasize about me, too."

"I didn't fantasize anything, Jazz!"

"OK. Calm down."

"How would I know about Leon? Explain that to me. You've never mentioned him. Or that your mother drinks vodka and Coke."

Jazz slowed her truck just before the end of the road and looked at him.

"Or that you drink, too."

Her eyes widened slightly. "You saw that?"

"Yes."

Jazz blew out a slow breath as she turned into her gravel and dirt driveway barely visible through a clump of trees, toward her house hidden from the street.

She set the gear to park and turned the key. "What happened in the story?"

"I'll tell you inside. I need to check something out first."

"You think you can eat something?"

"Yeah."

"By the way, my house is a mess. I'm not very tidy except in the lab. I've been living by myself for several weeks."

"Where's your mom?"

Jazz sighed. "She finally went to rehab. She's an alcoholic, which I guess you already knew."

"Sorry."

"I haven't told anyone she's gone. Most wouldn't notice anyway since she rarely left the house except to go to the bar. I thought she'd kill herself with how much she was drinking, so I finally convinced her to go."

Jazz opened the truck door and walked toward the log house, Hunter following close behind. Water dripped from clumps of snow stuck in the valleys of the roof. The front door opened into the mudroom where she removed her boots and jacket. Hunter did the same.

Jazz stopped and looked at the kitchen. "Holy shit! You don't realize how much of a mess you've made until you show it to someone else."

Her stove was covered in pots and skillets, while her counter and sink were full of dirty dishes. A metal trashcan sat in the corner, its lid propped up by folded food cartons, which didn't fit inside. A pile of laundry rested on the table, topped by a large red bra.

Hunter widened his eyes. "Whoa."

Jazz blushed and quickly grabbed the clothes. "Woops! Forgot to put these away last night."

"Don't worry about the mess. If I lived here by myself, the place would look worse."

She carried the clothes to another room.

Hunter walked to a wall to his left and moved his fingers near the doorjamb from chest-high to above his head.

Jazz returned. "What are you doing?"

"Here." His pinky finger fit into a hole at eye-level.

"What's that?"

"You don't know? You made it."

"How?"

Hunter saw the blank look on her face. The story had to be real because the bullet hole was there. "When did Leon leave?"

Jazz's eyes searched his face then moved to the ceiling. Her eyebrows scrunched together. "I don't remember."

"What's your last memory of him?"

"He came home from work, smelly and covered in dirt as usual. I was washing dishes. Mom was cooking dinner, but she burned it. He called her horrible names then disappeared into the bathroom for a shower."

"So why isn't he living here anymore?"

She tried to think. "Maybe you should tell me."

Hunter opened his computer and found the document. "You should read this."

Jazz sat at the table in front of the computer. As she read, her skin turned red, her breathing quickened, and emotions flashed hot across her face, like she was reliving the event. After a few minutes, she leaned back in her chair and pressed her head with her hands. After a few deep breaths, she stood. "OK, there's no way I would've forgotten that story, but I did. As I read this, the memory came flooding back into my brain."

She walked to the wall with the bullet hole and put her pinkie into it. After several seconds, she turned around with a jerk. "I got it! I was trying to remember when I might have thought about Leon and Mom around you. It was right after you told me about wanting to drive into the trees this morning. My mind flashed to my Mom crying about how miserable she was with Leon, claiming she just wanted to drive off a cliff. That was just before Leon came home that last time."

His blood rushed to his head as he lifted both hands. "Which means my stories are real, and they're prompted by people nearby who are thinking about the memory before I see it."

Jazz approached him. "Did you see Anthony today?"

"Yeah. He was crying in Patty's office when I left Bentley."

"Maybe the kids had teased him about being an arsonist. Kids have bullied him all year about the fire. So all three stories today were about people you saw."

"True, but why them? How many others did I see today? Fifty? A hundred?" Hunter plopped down in a chair at the table. "Why those three?"

"I don't know yet. It seems that when memories invade your mind, they evidently leave the brain that formed them. Don't ask me how, yet, but I'll figure it out. Hey, I need some food. I'll reheat last night's leftovers, if you don't mind. It's hard to keep my body looking this good without a lot of fuel," she scoffed. "I have spaghetti and meatballs or meatballs and spaghetti. Do you have a preference?"

Hunter chuckled. "Either one's good."

"Great. Easy to please. I like that in a man." She opened the refrigerator, pulled out a glass dish covered in plastic wrap, and slid it into the microwave. She walked back to him, looking at the ceiling, obviously thinking about something. "So let's recap. You wrote three stories today. Whose memories were they?"

"What do you mean?"

"Well, the one about me was obviously my memory of the event. I heard yelling and furniture scraping as I sat in the living room. I didn't see him attack her. Your story was from my point of view. If I asked Mom about the event, she'd still remember it. You took my memory, not Mom's or Leon's."

"It was Eric's memory. The story started with him outside. And the fire story was Anthony's memory."

Hunter remembered his father this morning and the look on his face as Hunter came into the room. His skin tingled as the explanation of that look unfolded in his mind.

"I wrote a story last night about a boy named Parker going into a dressing room only to find another boy still there. In his underwear. They had sex. I found Dad reading the story this morning, turning pale. He looked scared. Before I left, he asked me why the other boy didn't have a name. Why would he care? At the time I thought that was an odd question, but now I think he was worried I'd say the boy's name was Joe."

He felt blood rush to his face. "But the story was from Parker's point of view. That was Dad's memory! That would explain his reactions." He saw Jazz smiling at him. "But why'd he call himself Parker in his memory?"

"Defense mechanism," said Jazz. "Maybe in his mind he denies he was the boy who walked in the dressing room. It was someone else named Parker, who I'll bet was the real name of the other boy. He was scared you saw a deep secret of his, one he probably didn't want to remember."

"As he read that story, the memory came back to him?"

"Probably, which added to his fear. When I read your story about Leon, I had the weirdest feeling. It was like that event happened again for the first time. Usually memories fade so when you think about them, you don't experience the same emotion you felt originally. But when I read your story, I was there. I'll bet your father felt the same way."

The microwave dinged. She grabbed a towel and two forks then pulled out the dish. "Lunch is served." She put the food on the table and sat. "Hmm, looks remarkably like last night's dinner." She held the two forks in her fist. "Choose your weapon."

Hunter smiled and pulled one of the forks out of her hand.

Jazz stabbed a meatball and held the fork by her lips. "What was Eric doing when you walked into class this morning?" The fork disappeared into her mouth and emerged, minus the meatball.

"Staring at Tucker. Almost falling out of his chair as she walked around the room."

"He was fantasizing about her. That's the story you picked up on."

"I thought I was seeing memories." He twirled spaghetti around his fork and stuck the wad into his mouth.

Jazz's eyes widened in excitement. "Fantasies and memories are formed in the same place in your brain. A group of scientists at the National Institute of Health did brain scans of people performing a real task and of people imagining doing the same tasks. There was no difference in brain activity or location. What we imagine happens is no different to the brain than what actually happens. They both become part of our memories. Just like Bentley's version of his big shot in the game versus his fans' version."

"How the hell do you know that?"

"Because," she stabbed another meatball, "I've read hundreds of articles about memory for my science project. I'm supposed to know this stuff." She grabbed the meatball with her teeth, chewed a few times, then swallowed.

"Wait," said Hunter. "Ms. Tucker said her first name wasn't Vanessa. Eric made that up."

"Sounds sexier than her real name."

"Which is?"

"Mary."

"I'll be damned." Hunter twirled another wad of spaghetti. "Did you make this?"

"From an old family recipe of Ragu, frozen meatballs, and spaghetti noodles cooked until they stick to the cabinet door when I throw them."

He chuckled. "You throw the noodles?"

"Not all of them, silly. Just a few. In fact, I think there's one still stuck on the cabinet to the right of the stove." She pointed. "Now back to your other question."

"Which was?" He cut a meatball in half and stabbed one piece.

"Why these stories? Why did you see those memories from those people as opposed to someone else's?"

"I don't know."

"Do all your stories have sex in them?"

He blinked several times and scratched his face. "The one about Anthony didn't. No, that's not true. That's why Anthony had to stay outside. Yours didn't."

"It would have if I hadn't come out with a gun. He was going to beat her up while having sex with her."

Hunter choked a little while swallowing his food. "He'd done that before?"

"Yeah, but I didn't know it at first. When I saw her bruises, I talked to Mom. Told her to stand up to him and come to me if she needed help. She knew I kept a gun." Jazz ate another meatball.

"*You* kept a gun? Why didn't she?"

"Because they freak her out. I think we should look through your other stories."

"You could come over to my house after school."

"I'd love to." She stared into his eyes. "How many of your other stories have sex in them?"

"I don't know."

"Guess. Half? Most?"

"Probably most of them."

Jazz squinted her eyes. "Yet your Tremarian stories are about a genderless world that banished sex."

"They tried, but the Dumarians resisted, so there's a war."

"A war between those wanting to eliminate sex and those who don't. Which side do you want to win?"

"The Tremarians."

"Really? The last one I read was about the Dumarians struggling to survive. They weren't evil. I actually felt sorry for them."

Hunter dropped his fork and covered his face with his hands. "I don't know."

"Do you think sex is bad? You told me months ago that sex causes all of the world's problems. Do you believe that?"

"The Tremarians do."

"What do *you* think? All the sex in these four stories is illicit or forbidden or caused a fire or was an excuse to hurt a woman. Where's the good sex?"

Hunter leaned back and shook his head. "Is there any?"

"Can I ask you a personal question?"

"Sure."

"Have you ever had sex?"

Hunter heard a scream, a long "Ahhhh!" He covered his ears and grimaced.

"Hunter? Are you OK?"

He felt Jazz's hands on his as his head pounded.

"Hunter? Please! What's the matter?"

Hunter grabbed her hands in his, trying to breathe.

"I heard a scream and then a pounding sound. At the start of every story, I'm in a hallway outside a bedroom door. Just before I saw your memory, I heard a voice through the door. She said, 'I waited two weeks for this?' Then I heard a door slam."

"Who was she?"

"I don't know." Hunter stood. "I asked my dad this morning if our old house had handles on the doors instead of knobs because the door in my vision has a handle. He wouldn't answer. I think I'm standing in my old house at the start of each story."

"Could that voice be your mother's?"

"I don't know. I don't remember her."

"'I waited two weeks for this' sounds like she's upset about someone's sexual response to her, or lack of a response."

"What do you mean?"

"Like she wanted sex, but he wasn't interested."

He pushed his hair away from his face. "Why am I seeing other people's memories and not my own?"

"I think you're seeing some part of your memories. The woman yelled at the man for not being interested in her. Then you saw the memory where Leon yelled at my mom for being ugly and not sexually attractive to him. Maybe there's some connection between your lost memories and the ones you're seeing."

He sat down next to her. "I need to know what happened to me. Why my mother and brother died in a car wreck, *if* that's how they died."

A man's leering face flashed into Hunter's mind as Jazz closed her eyes.

She rubbed her face. "Maybe when you know, you'll wish you didn't."

Hunter almost described what he saw, but decided not to. He'd just embarrass her. He hesitated before he asked, "Have you had sex?"

Jazz blew out a breath. "Nothing I want to remember. Maybe if we keep hanging out, you'll see all my memories and take them away."

Hunter felt a rush of excitement. "Would you want that?"

"I wouldn't want you to know them, but I would like them to disappear."

"Maybe next time I won't let you read the story."

She stood. "Hunter, this is so freakin' weird!"

"I know. Why is this happening to me?"

"I don't know, but I'll figure it out. I'm sorry, Hunter, but I need a drink." She went to the cabinet where Hunter knew she stashed her liquor, took out a bottle of vodka, pulled a can of Coke from the refrigerator and poured it into a glass with ice. Then she added some vodka and stirred the mixture with a spoon. She drank about a third of the glass without a break.

Hunter felt his breath catch in his chest as he watched her. "Do you always drink during lunch?"

"No. And I'm sorry you're seeing me do this, but you're going to see lots more, Hunter. You probably won't like me very much once you do." She took another guzzle.

Hunter went to her side, shoving his hands into his pockets, leaning toward her, almost touching her shoulder with his, then pulling back. "Jazz, you're my best friend and the nicest person I know. I can't believe you would ever do anything bad on your own. Leon deserved having a gun pointed at him. Would you have shot him?"

"Yes, if he didn't leave."

Hunter swallowed and raised his brows. "You could do that?"

"I know I could. No doubt at all." Her eyes met his as she drank from the glass.

The strength of her answer left him lightheaded. *No doubt?* "Did he ever come back?"

"Nope." She guzzled the remaining liquid.

"He wasn't your father, right?"

"No. He was just one of the assholes my mother latched onto." She put the glass on the counter. "I never knew my father. I don't think Mom knew him either." She poured more Coke and vodka into the glass. "She said she was probably raped at a college party. Woke up with bruises and ripped clothes, smelling like vomit and sex." She swirled the ice around the inside of her glass. "She called her parents from college and said she was going to kill herself." She shook her head and took a sip. "They rushed up there and brought her home. Mom says they weren't very happy with her, especially when they learned she was pregnant with me." She scoffed and shook her head. "I decided to be conceived at a most inopportune time. They took care of Mom until I was born. We lived with them off and on until I was twelve." She took another drink.

He clasped his arms over his stomach. "Off and on?"

"Yeah. Sometimes we lived with one of Mom's boyfriends, but we always went back to her parents for one reason or another. Well, actually the same reason. The men were shits, and Mom couldn't keep a job 'cause of her drinking." She wiped sweat from her forehead.

The urge to hold her was almost overwhelming. He held his arms tighter. "Where do they live?"

"In Oregon."

"Why are you here?"

"Because something really bad happened and we had to move far away."

"Really bad?"

"I don't want to think about it, because you'll see it, and I don't want you to."

"OK, but why did you come here in particular?"

"She got a job at the base, then got fired. Then got another job at a restaurant bar, then got fired."

"How do you live?"

"She hooks up with men until I make them leave . . . or . . . something happens." She stared off and took another drink.

He felt a tear run down his cheek. "How do you buy food, especially now that she's in rehab?"

"Before we left my grandparents, MawMaw, my grandmother, gave me a credit card and a phone and told me I could use the card as much as I needed but not to let my Mom know about it. I call them every once in a while, and they send new cards to the school for me. After I convinced Mom to go into rehab, she said that maybe we should go see them once she got better."

"Would you like that?"

"Yeah. There's been a few times I wanted to leave Mom to go back to them, but I could never do it. She'd keep finding assholes to beat her up. She'd be dead if it weren't for me." She wrapped her arms around herself.

Hunter stared at her in a daze and slowly shook his head. "You must have a lot of memories you'd like to forget."

"Yeah." She wiped a tear away from her left eye. "That night with Leon wasn't too bad compared to others."

"Don't you get lonely living out here by yourself?"

"Are you kidding?" She laughed and stood. "I have parties every weekend. Kids come out here all the time."

Hunter scrunched his eyebrows then smiled.

Jazz leaned against the stove. "Actually, you're the first person from school to be in this house."

Hunter walked toward her. "I wish it had been sooner and under better circumstances."

"Me, too, Hunter. Me, too." She finished her drink and put the glass on the counter. "We should probably get back to school."

Hunter felt such sadness for his friend. He'd never expected her life outside of school to be so difficult.

He reached out for her hands. "I want you to know that whatever I see from your past won't change our friendship, and if it's bad, I won't let you read the story."

She pulled him to her.

"Oh, Hunter, you're going to see some horrible things. Including me with no clothes on."

He leaned back and smiled. "Why would that be so horrible? Your bra was pretty damn big. I had no idea. You're always so covered up."

She laughed. "My breasts don't stand out because everything on me is big. Boobs, butt, stomach, legs, everything. Which is a problem in our fat-shaming culture. If the only things big on me were my boobs, then I'd be hot. But since everything else is big, I'm not."

"Well, I think you're hot." He looked into her pretty green eyes and then at her beautifully full lips. "I like your smile, and your eyes, and how happy you are, or pretend to be."

"I *am* happy around you. I'm not pretending. I have fun with you. And I don't want that to change, but I know it's going to." She touched his cheek. "You're going to see some ugly things about me."

"Maybe some bad things that others did to you, but not ugly. You're a beautiful person, Jazz." He felt so good telling her that.

She hugged him. "I hope you always think so."

"Besides, I'm sure when I remember what happened to me, it won't be pretty. Otherwise, why wouldn't I remember? Why would anyone forget happy memories?"

They continued to hug each other. Hunter could feel the bulge of her breasts against his chest. He had to lean his head forward to put his cheek against hers. He also felt her stomach pushing against his. He moved his hands on her back and felt the bra strap underneath her clothes. He was amazed at how wide it was. His fingers explored.

Jazz pulled away and gave him a sly smile. "Yes? What are you doing, Hunter?"

"Your strap is . . . " He saw Jazz's face turn red.

"Is what?"

Hunter's eyes moved away from her face as he thought he heard a woman's voice. *Hunter, help me with this, please.*

"Hunter?" asked Jazz. "What's wrong?"

In his mind, Hunter saw an open back strap of a black lace bra and white skin underneath. His breathing quickened. He heard the woman's voice again. *C'mon, Baby. Please.* She laughed.

Hunter's arms dropped from Jazz. He saw his hands reach for the strap to fasten it. His fingers felt the warmth of her back, so much of it exposed. He fastened the clasps. *Thank you, Baby.* He felt her lips linger on his cheek.

"Hunter?" Jazz placed her hands on each of his cheeks. "What's going on?"

The vision faded, and he saw Jazz's face in front of his.

"What happened? Hunter, tell me."

He looked up at her, his face pale, his lips trembling. "A woman . . . "

"Who?"

"I don't know. She asked me to fasten her bra."

Gently, she asked, "Did you?"

"Yes."

"Did she wear a shirt?"

"No. Her dress was unzipped."

"Was the bra on when she asked you?"

"Yes. Kind of."

"So you fastened it. From the back?"

He nodded.

"Then what?"

"She said, 'Thank you,' then kissed me on the cheek. A long kiss."

"Was she your mother?"

He peered into her eyes. "I . . . I don't know. She was old enough to be. She called me Baby."

CHAPTER TEN

Joe bought a new computer for Hunter, a few flash drives, a Trac Phone, and had VPN apps installed on everything to hide his device location and ISP addresses. The technician at the computer store had assured him that the app would prevent anyone from locating his phones, including the old phone he had hidden from Hunter. Dr. Ru's warnings had made him paranoid about someone finding Hunter and exploiting his ability.

Though he didn't want Hunter to go through something so invasive, he was more concerned about others finding out about himself, his past behaviors, his role in his wife's death, or what he considered his role.

While Hunter's stories were being copied and bound into two spiral books, Joe sat in his truck, thumbing through old photos on his phone: Savannah, Hunter, and little Frankie back before the incident, before their world was destroyed. The last time he tried to view these pictures he was in a hospital room a year and a half ago while Hunter recovered from a procedure Dr. Ru had recommended.

Joe never tried therapy. He could get through this, he'd told himself and others. But mainly, he just didn't want to tell anyone the truth. Joe knew his shame was partly irrational, but pure reason rarely stood a chance against tears or screams or guilt.

His main worry, he told himself and others, was Hunter, who had attempted suicide several times and mutilated his arms with a knife.

Joe knew he wasn't fine. He realized now he should have found someone to help him.

When the boys were young, he and Savannah took them camping. Their favorite parks were Mount Rainier and Olympic. Every year Savannah would insist on taking the family on the ferry to Victoria and spend the day amongst beautiful flowers at the Butchart Gardens. He had hundreds of photos of his family in campgrounds, on trails, in the snow, being wild, and hundreds more in the structured, colorful fairyland of the Gardens. The pictures revealed a happy, young family.

Then he got laid off, and their lives changed. They left the city and Savannah's job, forcing her to stay at home with the boys in a cheap house in the country. Eventually, Joe got a job at Prudhoe Bay in Alaska, which paid great wages, but he would be gone for two to three weeks at a time then home for the same lengths. Even after paying for travel, Joe earned enough to get them free of the crushing debts, which had caused so many arguments during the early years of their marriage. Things seemed to be good in the Williams' household.

But they weren't.

The last photo he had taken of them was outside their home during the summer. Joe said he wanted to have a poster made to put up in his room in Deadhorse. Savannah wore shorts and a tank top as she sat on a painted bench with eight-year-old Frankie sitting on her right leg, his arms around her chest and head against her shoulder sporting a big smile. Hunter stood on her right side, her left arm around his waist, her face close to his stomach. Hunter, 13, towered above her, shirtless, wearing gym shorts, his right arm behind her head, his left hand holding a basketball. His body faced his mother while his head looked at the camera in what Joe knew now to be a smirk.

At the time Joe had no particular thoughts about the photo, other than his boys were handsome, and his wife seemed happy. However, when he got the poster-sized print in the mail and stuck it onto his wall in Deadhorse, he wondered about some of the details. When one of his buddies pointed out the obvious bulge in Hunter's shorts so close to his mother's face which now seemed to be laughing, even glancing down a bit, Joe ripped it down.

He told himself the photo was grainy, and the light was dappled through the trees, so what his buddy saw was not real. He stared at that photo now on his phone and resisted the urge to expand it. Why torture himself again?

He flipped through more photos until he found Stanley's. Joe's heart skipped. The man was beautiful, especially with no clothes. Stanley had been married to a woman for two years before he realized he couldn't pretend any longer. After Frankie and Savannah died, Joe stopped seeing Stanley. None of what happened was Stanley's fault, but Joe knew that the fight between him and Savannah had ultimately led to her death. He told himself many times he should have continued pretending, that he was selfish for wanting to feel passion and lust.

Other times he told himself he should have never pretended, that his cowardly denial of his essential self led to all the blood, the nightmares, the excruciating anguish that followed him and Hunter for nearly four years since that horrible day in May.

He hadn't seen Stanley since before the accident, though he'd talked to him a few times. Every time he'd tried to explain to Stanley why he couldn't see him, his heart burned and ached with such longing for the man. How could he feel such desire when his wife and child had died? He couldn't stand the thought that someone would point to him as the cause. He hid behind self-sacrifice, the guise of a father living only to keep his son alive.

Now he wondered if he'd made a mistake. Perhaps he should've told Hunter everything, introduced him to Stanley, admitted to his son that he had passions, too. That they were often uncontrollable, undeterred by rules or conventions.

But Joe hid his feelings from himself and his son and now lived in a purgatory of daily tasks, which led to more tasks until he wondered if he were even alive.

Until he read Hunter's stories and his passions were rekindled. Joe didn't think he could simply go back to the drudgery of his life before this morning.

The next pictures were what Savannah had found on his phone. She had complained that his two weeks of work had grown to sixteen days, allowing for a day layover in Fairbanks each way. She had accused him of having an affair, which would explain his lack of sexual interest in her. When she found the nude photos of Stanley, the fighting intensified, and the threats to expose him to his sons began.

When Frankie confirmed what Joe had begun to suspect between Hunter and Savannah, Joe's anger turned to hatred and such deep disgust. He knew a part of him was relieved when she died. And that part filled him with such shame and fear.

He was stuck with a son he barely knew, who sooner or later would learn the truth, forcing him to live in fear of exposure and guilt. He had thought about telling Hunter everything and being done with it all, but Hunter was seventeen, still Joe's obligation and burden, and though he could not in truth say he loved his son, he did not want him to suffer more than he already had. Joe couldn't imagine feeling more guilt; the glass was already brimful.

Options?

Reset the chip and hope for the best.

Continue to live with Hunter and hope his memories did not become his son's stories.

Tell Hunter that Joe's phone was traced after speaking to Ru, so he and Hunter had to live apart for a while. Nefarious people could find Hunter through Joe, so he would need to lead them astray by moving elsewhere, thereby preventing Hunter from seeing Joe's memories.

That seemed the flimsiest option.

He walked inside the store and retrieved the bound copies of Hunter's stories, which were now in chronological order.

He decided to find a music shop where he could pay someone to play one of the most famous guitar riffs backward while Joe recorded.

After that, he would finish reading the stories and decide what to do.

CHAPTER ELEVEN

J azz had begun to suspect that Hunter had been victimized by his mother. Every story contained sex, yet his fantasy world was gender neutral. At least that was the case for the first stories he'd showed her. But the last few had depicted a civil war between traditional procreation and artificial methods. Wouldn't a boy who had been sexually abused by his mother hide in a sexless world?

Especially if the only sex he'd known was illicit or forced.

And if the truth were so horrible, it would make sense that Hunter would have to approach the topic indirectly through the experiences of others. So all of his stories started with a brief glimpse from his own life before diving into another person's memory that in some way connected to his own past experience, which he couldn't yet see.

What other woman besides his mother would ask him to fasten her bra and call him *Baby?* He'd mentioned no other women in his life. And what mother would do that unless she had ulterior motives?

"How are you doing?" she asked Hunter who was silently staring out the windshield as she drove them back to school.

"I can't get her image out of my mind."

"Her face or back?"

"Her back."

Jazz could tell he was still seeing her body. His eyes were open but unfocused. "Was she wearing a dress?"

"Yes."

"How far down was it unzipped?"

"All the way." He looked at her then dropped his eyes. "I could see her underwear. I could see her shoulders."

"How did you feel?"

He sat up and turned to her. "What if that was my mother? Why would she do that?"

"I don't know, Hunter. How did you feel?"

"Scared. Excited. Really nervous. The same as now. My heart won't stop racing."

"Do you remember anyone calling you Baby?"

"Not until then. What mother calls their teenage son Baby? And what teenage boy would want that?"

Jazz waited for Kelly's ATV to turn into the school parking lot before she followed it with her truck. Kelly and Skylar were middle schoolers returning from eating lunch at home just like most of the kids at school did before afternoon classes. There were almost as many ATVs in the parking lot as cars and trucks.

Jazz drove past Eric and his girlfriend, Drew, seemingly arguing outside his truck.

"What's that about?" asked Jazz. She parked and quickly opened her door. Hunter jumped out on his side.

Eric reached for Drew's arms, but she hit them away then turned toward the school building.

"Lovers' quarrel," whispered Jazz to Hunter as they walked toward the school entrance.

"Stay away!" Drew shouted over her shoulder to Eric who slammed his truck door.

"Drew! Wait up!" shouted Eric.

She turned and glared at him, pulling her long black hair back from her face. "You're disgusting!" She ran to the school entrance, yanked open the door, and disappeared inside.

Jazz and Hunter stared at Eric.

"What're you looking at?" barked Eric from across the lot.

"Not much," Jazz smirked.

She and Hunter walked inside and headed toward the gym for their PE class.

Hunter stopped in the lobby outside the gym. "The pounding is starting. I need to sit down."

"I'll tell Mr. Harris you're feeling bad. Just sit here, and I'll check on you in a few minutes."

Hunter sat down and opened his computer.

"Do you know who the story's about yet?"

Hunter was breathing hard. His eyes closed. "Them."

"Are you going to be all right?"

"Yeah."

Jazz squeezed his shoulder and ran to the girls' locker room. If Hunter was going to write about Drew and Eric, Jazz wanted to see how Drew responded. Maybe she could get Drew to tell her what happened before she forgot.

Inside the girls' locker room, she found Drew sitting on the bench between rows of lockers, crying. Two other girls finished changing and left. She heard someone close the door to a toilet stall.

Jazz sat next to Drew. "Are you OK?"

"Why would you care?" she scoffed and turned away.

"Eric's an asshole. He pushed Hunter into the Pit this morning. We both have to serve detention after school."

"Why you?"

"Because I stomped on his foot and threatened to kick him in the nuts."

"They should be cut off," Drew snapped. "He's sick."

"Do . . . you want to talk about it?"

She drew in a long breath and turned toward Jazz. "We went to my house during lunch. My little sister, Kelly, and her friend, Skylar, showed up a few minutes later. I was making sandwiches for lunch when Kelly asked Eric to help get the snow off of the trampoline so they could jump. A few minutes later I went to the back door to tell him lunch was ready, and he's standing there on the porch, watching the two girls jump on the trampoline while taking a video of them as their sweatshirts bounced up to their boobs. Skylar doesn't wear a bra yet. They didn't know he was watching them. I called him inside, and he walked in with the biggest hard-on.

"I said, '*What the fuck, Eric!*' And he said, '*What'd I do?*' And I said, '*Why do you have that bone in your pants?*' And he said, '*I do not.*' And I said, '*Eric, I know when you're hard, dammit! You're gettin' off watching twelve-year-olds jump?*'

"'I said, '*First, you're gonna delete that video right now so I can see you do it.*'

"He cussed and said, '*You're crazy, Drew. I didn't do anything.*'

"Then after he deleted it, I said, '*You take me back to school right now and never come here again.*'"

She covered her face with her hands and cried. As Jazz held her shoulders, she thought she heard someone vomiting, very quickly followed by a toilet flush.

"I'm sorry, Drew. At least you caught him doing it so you can warn the girls about him. You should report him."

She stopped crying and looked at Jazz with a quizzical look. She shook Jazz's arm off her shoulders and stood. "Why were you hugging me?"

Jazz heard a toilet flush again. "You were crying."

"I was?"

Tatiana walked past them and opened her locker. Jazz watched her put a toothbrush on the top shelf and grab a water bottle then close the door. She must have sensed Jazz watching her because she turned to Jazz, raised her brows, and said, "What?"

Jazz shook her head. Tatiana turned and walked away while unscrewing the bottle and guzzling some water.

Jazz turned back to Drew. "You were upset with Eric?"

"What'd he do?"

Jazz stared at her. Drew had forgotten everything she had told her. Had Hunter finished typing the story and thereby stolen Drew's memory? The same way he had stolen the memory of Jazz shooting at Leon? *What should I say now?* "Eric pushed Hunter into the Pit this morning."

Drew shook her head and frowned. "Why'd he do that?"

Molly opened the door to the locker room. "Hey, Coach wants to know why you guys are late."

"Give me a minute," shouted Drew. She looked at Jazz. "Aren't you going to change?"

"No, I have to check on Hunter."

"Whatever."

Jazz ran out of the locker room.

"Jazz, where are you going?" shouted Mr. Harris.

"Hunter was sick before lunch, and I left him in the lobby. I need to see how he is."

"Maybe he should go to the nurse," said Harris.

"I'll tell him." Jazz exited the gym and found Hunter typing. "Show me."

Panting, he gave her the computer. "I just finished."

Jazz skimmed through the story about Drew and Eric. "Drew told me about this in the locker room. Then she forgot she told me. You hijacked her memory, Hunter." Jazz pressed keys to print the document in the library. "C'mon."

"What are you doing?" He stood and followed her.

"She needs this back."

They hurried down the hall to the library and stood by the printer as it rolled out Hunter's story.

Jazz picked up the pages. "I'll show this to her after class."

"And tell her what?" he asked in a tense voice. "Hunter stole your memory, but you can have it back?"

"What else should we do? Eric knows this happened. He'll expect Drew to be angry with him. What will he think when she kisses him by his locker between classes like she always does? And besides, Eric's a pervert who shouldn't be anywhere near Kelly or Skylar."

"OK. But if you tell Drew about me and the stories, then everyone else will know."

Jazz thought for a second. "Maybe I could tell her I wrote this based on what she told me. I typed it up because she blanked out in the locker room, and I was worried."

"I don't know." Hunter seemed unconvinced.

Hunter's phone dinged. He pulled it out of his pocket and noticed the message on the screen. "Dad." Hunter typed in his code and opened the message. He and Jazz read it together.

I am driving home from Fairbanks, so I'll be later than usual. I took all your stories with me because I wanted to read them and to make sure they stayed safe.

You need to be very careful with who knows about them. I found at least three stories that appear to be real memories from people who shared something of their past with me. Maybe all the stories are real. I have no idea what's happening to you or why, but you can imagine what might happen to you if your ability becomes known.

I bought you a new computer. I don't think it's wise to have these stories on your school computer. If you have a flash drive, you should transfer the files ASAP and delete the originals. We'll talk about all this tonight.

Maybe you should go home early today.

"Whoa," said Hunter. He locked eyes with Jazz. "Life just got more complicated. You sure you want to be part of this?"

"I want to help you." She gave him a wry smile. "Besides, I have some memories I'd like to get rid of."

"Thanks, Jazz." He leaned his forehead against hers while he held the back of her head. "You're a good friend."

Jazz grinned. "You're dripping on my chest."

"Shit. I'm sorry." He tried to wipe his sweat off her chest, then realized he had just touched her neckline. He jerked his hand away, staring at drops disappearing into her shirt then glanced up at her eyes. "I'm so sorry."

Jazz chuckled.

He touched her glasses. "Your lenses are wet."

Still smiling, she said, "Did you drip on the outside, or did I steam them up from the inside?"

"I don't know. Maybe both. You should wipe them."

She pulled off her glasses and dried them with the tail of the open shirt she wore over her stretch top.

"So what do we do now?"

She put her glasses on. "Text your dad and ask him to call Patty about you needing to leave early. I'll go back to PE and find a way to talk about this story to Drew. She can't forget this happened. I'll follow you home after class."

"You have detention."

"Shit." She stomped her foot. "And it's with that asshole, Eric."

He held her shoulders. "I can go to your house and wait for you. Dad said he won't get home until much later. I can clean your kitchen."

She laughed. "He'll be home tonight, not a week from now."

"I'll clean what I can. Do I need a key?"

"No. I never lock it except at night."

"Do you have a flash drive?"

"Actually, I do." She fished one out of her jeans pocket. "I back up all my lab files on this, so don't lose it."

"What about your worms? I don't want to mess up your experiment."

"You're very thoughtful, Hunter. Seriously. But I think I'd rather work with human memories from now on. They're a lot more interesting."

Hunter stuffed the flash drive into his pocket. "So I've written another story about sex, though sicker than normal. If there's such a thing as normal."

"There's got to be somewhere." Her eyes met his.

"I hope so."

Their eyes wandered around each other's faces. Her eyes found his beautiful cupid bow upper lip and a full, pouty lower lip. Then his brows—extra thick—and his eyelashes—so long. Then to his dimples. He was the cutest boy she had ever seen.

And he seemed to like looking at her.

Yet both of them were struggling with demons from the past. Her stomach churned. What would he think when he saw hers?

She touched his cheek. "Don't forget to text your dad."

"OK."

She left for the gym.

CHAPTER TWELVE

Hunter walked to the Pit, sat down, and downloaded all his stories, plus everything he'd written about the Tremarians, onto Jazz's flash drive. He removed the device, reinserted it to make sure the documents were there, and opened a few. Satisfied that the files were safe, he then deleted every document from his computer.

"Hunter!" shouted Patty from her office behind him.

He stood.

"Your dad called and wants you home."

"OK."

"You sick?"

"Yeah. My head's messed up."

"I hope you didn't give it to me. Get! And don't come back tomorrow if you're still sick. I just got over the flu last week."

"Yes Ma'am."

"I hope you feel better, Hunter."

"Thanks."

Hunter walked out to his truck and climbed in. As he drove to Jazz's house, he thought about the prelude to Drew and Eric's story. This time, when he'd moved to the hallway door, he'd heard a woman moaning in pleasure and breathing rapidly, then music, or something like music. Rapid percussion in the background and then the sound of bees swarming in waves while another voice repeatedly screamed, "Ahhh, ahhh, ahhhh!" Followed by a machine gun, or maybe rapid drumming. Then the sounds disappeared.

Somehow it seemed familiar, but he couldn't remember the context.

He needed to confront his father about his past. Hunter was hallucinating and hearing voices. Something horrible must have happened to him years ago. Otherwise, why would his memories have disappeared?

The voice who thanked him for fastening her bra was the same voice moaning behind the door. At least, they sounded the same.

An immense foreboding lurked somewhere near, a suffocating presence ready to pounce and crush him. He knew it was there, but he had no idea what it was.

He pulled into Jazz's driveway and took his pack and computer inside where he noticed a smell of flowers; that was Jazz's scent—rich, sweet, and fruity—mixed slightly with sweat.

She always wore heavy clothes—sweatshirts, velour tops, and long-sleeved dresses. The only skin she revealed was her neck, face, and hands. Jazz dressed differently than any other girl at school.

He laid his things on the kitchen table and approached the sink. Almost everything was encrusted with old food. After opening cabinets, he determined that every plate, pot, and utensil she owned was dirty. Hunter chuckled. Jazz cleaned up only when she had to. He'd been taught to clean everything as he used it, which meant that most of the dishes and utensils in his house were never used. Jazz evidently believed in equal dirty time. Or maybe her mother's absence had caused this.

Despite her apparent confidence and aggressiveness, Jazz seemed as lonely and desperate for friendship as he was.

He filled the sinks, pots, and pans with warm soapy water to let everything soak for a while before he tried to scrub them. He emptied the trash, which required another bag to contain all the food scraps and boxes the first bag couldn't hold. After he removed the overflow, he found an empty vodka bottle, neck up, in the bag.

How much did Jazz drink every day? And when did it start?

He had some idea about why she drank. Having to deal with her mother's men, all similar to Leon, must have taken a toll. Her warning that he would see her do horrible things, that she would be naked suggested . . . what? Sexual abuse by Leon or others? Recalling Jazz handling her gun made him wonder how anyone would get away with abusing her. But maybe she got the gun afterward.

Hunter opened the cabinet with the liquor and found three bottles, two unopened and one half empty. A shot glass sat to the side. He remembered drinking his father's whiskey and being surprised it didn't choke him. He poured a little vodka into the glass and sipped it.

His throat felt warm as the liquid seeped along his tongue, and he realized he had tasted this before. But when?

He filled the shot glass and tossed the liquor into his mouth, his eyes closed as he swirled the vodka around and swallowed. His neck loosened, and the relaxing numbness spread to his shoulders. He'd had no idea he was so tight.

He poured more into the glass and walked down the hall, which he knew led to Jazz's bedroom.

He stood outside the open door and leaned in. Her clean clothes were piled on the bed—a tangle of sheets, a blanket, a large teddy bear, and some pillows—and random piles of underwear lay on the floor. Hunter sipped more vodka.

Bulges of her clothing rose above the open drawers of her dresser. A stack of books leaned against a lamp on her nightstand. Standing in an almost-dried puddle of liquid was a glass, a third full of what looked like diluted Coke, possibly left over from last night.

She drank at night to fall asleep, just like he'd done the night before.

Then he saw the poster fastened to the ceiling above her bed—a muscle-bound guy, pecs and abs hard and bulging, naked except for a g-string, smiling down at him.

Jazz's dream guy? Someone she wished she could be with? Or have sex with?

What must Jazz have thought about him writing stories about a land without sex now that he saw what she slept under every night? She'd talked about the gender disparity in orgasms during their first conversation while at the time he had never considered the overwhelming desire for sex being a factor in resistance to the Tremarians.

The realization that he'd never thought about sex punched him in the gut. He was seventeen years old, and he couldn't remember having fantasized about a girl—or woman. He couldn't imagine sleeping under a poster of a nude female.

Why?

When he'd seen Jazz's bra on the table and later felt it under her shirt, he'd had a flashback of a woman, possibly his mother, asking him to fasten her bra. All his senses electrified when he felt Jazz's breasts against his chest, but he'd felt more when he saw the woman's bare back. The vision had left him breathless.

It was obvious to him that he had stifled any sexual feelings or desires for years. Why?

Because of something that happened to him. Something sexual that he had forgotten or blocked out of his mind.

Then he noticed two posters of Einstein hanging on the wall across from her bed. One with his tongue touching his chin—nutty and rebellious. The other with a pipe in his mouth—serious and intelligent.

Jazz's personality was complex, to say the least.

Down the hall past the bathroom, he saw another door, slightly ajar—her mother's bedroom. He pushed it open and was immediately hit by the choking smell of stale cigarette smoke. He turned on the light.

He saw two multiple photo frames hanging on the far wall filled with pictures of Jazz and her mother at various ages. He couldn't help walking inside the room.

In the center of one frame was a 5x7 of what must have been Jazz's grandparents holding a baby. A much younger, thinner Jazz and her mother stood next to them.

Who was the baby?

He drank the last of the vodka as he turned around to see if more pictures were displayed. He noticed a pile of CDs and a dusty boom box on the dresser.

Excitement trickled into his chest, fluttering his heart.

He felt an uncontrollable urge to look at the CDs. His trembling fingers pushed through the pile until he saw the blood-red cover for the *Mothership* album.

The name pulsed in his brain, edged by flashing lights and gyrating bodies.

He removed the disk and read the song titles, hearing beats and a voice embedded in each of the words.

The title of number five—"Whole Lotta Love"—thumped his chest and he held his breath until he could slip the disk under the slowly rising lid and slam it down before it reached its apex.

Hunter pressed the button until "5" appeared on the screen, hit 'Play,' and cranked the volume knob all the way to the right.

* * * * * *

When Jazz jogged through the gym into the locker room, she noticed Drew laughing with Eric as Coach Harris led the group in stretching exercises.

Eric must have come in while she was talking to Drew and walked right past Hunter while he typed his story.

As she sat in front of her locker unlacing her boots, Hunter's story on the bench next to her, she heard the toilet flush right after a retching sound. A few seconds later, she heard another flush. Tatiana came out of a stall holding a toothbrush and saw Jazz. Tatiana palmed the brush against her arm as she smiled at Jazz.

"Are you sick?" asked Jazz as she pulled on her sneakers.

"Something I ate, I guess." She seemed a little unsteady as she walked to her locker. Hiding the opening with her body, the hand holding the brush darted to the top shelf. She shut the door and turned to see Jazz looking at her.

"Questions?" Tatiana asked.

Jazz shook her head. She thought Tatiana could be a model: tall, thin, pretty. She didn't know she purged until today, using a toothbrush to make her gag. Now she knew why Tatiana was often late to PE or had to use the restroom frequently during class. Jazz wondered why she'd started. But then why did anyone start anything? Something happened to her.

"Did you hear what Drew told me earlier?" asked Jazz, wondering if she noticed Drew's loss of memory.

"About Eric, the pervert? Yes. And then she seemed to forget what she'd just said."

"She's out there giggling with Eric right now like nothing happened."

"Weird." As Tatiana walked past Jazz, she bent down a little toward the papers on the bench.

Jazz noticed and grabbed the story. "Questions?" She pasted a smile on her lips.

"What's that?"

"A story Hunter wrote. He wants me to read it."

"He wrote about Drew and Eric having a fight?"

Jazz felt a chill spread under her ribs. She couldn't think of anything to say.

"He's a cutie," said Tatiana, "but a little strange for my taste. Toodles." She walked back to the gym.

When Jazz appeared on the court, Harris ordered her to run five laps. Ugh! She was not built for running. As she circled the court, she kept an eye on Drew, trying to decide when and how she would talk to her about the trampoline incident. The angry, disgusted girl who had stomped through the front entrance half an hour ago was now her usual flirty self, taking every opportunity to make sure Eric kept his attention on her.

After the laps and drills to prepare for the upcoming track meet, Harris gave them a water break. Drew walked into the locker room, so Jazz followed.

She headed toward the sink as Drew closed a stall door. Jazz splashed some water on her face and pulled out a few paper towels.

"Hey, Drew. I've been thinking about that story you told me before class."

"What're you talking about, Jazz?"

"About Eric watching Kelly and Skylar jumping on the trampoline."

"OK. When did this happen?"

"You told me before class. You yelled at Eric in the parking lot and ran in here."

"What're you smokin', Jazz? Hey, I got to crap, so could you hurry up and leave?"

"Sure, Drew."

Jazz left the room and headed for the court.

Eric walked toward her. "Where's Drew?"

"Taking a dump."

"Why don't you ever change clothes for PE? It's disgusting to sit in your sweaty clothes all afternoon."

"And have you ogling my boobs? Oh, that's right, you like looking at little girls' boobs. Especially when they bounce." Jazz walked away.

"Hey! Bi ...."

Jazz turned. "Please say it, Eric. Then none of us would have to see you tomorrow. Maybe for three days."

She had been needled about not changing for PE for years. But wearing a gym uniform would cause even more comments. Her mother had finally talked to Patty, explaining that Jazz had an embarrassing skin condition, so staff stopped bothering her, but kids like Eric still gave her a hard time occasionally. She wished the problem were merely a skin condition.

Jazz heard a swarm of kids enter the gym and turned around. The 7th graders grabbed basketballs from a rack and launched them toward three baskets on the far end of the court. Various grades shared the court during the day, especially when snow covered most of the playground.

She saw Kelly and Skylar playing one-on-one and walked toward them.

"Hey, Kelly! Drew told me you got to use your trampoline at lunch today. Bet that was fun." Jazz wondered if the girls had noticed Eric watching them.

Kelly held the ball and seemed ready to blurt out an angry comment, but swallowed it. She sighed. "It was OK."

Jazz let out a breath and took a chance. "Would've been better if Eric hadn't stared at you, huh?"

Kelly's eyes widened. "How'd you know?"

"Drew told me. Did you know he shot photos of you?"

"No! That creep!"

"Drew made him delete them."

She ran up to Jazz. "You sure?"

"You want to ask her? Let's go."

As Jazz led the girls toward the locker room, she noticed Eric was playing basketball at one of the side baskets.

Drew had just emerged from the locker room. She smiled at her sister. "Hey, Sis! What's up?"

"Eric was taking pictures of us while we jumped on the trampoline?"

Drew's brow wrinkled in confusion.

"Yes," said Jazz. "Drew caught him doing it from the porch."

"Your boyfriend's a creep, Drew," said Kelly. "After he got the snow off, he wouldn't leave."

"Yeah," said Skylar. "We told him to go away a bunch of times before he actually did."

"That's what you told me before class, Drew," said Jazz. She pulled the folded papers from her back pocket and held them out. For a second, she hesitated, wondering whether Drew needed to read the story, but she worried her full memory wouldn't return unless she did. "Please go read this . . . by yourself. I typed up what you told me."

Drew took the papers slowly then looked over at Eric.

Jazz noticed Tatiana watching them out of the corner of her eye.

"C'mon, girls," said Jazz, "let's get back before Ms. Sally gets mad." She walked with them back to their class.

Tatiana walked up to her just as Jazz turned around.

"Well, that was interesting," said Tatiana. "I thought Hunter wanted you to read that story, not give it to Drew."

Jazz cleared her throat and tried to smile. "His story's in my locker."

"So Drew told you about Eric then forgot. And the first two lines of Hunter's story are about Eric and Drew having a fight. At least that's what I read. Is Drew going to remember now?"

Jazz wiped her sweaty hands on her pants and looked around to see if anyone looked their way. "I hope so, for her sister and Skylar's sake. Don't you?"

Tatiana moved closer to Jazz and reduced her volume. "Yeah, but why did she forget what just happened? She was mad about what he did at her house. Then she came to school and told you. Then forgot. And now you give her a story that Hunter wrote . . . When did he write the story?"

Should she deny and walk away? Or would that cause her to talk to Drew about what had happened? She looked at pretty Tatiana whom no one would suspect to be purging every day and knew she had something she'd like to forget. Jazz weighed her desire to protect Hunter with Tatiana's obvious need for help. "He wrote it while Drew was telling me the story."

"He was in the locker room?"

"No, he was in the lobby outside the gym."

"Then how could he . . . ? She looked away from Jazz then back at her. "What are you and Hunter doing?"

"Maybe something you'd like to know about, Tatiana. Maybe we can talk later about it?" She searched Tatiana's eyes, trying to break through the happy façade she always projected. "We both hide things we do to ourselves from other people. For reasons we don't want others to know. Reasons we'd like to forget."

Tatiana's face relaxed, losing the ever-present smile and cocked eyebrows. "Can we?"

"Maybe. I'll talk to you later. Can we keep each other's secrets for now?"

"Sure."

Later, Jazz noticed Drew shouting at Eric by her locker, calling him a pervert. Tatiana watched as well then walked over to Jazz. "Guess she remembered, huh?"

During the next two classes, Jazz could feel Eric's glare burning her back.

After school, she made sure she got to Bentley's office before he did to avoid any confrontation with him in the hall. Bentley told her to sit down in one corner of his office. A minute later, Eric entered.

"You're late," Bentley barked.

"Had a problem with my girlfriend. Sorry."

Bentley pointed to a chair. Eric sat.

Jazz had opened her computer and began a search about memory loss. She noticed that she hadn't closed Hunter's story about Eric, which she'd read in math class. The Word document appeared on the left side of her screen, overlapped partially by her Safari window.

Eric jerked his computer lid up and stabbed his trackpad.

After another minute, Bentley stood. "I'll be right back. No talking while I'm gone." He left his office.

Eric glared. "What did you tell her?" he growled.

Jazz looked up and smiled. Then put her finger to her lips. "Shhh."

"She was fine until you talked to her! Bitch!"

"Eric!" yelled Patty from her desk. "Shut your mouth. I just added ten minutes to your detention."

Eric ground his teeth and turned his desk toward the wall.

Jazz inadvertently clicked on Hunter's story, bringing it to the front. She looked over the story for a few seconds.

Bentley returned, sat at his desk, then opened his computer. After a few minutes, he looked at Jazz. "Where did you get that, Jazz?"

Jazz's stomach locked and fear burned her chest.

"Don't lie to me. I can see it on my screen."

Eric turned toward Jazz.

"I got it in an email," said Jazz.

"I told Hunter to delete his file," said Bentley.

"He did, but he'd already sent me a copy. I'm sorry. I should have deleted it."

Bentley looked at both of them. "Since you're both here, I want an explanation about this story. Eric, what do you know about this?"

Eric shook his head. "I have no idea what you're talking about."

Bentley nodded to Jazz. "Send it to my printer."

Jazz pressed keys and soon the printer behind Bentley churned out the document. He picked up the pages, looked them over, and gave them to Eric. "This is the story Ms. Tucker read on Hunter's computer this morning."

As Eric read the first page, his face turned red. He looked up briefly after turning to the second page, then hid his face behind the papers. Slowly he put the papers down on his desk and looked to the ceiling.

Jazz felt her chest pounding as she snuck a few quick looks at Eric reading.

"Eric?" asked Bentley. "Where did Hunter get this story?"

"From my head, sir. I never talked to him. I don't know how he could possibly have known . . ."

Bentley sat forward in his chair. "That you fantasized about Ms. Tucker?"

"Yes, sir. But I said nothing to him. Or to anyone." He glared at Jazz.

Bentley turned to her. "Why did he send you a copy?"

Jazz swallowed and tried to keep her voice calm. "I think he was scared when Ms. Tucker started to read it. We're friends."

"Who else knows about this story?" asked Bentley.

"Just Hunter, me, Ms. Tucker, and Eric," said Jazz. "No one else."

"And it will remain that way," said Bentley. "Jazz delete that file and the email. Eric, give that back to me." Eric handed him the papers. He looked sternly at both of them. "Neither of you will speak about this again. Jazz, you will tell Hunter the same."

"Yes, sir," Jazz replied.

"Jazz, your time is up. You can leave."

Jazz rose and left the office. As she walked to her car, she realized she had made three big mistakes: Tatiana saw the story about Eric after lunch, Drew read it, and Jazz was caught reading the one about Eric and Tucker. Why did she have to do that? She hoped she hadn't made Hunter's life more difficult.

"Jazz!" Tatiana waved her hand out of her car window then opened the door. "You said we could talk later, so I waited for you."

"Hey, Tatiana."

"I'm sure you noticed Drew and Eric after you gave her that story."

"Yes."

"Would she have remembered what happened during lunch if she hadn't read it?"

"Probably not. We're not sure yet."

"We? As in you and Hunter?"

"Yeah. Listen, Tatiana, this is all new for us. We're still trying to figure things out. Maybe after another day we'll know more about this. Can you come to my house for lunch tomorrow?"

"Sure. Did you and Hunter make Drew forget what happened?"

"Hunter did, but he wasn't trying to. He saw Drew's memory in his mind."

Tatiana sucked in her lips and scrunched her eyes. "How?"

"We don't know, but it keeps happening."

"Can Hunter take a memory from me?"

Jazz watched her bite her bottom lip as she locked onto her eyes. *This girl is desperate.* Would Hunter want Jazz to protect his secret or give him the chance to help her? She thought she knew the answer. "I think so. He can try."

Tatiana grabbed Jazz's hand. "OK. I'll be there tomorrow."

"Can we keep this between us?"

"Yeah. Just like you'll keep my secret?"

Jazz nodded.

"Thanks." She squeezed Jazz's hand then returned to her car.

Jazz waved as she pulled away. *Will she tell anyone else?*

CHAPTER THIRTEEN

The most famous riff in the world (how did he know that?) pounded from the speakers: Jimmy Page on guitar first, then John Paul Jones on bass, then the voice of Robert Plant screaming the words. He was surprised he knew their names. By the time John Bonham crashed into the mix with his drums, Hunter's hips were undulating to the beat beneath hands reaching to the ceiling, nodding his head, mouthing the lyrics.

He turned around, still dancing, closing his eyes, feeling the music fill every part of his body. He felt loose, lithe, electrified!

He turned again, opened his eyes, and saw her dancing in the mirror—a beautiful blonde woman, shaking her long hair from shoulder to shoulder, piercing him with her dagger blue eyes as she directed every word of the song to him through blood-red lips, jerking her hips with each lift of her heel, pointing at him with long, red fingernails.

Her large breasts swayed unrestrained beneath her cut-off t-shirt. She turned, put her hands on her hips, and shook her ass, barely covered by yoga shorts.

Hunter was hypnotized, staring at her, panting his breaths. She moved out of the mirror during the instrumental section like an animal on the prowl, grinning with malice and seduction, shimmying so close to him he could feel her warmth and inhale her scent of patchouli and rose petals. She bent toward him, forcing him to lean back with her hands on his chest. Then he leaned toward her as she bent back, shaking her shoulders, moving her breasts beneath her shirt.

They both held their hands above their shoulders as they turned around slowly, rotating their heads, humping their pelvises as Plant's orgasmic shouts filled their ears. When Bonham brought the simulated sex to a close with a roll through his drums, Hunter and the woman jumped side by side and thrust their hips toward each other with each pair of crashing drums and guitars before Page launched into his solo. They jumped around and did the same hip crunch from the other side—six times—before Plant's voice rose above the din.

Hunter and the woman twirled around each other, eyes locked, as they shook and shimmied. The woman's hands flung wildly, often raking across his ass or his genitals. When Plant roared in ecstasy toward the end, the woman screamed, "Shake for me!" The woman shook her shoulders and hips. Hunter stared at her chest, hypnotized.

"Shake, Baby!" she screamed at him. She reached for his hips and jerked them back and forth, allowing her hands to wander. Hunter gasped, backed away, but she followed, repeating everything she'd done previously.

As the song ended, the woman smiled at him slyly as she looked directly at his erection. She moved back into the mirror, purposely swaying her hips, and laughing. Hunter couldn't help watching her butt as the quiet strumming of the next song started.

He was about to shout something at her—

"Hunter?"

He jerked his head around to see Jazz standing in the doorway, smiling as her eyes moved below his waist.

Now she was staring. "What were you doing?"

Hunter looked down and realized his erection was pushing out his pants.

He lunged toward the boom box and stopped the music.

"I'm sorry." He kept his body facing the dresser, trying not to think of what pressed against the drawer handle.

"How come you never told me you could dance? You were amazing."

"How long were you standing there?" he said as he fumbled with the disk and placed it into the case. He felt lightheaded as he shuffled his feet.

"Since the guitar solo. My mother played that album all the time."

"Oh my god." He grasped his head. "I'm so sorry. I shouldn't have come in here."

She leaned against the door jam. "True, but I would have done the same. After you left, I thought what I would do if you sent me to your house by myself. I'd have to look around because I care about you and want to know you better." She moved toward him. "You're a good dancer, Hunter. Did you teach yourself, or did someone . . . "

The realization of who the woman was slammed into him. He looked at the mirror and saw the horror on his face—his eyes bulging and his mouth open to scream. His heart raced while his stomach churned. His knees buckled, and he slumped to the floor.

He and his mother had danced to that song all the time.

"Hunter!" Jazz blurted as she ran to him. "Are you sick?"

"My mother," he cried. "She taught me. We used to dance together to that song almost every day."

He could feel the shock sparking through Jazz's brain.

"You danced like that with her?" Jazz said slowly with barely a hint of the disgust Hunter thought she felt.

"I saw her in the mirror, and then suddenly she was dancing next to me. I couldn't remember what she looked like before now."

Jazz reached for him.

"Don't touch me!" he shouted, moving away from her. "I'm sorry, I just . . . I can't." He ran a shaking hand through his hair. "I felt so good dancing. Then she kept touching me like it was an accident. She was trying to arouse me, teasing, like she wasn't doing it on purpose. She wore no bra and short shorts." His face twisted in pain. "I didn't want her to leave, but I felt so embarrassed. I felt dirty, but she laughed at me. What the hell? She wanted her thirteen-year-old son to get a boner over her!"

"I'm sorry, Hunter."

"Do you think that's really what my mother did to me? Or maybe that's what I wanted her to do and felt guilty for wanting that?"

"I don't know, Hunter. I think it means you knew her behavior was wrong. Did you try to touch her?"

"No. But I wanted to. I kept staring at her body."

"Maybe it was the vodka you drank."

Hunter's eyes widened as he jumped to his feet. He saw the shot glass and quickly grabbed it.

"I already saw it, Hunter. How much did you drink?"

"Not much." He looked to the floor. "I think I used to drink back then. I think she drank more. I don't know whether she gave it to me or maybe I sneaked it. How did you start?"

Jazz looked away. "I snuck it at first just because Mom and her boyfriends drank and partied all the time. Then it got to be a crutch because of . . . things that happened to me."

"How much do you drink now?"

Jazz averted her eyes. "More than I should."

He watched her face turn red. "I'm sorry, Jazz. I'm not judging you. I'm just surprised."

"Yeah," she scoffed. "Guess I'm just like my mom." She sat on the bed. "I drink at night so I can sleep. No other time. Well, today at lunch, but usually just at night. I can't stop my mind when I get into bed. Things from the past keep swirling around. Now four shots of vodka and Coke knock me out until morning."

He sat on the bed next to her. "I found my dad's whiskey yesterday and drank some for the same reason. I wondered why it was easy for me to drink. Then I tried the vodka. Same thing. Easy."

"Did your mother drink?"

"Yeah."

"Maybe she was drunk when she danced with you."

"Would that have made it better?"

"No, but it might mean she realized what she did was wrong." She reached for his hand. "Everyone feels their own pain, Hunter. But we all respond in similar ways. We either hurt ourselves, or others, or both. The one thing you can count on in life is feeling pain."

"Or nothing."

"Or nothing. Which can be worse." She shook her head. "I recently read a survey of teens. Seventy percent consider anxiety and depression to be major problems with their peers. I wonder who that thirty percent are who have happy friends."

They stared at each other through the mirror. Hunter wondered what she really felt about him.

Jazz stood up from the bed. "But feeling hunger is usually easier to deal with. You hungry?"

Hunter laughed. "Even if I was, you don't have a clean plate in the house."

"Then help me wash them. I was expecting to come home to a clean kitchen. You can imagine my disappointment." She grabbed his hand. "Let's get out of here. I can't stand the smell of cigarettes."

She led him down the hall to her room and stopped, raising her brows and giving him a sly look. "Did you go in here?"

"No, but I looked inside."

"So you saw Alessandro?" She pointed up, laughing. "He's seen . . . way too much. Lucky he can't talk." She said wistfully, "Though sometimes I wish he could."

"What would you want him to say?"

Jazz sighed deeply as her eyes found Hunter's then looked to the floor. "I'd want . . . I'd want him to say, 'Despite everything, I love you.'" She held his hands and blinked a few tears from her eyes. "Hunter, I hope when you see my memories, you won't run away."

"You didn't run from me when you saw mine. Despite everything so far, you're still my friend." He kissed her hand.

She smiled. "And I am yours—so far." She kissed his hand.

CHAPTER FOURTEEN

During their dinner of canned beef stew and bread, Jazz told Hunter what had happened with Tatiana, Drew, and Eric. She was worried Eric would confront Hunter the next day, and she thought Bentley would be extra nosy watching their computers. What would happen when Hunter wrote another story at school?

Hunter washed their bowls in the sink. "I won't go tomorrow. Patty thinks I'm sick, and Dad wants me to stay home. But once he finds out I see memories from people near me, I don't think he'll want us to be in the same house." He gave her a bowl.

"Why?" She dried the bowl with a towel.

"He doesn't want me to find out what happened. I'll see it, just like I saw him having sex with Parker."

"OK. You two are in the same house tonight, and he leaves for work. Then what would you do?"

"I'll drive over here." He gave her another bowl and some spoons.

"Why?"

He flung water and suds off his hands. "Think I'll find out what Alessandro knows."

She dried the bowl. "He's not real, silly."

"But you are. You can stay home, too."

Jazz put her hand on her hip and raised her eyebrows. "Are you asking me for a date?"

"Yup. We can sit in the living room. You'll relive your horrible memories, and I'll try to get rid of them."

"You really want to try?"

"Yes. And I promise not to run away."

"Cool. I'll make us breakfast." She hung up the towel, put away the bowls, and closed the cabinet. "I invited Tatiana for lunch. She wants you to try and delete a memory. Wonder what it's about?"

"What they're all about. Something bad that she did or someone did to her." He dried his hands. "Do you have any explanation for why this is happening to me?"

"Actually, I think I do. I revisited some of the articles I used for my project and found others during sixth period. Most scientists believe memories are stored in the brain, that each experience causes the formation of neural networks, but no one has found a specific area of the brain where specific memories are stored. Others think memories are holographs—like the projection of Princess Leia in Star Wars—formed by the entire brain. And like holographs, each part of the memory contains the entire memory, so brain damage doesn't necessarily result in a loss of memory."

Hunter scratched his head. "Which theory do you believe?"

She felt a surge of adrenaline as she moved toward him. "Well, there's another interesting idea. Memories might be stored outside the brain in another dimension like a halo around us and are linked to every other memory, forming a collective unconscious or a source of dreams where memories interact. I love this idea!" Her scalp tingled.

"So the brain transmits and receives memories. Once you form a memory, it remains linked to the brain that experienced it. Your memory or fantasy is entangled with your specific brain, so when you recall it, the memory plays again in your head. It's like backing up your movies to the cloud and then restoring them on your phone. You get *your* movies back, not someone else's, because each digital sequence begins with your specific combination of 1s and 0s. Does this make sense?"

"Yeah. It's amazing."

She clapped her hands. "Cool. Your brain, for whatever reason, can't recall its memories. The codes no longer match between your memory and your brain. Or, actually, your brain no longer seeks a specific code. It now accepts almost any code. But—and here's the really interesting part—the only memories you receive have some connection with the content or theme of the memories you lost."

She felt a flush of excitement as an idea hit her. "Which is why so many of your stories deal with sex, but not just any sex. Your mother may or may not have abused you, but something happened which is abnormal between a mother and son, so the memories you capture deal with sex between a teacher and student, or creepy Eric getting off on twelve-year-old girls. There's a reason why none of your memories, so far, have depicted a happy reunion or a big sports victory. They don't connect to your lost memories."

She looked at him thoughtfully. "It's like your brain is searching for your memories but can only find related ones."

"Then why did I see my mother dancing with me?"

"Because that song was a trigger. It was so strong it overrode whatever your brain does to block your memories."

Hunter threw up his hands. "Which is why Dad got rid of all the photos, or hid them. And my old clothes. And the CDs. He wanted nothing to trigger my memories."

She nodded. "All of your stories came from someone you were next to at one time or another. And they were probably thinking about that memory which then appeared in your mind. You're not grabbing memories from someone in California, for instance. You saw Drew's memory because we were near her, and she was obviously thinking about what had happened."

"So why did I see your memory of shooting at Leon?"

She took a breath and pondered his question before replying. "Some possibilities might be because I was defending my mother. Because she was drinking. Because the sex between her and Leon would be abusive, and I prevented that from happening. Maybe you prevented your mother from being taken advantage of—"

"Or maybe someone prevented me from having sex with her. Maybe Leon is me. That'd be ironic as hell wouldn't it?" He shook his head.

"We won't know until you regain your memories, or I read through all your stories and try to decipher the connections."

"When I receive a person's memory, they forget it. Why?"

"Just an idea, but I think once the memory plays in your head, it becomes entangled, meaning the memory becomes yours. It's now linked and coded to your brain only. When you received Drew's memory and Eric's fantasy, they wouldn't recall it anymore. Like they sent a video to your phone and can't grab it back."

"But phones send a copy, not the original. So they keep the video.

"True. But if the brain doesn't store memories, then it has no copy. So they lose the memory until they read your story. Once their brain sees the event, it's now coded to that brain. You each have a copy in your separate minds."

He nodded and smiled. "You're a genius. But if this happened to me, surely it's happened before. How can I be the first?"

"We don't know that you are."

"OK. Then why me?"

"Ask your dad what treatment you received. You said you don't remember anything from more than a year ago, so why did that happen? How? I looked that up, too. There are different methods to treat PTSD, but the most extreme is electroconvulsive therapy—shock treatment. You don't remember an operation or being in the hospital?"

"No. Shock treatment? How bad was I that Dad thought I needed that?"

"You should ask him."

"*We* should ask him."

"You want me with you?"

"Yeah. First, I don't trust driving by myself right now. I could hallucinate again or decide to run off the road. Second, I need you with me. I don't want to do this by myself."

Jazz felt happy he wanted to be with her. She had no desire to be alone either. She smiled and grabbed her pack then stopped. "What happens when you bring me back here? You'd still have to drive back to your house after dropping me off."

"We'll see. Just ride with me. Please."

"Does your dad even know who I am?" She hoped he did, that Hunter had talked about her.

"I don't think so. We barely talk."

"Is he going to be upset that I know about your stories?"

"I can't remember the last time I saw him happy, so more unhappiness shouldn't bother him. Wait a minute." He ran back to her mom's bedroom and returned with the *Mothership* album.

"I don't think you should play that while you're driving."

"I don't intend to. I want to show it to him."

"Why?"

"To prove that I know something about Mom. Maybe he'll tell me more."

They climbed into the truck, and soon Hunter drove out of town. Jazz had never been driven by a guy and never gone on a date before. Of course, she'd also never had a boy in her house either.

Watching him dance was amazing. The only thing that kept her from joining him was embarrassment. It was one thing to dance alone with Alessandro. It was quite another to shake her body in front of a real boy, especially one she liked. She always hid her figure behind clothes and forced others to focus on her big personality full of wit and sarcasm and intelligence. But dancing put her body front and center. She had tried practicing moves in the mirror, but soon grew tired with self-disgust. Being large and luscious was one thing. Being scarred and scabbed was another.

How wonderful it must feel to move your body to music without inhibitions, without any worry of criticism! That feeling shouldn't be restricted to the beautiful and talented.

Her phone buzzed. She pulled it out of her pack and looked at the screen. She'd received a news alert about a school shooting.

Jazz scanned the headlines. "There's been a shooting at a school dance in Washington, outside Bremerton."

"I used to live near there." He passed a slow-moving sedan.

"The shooter was a sophomore. He brought a pistol to a dance in the gym. Shot students and adults. Doesn't say how many."

"Did they catch him?"

"He's dead. Though it doesn't say whether he killed himself or the police shot him."

"That's crazy. Did he have mental issues?"

She looked over her phone at him. "We all have mental issues, Hunter."

"Yeah, but not enough to shoot students at a dance."

"Hopefully, that's true."

Hunter frowned. "You think something like that could happen here?"

"Easily."

"But you can't get into the school building without Patty checking you out on the video screens."

"How does that keep a student from bringing a gun to school in his pack? I've done it a few times by accident."

He jerked the wheel as he snapped his head toward her. "You brought a gun to school?" The wheels bounced over the rumble grooves.

"Stay on the road, Hunter." He moved the truck back to the left. "I always carry my pistol." She lifted her pack. "I usually leave it in the car during school, but sometimes I forget."

"Whoa. You're full of surprises, Jazz."

"And you aren't?"

"OK, but I don't carry a gun."

"Then I'll protect you. I will never be helpless against an attack." *Not again*, she thought.

Jazz saw Hunter glancing at her from her periphery. She propped one foot against the glove compartment, chewed on her thumbnail, and stared out the windshield. "A lot of people carry guns in Alaska, Hunter. In the grocery store, Subway, the bookstore, strapped to their leg or stuck in their belt."

"When did you get a gun?"

"I took it from my grandparents when I was twelve."

"You took it?"

"Yeah. I needed it." She looked at him. "That's one of the memories I want to forget." She broke eye contact and looked down the road. "The mountain's out."

Denali, the highest mountain in North America, shone pink against the sky thirty-five miles away. Covered with snow year around, it rose 18,000 feet from base to peak, a higher rise than Mt. Everest. A single dark cloud hid its peak.

Hunter slowed the truck and pulled onto the shoulder. "That's pretty. I've seen it just a few times."

Jazz sat up. "You never know when the mountain will reveal itself. It can stay hidden for weeks, then boom, it's in your face, filling up the sky." She turned toward him. "Kind of like the truth. It may hide for a while, but it'll jump out and bite you when you least expect it to."

Hunter looked through the windshield. "Like finding out how my Mom and I danced together."

"You're not sure that's the whole truth. I think it's a lot more complicated than what you think."

"Whatever it is, I want to know." He checked for traffic, and pulled back onto the highway.

Jazz removed her glasses to wipe the lenses. "Have you ever been to the park?"

"No. Just my house, the school, and Fairbanks."

"Mom took me a couple of times. We should go to Wonder Lake together in June. The mountain sits right across from the campground. At dawn, it's pink like that and so much bigger." She put her glasses back on and gazed at him. "I would love to see it with you."

"Did you just ask me for a date?"

"The second time today."

Hunter scrunched his brows.

Jazz smiled. "Lunch?"

"Oh yeah. And now I'm taking you to my house to meet my dad. We're getting to be a regular couple."

They smiled at each other as Hunter turned off the highway toward his house. After a few minutes, he pulled into his driveway.

"He's not here."

Hunter parked his truck and got out.

Jazz opened her door and saw a small, one-story manufactured house, faded blue with an old composition roof held together by clumps of moss. Snow lay in patches around the sides, punctuated by birch and spruce.

"Come in," called Hunter, holding the door open for her.

Once inside, she saw bare walls separating a few windows covered with mini-blinds and short, ragged curtains. The ceiling was suspended with several panels stained yellow and brown from leaks in the roof. The place looked neat due to the absence of things, not their arrangement.

"Certainly much neater than my house," Jazz said. "You must've been horrified walking into mine."

"I liked it. Your personality is everywhere."

Jazz walked around, looking. "You've lived here for how long?"

"About nine months."

Jazz realized how blank a slate Hunter's life was. Nothing she saw gave clues about the people who lived there.

"Show me your room."

Hunter opened his bedroom door and switched on the light. His bed was unmade, but otherwise his room could have been inhabited by hundreds of different people. Nothing indicated Hunter, other than the void in that room.

"Where's all your stuff? Do you have things in storage, or is this everything?"

"What we had in storage burned before we moved up here. At least, that's what Dad claims." He sat on his bed. "I don't believe him." He pointed to the opposite wall. "I had dozens of stories pinned to that wall this morning. I wonder if he read them all."

Jazz walked to his dresser and opened the top drawer.

"Looking for something?"

She turned to him revealing an evil smile. "Your secrets."

She removed a pile of underwear and unfolded a few pair. They were stretch boxer briefs in gray and steel blue. "Hmmm." She held one up. "Size medium. Gray, gray, gray, blue, gray, gray. Where's the striped red ones? Or the skimpy tight briefs?"

"Sorry."

"Well, that's not very exciting." She opened another drawer. "Oh, t-shirts. And look at the colors. Gray, gray, gray, brown, tan, gray. Mostly long-sleeved."

Hunter suddenly grabbed his head.

"What's happening?" She went to him.

He looked at her with pained eyes. "Another story. I need to sit down."

He pulled his computer out of his pack and put it on his desk. Jazz stood behind him, lightly massaging his shoulders.

She tried to see what he typed as beads of sweat gathered on her forehead. It had to be one of her memories. But which one?

And what would he think of her afterward?

CHAPTER FIFTEEN

Hunter didn't just hear pounding this time. He heard the opening riff of "Whole Lotta Love" accented by a ball slammed against a wall, repeatedly. He saw himself walking down the hall and stopping at the door. From inside, he heard his voice yelling, "No!" And scuffling. Then her voice: "Dammit, Hunter!" Then silence. Hunter turned away from the door and walked to the end of the hall, which turned into another long hallway. He saw a frightened girl standing at the edge of a kitchen, listening.

She wore a robe, which she clutched tight against her pre-teen body. She heard a slap and her mother screaming at the other end of the mobile home.

"Mom," she said through gritted teeth. Her mother yelled again. The girl bit her fist.

Hunter stopped. That was Jazz, much younger. "You need to sit on the bed."

He turned his head to look at her.

"Why?"

"Please."

Jazz sat down and watched him. Hunter angled the computer screen away from her.

Jazz heard her mother again. "Micah! I don't feel good. Please wait 'till after the baby is born. Please."

"You look like shit anyway. Why would anyone want to screw you?"

The girl heard the door slam and the woman crying. At the sound of footsteps, she backed down the hallway.

She heard the sounds of Micah stumbling in the kitchen and kicking a chair. "Dammit!" he yelled.

She heard ice fill a glass, maybe two. Then a soda can popped open. She knew those sounds. He would drink then come to her room.

Her heart raced as she walked silently and quickly down the long hall and into her bedroom at the opposite end of the mobile home. After closing the door behind her, she reached under the pillow and pulled out a pistol. Shaking violently in one hand, the gun pointed toward her door as she gritted her teeth.

"Jasmine," Micah sang the word. "Jasmine. Such a beautiful name for such a beautiful girl."

Jasmine couldn't stop shaking. What would they do to her if she shot him? Maybe she could talk him out of wanting sex with her. She'd done it before. She pushed the gun under her pillow.

"Jas . . . mine." He knocked. "Hey, you up, sweetie? I brought you a drink. Thought we could share a little drink together."

Her voice quavered. "I'm really tired, Micah. Think I have a fever."

"That makes two of us, sweetie. Thinking about your beautiful ass makes me burn all over." He opened the door and staggered into her room. "Brought you something." He put the vodka bottle and two glasses of ice and Coke on her dresser.

Jazz thought he looked disgusting with greasy long hair, scraggly beard framing his jawline and wide lips, which never seemed to close entirely.

"Momma's due any day, Micah," Jazz whimpered.

"Yeah, but she said that two weeks ago." He poured vodka into each glass.

"She's overdue. The doctor said if she doesn't start labor by tomorrow, he'll induce her."

"Good to know," grumbled Micah, "but that doesn't help me tonight."

Jasmine shook she was so nervous. A tear ran down her cheek as she gripped her robe tighter together.

He held out a glass to her. "Go on. Take it." He smiled. "And why are you looking so scared? You act like this is the first time, Jasmine."

She squeezed tears out of her eyes as her heart tried to jump through her chest. She'd told herself she would never let him screw her again. Her mouth was bone dry. She reached for the glass and took a sip.

"There you go. Drink whatever you want. Loosen up, girl." He downed his drink and began to unbutton his shirt.

The glass clattered against her teeth as she took another sip. "You told me you wouldn't do this again. You promised me you'd leave Momma alone if I did it."

"Yes, I did, but you felt so good." He moved his eyes from her waist to her face, his head bobbling on his neck. "And you seemed to like it." He struggled with the buttons. "I can still hear you groaning." He chuckled then yanked his shirt open, sending buttons bouncing on the floor.

She backed away. "It hurt like hell, and I'm still bleeding!"

"It always hurts the first time." He unbuckled his pants.

"It hurt more the second time!"

"Get drunk enough and you won't feel anything." He pulled down his pants.

"You promised me!" she screamed.

"She promised she wouldn't be pregnant by now. Take off your robe. You know you want to. You just want to scream a little so you can tell yourself you tried to stop me. 'Cause you don't want to admit the truth. You liked it, Jasmine. I could tell."

He chuckled to himself as he tried to pull off his pants, stumbling as he pulled his feet out. Then he smiled and walked closer.

She drank a big swallow and tried to control her breathing. She wanted her hand to stop shaking.

"There you go. Finish it off."

She drank the rest and felt ready. She smiled at him. "You were right, Micah. I really want to do this. More than anything I've ever done."

His grin spread across his face as his tongue hung on his lower lip.

She let her robe fall open, revealing her underwear. She watched his eyes leer at her. It was so easy to distract this scumbag.

Forcing her voice to sound smooth and alluring, she placed a hand on her hip. "There's some lotion on my dresser. Can you get it, Micah? It would make it easier for both of us."

"Sure thing, sweetie."

He turned around and walked toward the dresser. Jasmine reached under her pillow and pulled out her pistol.

"Where is it, Jasmine? I don't see—"

She pulled back the hammer and held the gun in front of her with both hands, focused, eager to pull the trigger.

He jerked his head around, saw the gun, and pointed at her. "What the hell?"

She snarled. "That's where you belong, Micah."

She fired at his chest. The sound was much louder than she'd expected, but she didn't drop the gun.

He grunted and staggered back against the dresser. His eyes widened as Jasmine took two steps closer. His blood seeped into his shirt and through his fingers.

"Please . . . don't . . ."

Her throat burned as her eyes bored into him. Her finger tightened on the trigger as she spoke slowly, hatred dripping from each word. "How many times did I say, 'Please don't' to you?"

He held out his hand, trying to block the bullet. "I'm sorry, Jazz. I'm sorry!"

"Not sorry enough."

She fired again, and he fell to the floor with a bloody grunt.

Jasmine held the gun in front of her, pointing at him. His leg twitched. He moaned. Then silence.

She wanted to scream, to hide under the covers, but they had to leave. Now.

"Jazzy!" her mother shouted. "Were those gunshots?"

Jasmine looked down the hall at her mother struggling to move toward her in her nightgown.

"I killed him, Momma."

Her mother's eyes widened.

"Why? What did he do to you?"

"He raped me twice, and I wouldn't let him do it again." Her chin quivered. "I . . . tried to keep him away from you, but he . . . he wouldn't stop hitting you or raping me." She gulped air.

Her mother walked into the bedroom and saw Micah dead on the floor. She pulled Jazz to her. "I'm so sorry, Jazz."

Jazz wept against her mother.

"We have to leave now, Jazz. Change your clothes. I'll get my hospital suitcase." She pulled Jazz's face away from her and looked into her eyes. "You are so brave, Jasmine. I should've done it myself. Now hurry."

"I'm going to burn him and the trailer." She picked up the vodka bottle.

Her mother held her chest, her eyes bulging. "Yes. That's what we have to do. Wipe your prints off the bottle, Jazz then put it near his hand. But you need to change first."

Her mother hurried down the hall, bracing herself with her hands against the walls.

After changing clothes, Jazz wiped the vodka bottle with her robe and poured the remaining liquor on Micah's clothes. She lay the bottle on the ground next to him then picked up his hand and placed it on the bottle.

She struck a match and tossed it into her room. The whoosh of fire covered Micah instantly. Jasmine ran down the hall, grabbed her mother's suitcase, gave her the car keys, and led her to the front door. "Let's go."

By the time Jasmine threw the suitcase into the back seat and climbed in next to her mother, the end of the trailer was in flames.

They both stared out of the windshield at the fire. Her mother started the car. "Burn in hell, Micah." She backed up, turned around, and accelerated down the driveway.

Jasmine turned around, watching the flames engulf the trailer. Once they left the hills, she could see only a yellow glow, soon swallowed by the dark.

Hunter felt the vein in his neck pulsing. He looked at Jazz and saw her as the little girl she used to be. How could she have lived through that? His skin chilled, forcing him to shudder. His eyes brimmed with tears.

"Are you going to print it?" asked Jazz.

"Not now." He pressed the lid closed.

"Are you stealing one of my memories, Hunter?"

"For now."

"Was it a bad one?"

"They're all bad." He pushed back his chair and stood. "How do you keep from crying all the time?" He wiped a tear and moved to her. "How do you keep from dying?" He held her hands.

Tears gathered in her eyes. "I cry at night. I drink. Sometimes I do other things. But I don't think I need to as much when you're with me."

He held her head and brought it to touch his. "You must be so strong to live with those memories."

"You could take them all away."

"Would you want me to?"

"I don't know. Maybe I could sleep better. But you'd have them instead of me. You're taking everybody's worst moments, their nightmares. How much can you take?"

"I don't know."

"Let me read it, Hunter."

"No. Not now. Maybe not ever. I don't want that in your head anymore."

A flash of headlights crossed the window. They heard tires biting gravel.

"He's home." Hunter grasped her hand and led her to the living room where they stood awaiting Joe's entrance.

CHAPTER SIXTEEN

Hunter felt much more confident dealing with his dad with Jazz by his side. Right now, his father was not helping him. Why would he keep Hunter's past a secret? What was he hiding? He wasn't a caring parent to Hunter. He was the enemy.

Carrying a large bag in one hand, Joe opened the door and stared wide-eyed at Jazz. "Who's this?"

Hunter felt his hands tremble then Jazz's fingers grasping his. He took a deep breath. "Jasmine Williams. Everyone calls her Jazz. She's my best friend. We're in the same grade at school."

"Hello, Jazz. My name's Joe." He reached out his hand.

Jazz smiled and walked toward him. They shook hands. "Nice to meet you, Joe. Your son is an amazing guy."

"Oh really?" He kicked the door shut and put his things on the table. The kitchen was silent except for the lurch of the refrigerator starting another cycle. Joe scrunched his brows at Jazz. "And why is that?"

"One reason among many is that he's seen me at my worst and still wants me as his friend."

A flash of fear crossed his face. "Meaning what?"

"He saw some of my bad memories."

Joe tightened his eyes as he looked at Hunter, shook his head slightly then turned back to Jazz. "You know about the stories?"

"He's written four today."

"Not including the one you were reading this morning," blurted Hunter through gritted teeth. He felt his chest tighten as he looked at his father.

Joe shot a panicked look at Hunter then turned back toward Jazz. "How long have you known about them?"

"Just today."

He looked at Hunter. "Why was telling her a good idea?"

"Because she's my friend, and she cares about me. We actually talk with each other." Hunter couldn't help throwing that dig at his father. They locked eyes.

Joe turned his eyes toward Jazz. "Anyone want coffee? I need some." He inserted a fresh pod into the machine, positioned a cup, and pushed the button.

"I'd like a glass of Jameson, with ice," said Hunter with obvious sarcasm.

Joe coughed and turned around. "When did you start drinking?"

"You know the answer," said Hunter. "Years ago. I just don't know whether Mom gave it to me or I stole it from her."

Joe tried to clear his throat. "You went through my things?"

"Not today. But, yes, I did. Trying to find some answers but found nothing that meant anything to me." Hunter noticed his father relax slightly and smiled, knowing what he was about to throw at him.

"What brought on this need for answers?"

"Because I've been seeing events, or parts of events from my past. That bedroom door with the handle I asked you about? I heard Mom's voice behind it today."

He tightened his lips. "How would you know her voice?"

"Because I saw her today." He pulled the *Mothership* disk out of his shirt pocket and place it face up on the table. Hunter watched his father's eyes bulge. Hunter's voice was less than a whisper, but the silence made it sound like a shout. "We used to dance to this, particularly number five."

Joe gulped a few breaths as he stared at the disk. "Did you find that here?"

"No, you *burned* everything that might be a trigger for my memories. I found it at Jazz's house. In her mother's bedroom."

Joe's hand shook as he spooned sugar into his coffee. "Hunter, please believe me when I tell you that you don't want to know the answers. It's better that those memories are gone." He tossed the spoon onto the counter too hard so it fell onto the floor. He grabbed his neck and squeezed.

"Did my mother abuse me?" Hunter pounded the table. "When we were dancing to 'Whole Lotta Love,' she tried to seduce me. She tried to arouse me. How long did you know about that?"

Joe rubbed his face firmly like he wanted to squeeze out all his pain. "Please, Hunter. Trust me. You don't want to know."

"Trust you?" Hunter felt his heart pounding inside his chest. "I'm sure you lied about the fire. And about your phone." He shoved one of the chairs. "Why should I trust you?"

Joe's hand shook as he tried to sip from his cup. He reached up to hold the cup with his other hand then placed it on the counter. "Has he shown you his scars?" Joe asked Jazz.

Jazz folded her arms. "No."

Hunter was not expecting this question. "What do my scars have to do with anything?"

"So you haven't seen him without his shirt."

Jazz shook her head.

"Hunter," commanded Joe, "take off your shirt."

"Why?" he sputtered. "What does my shirt have to do with what my mother did to me?"

"Please do it. I want you to see one reason why you shouldn't know the answers. Take off your shirt."

Hunter looked at Jazz, who nodded back at him. He slowly unbuttoned his shirt and dropped it to the floor.

Joe folded his arms. "And the t-shirt. Please."

Hunter's chest heaved as he breathed and slowly pulled off his long-sleeve t-shirt. Jazz gasped and covered her mouth with her hands.

Hunter flinched at her sounds and looked at the scars on his arms and chest, rows and rows of discolored ridges and welts.

He turned to Jazz. "I fell off my bike riding downhill on a gravel road. I don't remember when."

"No, Hunter." Jazz walked over and hugged him. "That's not what happened."

"How do you know?"

"Because I have the same scars on my body."

"How?" gasped Hunter.

She touched scars on his chest. "I cut myself, Hunter. You did the same."

"When?" Hunter gaped at his father, who pressed fingers into his eyes and turned away.

Joe blurted the words over his shoulder. "Some before she died. Most afterward. Twice I thought you would bleed to death."

Hunter reached out shaking hands to hold Jazz's shoulders. His throat ached. "You have scars like mine?"

Her face turned red. "More than you. I have them on my legs all the way to my ankles."

Hunter shook his head slowly, his mouth open, trying to speak, but coughing instead. He felt tears filling his eyes. "Why did you cut yourself?"

Her chin quivered. "Because it stops the pain."

He tried to swallow. "How could it stop your pain?"

"Because I can focus on the cut and stop thinking about what's in my head." She clutched him, crying into his neck.

"I'll take every memory of every cut." He touched her arms gently. "I'll see every night or day you did these, and you won't remember anymore."

Jazz smiled through her tears. "Maybe someday you can tell me I had an accident long ago, just like your father told you. He took your memories for the same reason you won't give me back the one you just saw."

Joe turned around. "How did he take your memory?"

Jazz stroked the back of Hunter's head. "When he wrote about my memory, I lost it. I had no recollection of the event. When I read the story, the memory was restored. It's happened three times today."

Hunter pulled back from Jazz and looked at his father. "If you hadn't read that story this morning, you would've forgotten about Parker."

Joe's face lost color as he stared at his son then shot a glance at Jazz before looking to the floor.

"You walked in on a boy in his underwear when you were a teenager. I guess you're ashamed of that and didn't want me to know it, but at least you and the boy agreed to have sex. No one raped you or abused you like I've seen in so many other memories, including my own. Whether you tell me the truth or not, I'll see your memories eventually. When I write them down, you'll forget them, and I'll know the truth." Hunter locked eyes with Joe. "One way or another I'm going to learn the truth. So why don't you tell me?"

Joe gestured toward his son's scars. "Because I don't want to be responsible for more of those, or worse." He rubbed his face. "Look, there may be a way to stop all this. I spoke to your doctor today and described the stories. He told me how to reset your implant."

"He has an implant?" asked Jazz.

"Yes. Don't ask me how it works, but it's supposed to keep those memories from coming back. Ru . . . I mean your doctor said that resetting the chip would eliminate the stories and your memories." Joe wiped his mouth. He clearly had not wanted to say that name.

"Ru?" asked Jazz. "Is that the doctor's name? How did Ru remove his memories?"

"It took three years of therapy. And several different doctors."

"What else? Shock therapy?" asked Jazz.

He sighed and sat down. "Only because nothing else worked."

"Eliminate memories from when?" asked Hunter. "Three years ago or from the time of reset?"

"I don't know, Hunter. After the procedure, you were practically a blank slate. So maybe it would wipe out everything before the reset." He looked at Jazz. "Probably just what was erased last time. I think that's what he said." He moved closer to Hunter. "Do you want the stories to continue, or not?"

Hunter thought his father was trying too hard to sell the reset. Why? Slowly, he asked his father, "Wouldn't you want me to take your memories? How much pain have they caused you?"

Joe rubbed his face. "I would certainly like to forget. I almost asked the doctor to do the same to me as he did to you. But one of us had to know who we were."

Hunter moved toward the table. This didn't make sense. Why wouldn't his father want to forget the same memories that were so damaging to Hunter? Unless his father was hiding something. "OK, but eventually I would see everything you remembered about that time, and your mind would be clear."

Joe looked at his son then picked up one of the spiral-bound books he had made of Hunter's stories. "I read all of these stories today. And now I know that all these bad memories for these people are gone. Are they better off now? We don't know, and how would we find out? But let's assume that not having to remember and relive the night you were raped is a good thing. Are *you* better off for knowing these memories? I don't think you can take on everyone's sins and failures and horrors and remain unaffected. I think we should try the reset."

Hunter shook his head. "Not yet. If nothing else, I'll help Jazz. She doesn't deserve what happened to her. She's a victim just like most of the people in that book." He looked at Jazz. "Can I stay at your place?"

Her eyes widened. "What do you mean?"

"Move in with you. Just for a while."

"Because?"

"For one, Dad doesn't want me seeing his memories. And I want to help you." He reached for her hands. "Also, I need you to help me."

She squeezed his fingers and nodded. "Yes."

"I'll take some of my things tonight and come back tomorrow for some more. Dad, you won't have to worry about me seeing what's inside your head. Is that OK with you?"

He looked at both of them and sighed. "Maybe for a few days." He opened the bag. "There's a new computer in there. You can't be writing these things on school property. Your original stories and another copy of the booklet is in there. Does anyone besides Jazz know about the stories?"

"No," said Jazz quickly. Hunter glanced at her.

Joe stood. "Good. You need to be extra careful about keeping this a secret."

"Why?" asked Hunter.

"Because people will fear you and want you dead or in jail. They'll make an experiment out of you, or line up to have their bad memories deleted. You need to be careful. I'll call Patty tomorrow and say you'll be out for a few days. And here's some cash." He pulled out his wallet and removed some bills. "Jazz's family doesn't want to pay for an extra mouth to feed, I'm sure."

Hunter shook his head. "Jazz doesn't—"

Jazz cut him off. "Thank you, Joe. My mother will appreciate that."

Jazz raised her brows at Hunter.

"You sure she won't mind?" asked Joe.

Jazz smiled. "She likes Hunter. She'd love him to stay with us."

"OK."

Hunter grabbed her hand. "C'mon, Jazz, help me pack." He started to lead her back to his bedroom.

"Hunter." Joe had picked up his shirts. "Why don't you put your shirts back on?" He tossed them to Hunter.

"For you or for Jazz?"

"Both."

Hunter pulled Jazz toward his room. As soon as he closed the door, Jazz grabbed him in a hug. "I can't believe you."

"As soon as I wrote that last story, I knew seeing your memories wasn't a curse. I can help you, Jazz."

"You already have." She touched his cheeks and hair. "Can I kiss you?"

Hunter looked into her green eyes and smiled. "Yes." At that moment he realized he had never been kissed on the lips because he had no idea what to do.

They pressed their lips together gently for several seconds, forcing heat throughout his body, until Jazz moved her cheek against his.

Hunter pressed against her. "I'm sorry. I'm kind of clueless."

She squeezed him a little harder and sighed. "That was better than all the imaginary kisses I got from Alessandro put together." She pushed herself back from him. "I think I'll take him down tonight."

She stared at his scars and touched some on his chest. "You never knew what these were?"

"Only what he told me. He said kids would be grossed out by them so never show them to anyone. As you've noticed, I always wear long-sleeve t-shirts."

He slipped on both of his shirts.

"I've got a suitcase." He opened his closet and pulled out an old green duffel bag on wheels. He set it on the bed and unzipped it. "Grab some of my underwear and t-shirts. And some socks. I'll get some pants and shirts."

After a few minutes of stuffing his bag, Hunter took down the whiteboard and removed his Tremarian folder. "I didn't want him to know about this. I was afraid they'd end up burned like everything else." He stood on the bed and retrieved his liquor thermos from the ceiling.

"Anything else?" asked Jazz after she put both items in the suitcase.

"Yes." He lifted his mattress and pulled out the baleen, book of matches, and the knife.

"What are those?"

"What I found yesterday looking through his stuff. The only objects from my past to survive the fire. And I don't remember anything about them." He tossed them into his duffel. "Oh yeah. My printer and paper. I'll carry them out to the truck. Can you bring the suitcase?"

"Sure."

As they walked out of Hunter's room, Joe looked up. "Need a hand?"

"I think we got it," said Hunter.

Jazz put down the suitcase and held out her hand to Joe. "Very nice to meet you, Joe. Thanks for taking care of Hunter."

He stood up and shook her hand. "Thanks for caring about him."

Hunter nodded to his dad. "I'll be back in a second."

They walked out of the house and put everything inside the truck. Jazz climbed into her seat with a smile stretched across her face.

"Give me a minute," said Hunter. He walked inside to find his father rinsing out his cup.

"Did you get everything?" Joe said without turning around.

"No, but I have all I need for now." He gazed at his father's back. "You're hiding something, Dad. You didn't object at all when I said I'd go to Jazz's. It doesn't make sense that you wouldn't want to lose those memories. Unless there's something you really don't want me to know."

Joe turned around revealing a sagging, tired face. "I don't want you to know any of it. That's why I mentioned the reset."

"And if I agreed to that, I would never know what you're hiding. But once I know it, you'd have no memory of it. Makes no sense."

Joe's eyes avoided Hunter's face. "It . . . it will when you know it." He turned back toward the sink.

"Well . . . I'll call you sometime. Thanks for the computer." He started to leave.

"Hunter." Joe turned around. "I know we haven't been very close, and you needed . . . more than I've given you. Jazz seems like a good girl. And she cares about you. Take care of her."

"I'm going to save her."

"And who will save you?"

"Maybe she will."

He left the house.

CHAPTER SEVENTEEN

Jazz bit her thumbnail as she watched the sky bleed into a sunset. Hunter would stay in her house tonight. Where would he sleep? Did he feel the same excitement, the same flutters of nervousness? She could think of no other boy in her entire life she would allow to sleep in her house. Alone with her. But that situation had never arisen, would never. She'd always worried that no boy would want her, even if all her secrets remained hidden. If she found a boy who could accept her public appearance, how could he possibly not be appalled and repelled by her scars? Even she had trouble looking at them.

But Hunter had similar scars.

He'd cried for her, not run from her. They already had so many dark secrets, yet he wanted to stay with her.

Unbelievable.

Hunter emerged from his house and smiled as he walked toward her.

"How'd that go?" asked Jazz as Hunter started his truck. The bound book of stories lay in her lap.

"A little awkward. He thinks you're a good girl and ordered me to take care of you."

She laughed. "Will you?"

He grinned. "I told him I would save you." He guided the truck along the driveway.

"By filling up another one of these books with all my bad memories?"

"If that what it takes. Why should they haunt your life any longer?"

She tried to imagine waking up tomorrow and not remembering the nightmares of the past. She had tried to pretend, hide behind the facade of confidence and sass, think of nothing but science and her lab work. But some little thing would recall an event. And even if it didn't, she went home to emptiness, to Alessandro—fake love, fake sex, fake peace, until the only real thing in the now of her life was a blade leading a trail of blood.

What if all the bad times were gone? Could Hunter do this for her? Maybe, but how could he stand the burden of hers and his memories? Would she want a friend to take away her stomach flu or disease if that meant he would succumb to her illnesses?

But he wanted to do this for her. He wanted to remove her suffering.

She gazed at his beautiful profile. "What about you? How can I save you?"

He stopped before turning onto the road. "By being there when I remember my past."

"I'll be there."

"And still caring about me when you know the worst."

"I think the more we share, the closer we'll be."

Hunter looked deeply into her eyes. "Despite everything?"

Jazz felt such warmth in every part of her body. "Despite everything."

As they moved down the highway, Jazz opened the book of Hunter's stories and began to read. The first story was about Stewart Face-Timing Molly late at night, masturbating together. His mother had walked into his room at a most inopportune time. Embarrassment, guilt, disappointment, shock, and screaming followed. Jazz wondered if Stewart without this memory was now more uncomfortable around his mother, not knowing why she looked at him so differently. His memory of the event was gone, but his mother's reaction surely lingered.

This was the story that had started it all, the first to push into his brain and keep him from writing about the Tremarians. All of these stories related to Hunter's forgotten memories in some way.

Was the girl a substitute for his mother? Fantasies that Hunter wished could happen? Did Hunter's mother catch him masturbating about her and shame him? Or did the mother's reaction in the story stand for Hunter's guilt at what he and his mother actually did?

She remembered Hunter saying he'd been homeschooled. Which meant he was home with his mother and brother all day while his father worked. Something happened when Joe was away from the house. Something which probably fed Hunter's guilt.

And how did the mother and brother die? Why wasn't Hunter in the car with them? Jazz suspected their death was more complicated than simply a driving accident.

The next story was about a girl who was caught wearing a very skimpy outfit at the State Fair by her father. She hadn't expected him to be there. He caught her flirting with older guys, practically exposing everything. Interestingly, she felt anger at him, not shame. She accused him of ruining everything, as always, keeping her from having fun, and spying on her, like he was the pervert for watching her.

Perhaps the father in the story was similar to Joe, catching his wife and Hunter engaged in . . . what? Interestingly, the girl in the story did not deny her behavior. She hadn't acted inappropriately. *He* had for watching her. What arguments had occurred between Hunter's parents?

"Someone's here," said Hunter as he pulled into Jazz's driveway. "Were you expecting anyone?"

"Are you kidding?" Jazz sat up and peered out the windshield. "That's Eric's truck. What does *he* want?"

"Probably nothing good."

As soon as Hunter parked his truck, Eric emerged from his and walked determinedly toward Hunter.

Jazz jumped out her door. "What do you want, Eric?"

"I need to talk to Hunter, not you," Eric snarled.

Hunter opened his door and stared at Eric. "Whatever you need to say, you can say to both of us."

Jazz glared at Eric as she walked past him to Hunter's side.

"You two living together now?" Eric sneered.

"Just visiting," said Hunter.

"I didn't know where you lived, Hunter, so I asked around to find out where Jazz lived. I thought she might know where your house is."

"Such an analytical mind, you have, Eric," Jazz taunted. "You have a future as a stalker."

"And I figured something else out, Hunter. You wrote a story during first period today then Tucker chewed me out after class. I had no idea what she was talking about. Then I saw you typing up a storm outside the gym during PE. I'm expecting Drew to be mad at me, but as soon as she comes out of the dressing room, she's like normal. Like nothing happened during lunch. But then Jazz says something to her, and she's angry again. Plus," he pulled some papers out of his pocket. "I found this in Drew's locker after I left Bentley's office. I figure you wrote this story, too. When Bentley showed me the papers Jazz printed during detention, I remembered my fantasy about Tucker. So when Jazz showed these papers to Drew, she remembered.

"Which means," he said, poking Hunter's chest, "you can get into people's heads and steal a memory."

Hunter smiled. "And how would I do that, Eric?"

"I don't know, but I need you to do it again."

They locked eyes for several seconds. Jazz saw Eric's eyes change from anger to pleading.

Hunter shifted his feet and looked down. "I can't control what I see. The stories just invade my head."

"Drew ran right by you, and two minutes later you were typing this." He shook the papers. "You can do the same for me!"

Eric seemed ready to fight, but then his shoulders slumped. "Please. You need to help me."

"You have a memory you need to get rid of, Eric?" Jazz asked softly.

"This is between me and Hunter, Jazz. You butt out!"

Hunter put his arm around Jazz and pulled her to him. "Don't mess with Jazz. We're partners in this. Look, I've never tried to steal a memory. It just happens. I don't know if I—"

"You can try! Or I'll take this to Bentley tomorrow and tell everyone what you're doing!"

"You want Bentley to read that story?" asked Jazz. "I don't think so."

Eric gritted his teeth and kicked a rock into the trees. "Look, I need help. I need you to try. Please."

"We're not sure how this works," said Jazz. "Were you thinking about sex with Tucker at the beginning of class this morning?"

"Who doesn't?" scoffed Eric.

"Why don't you two sit in the living room for a while," said Jazz, "and see what happens?"

Jazz opened the back door of the truck and pulled out the printer. Hunter took it and headed for the house. Jazz reached in to pull out the duffel.

"I'll get that," said Eric.

"You don't have to."

"I said I got it." He reached around her and lifted the bag. "Why'd you give that story to Drew?"

"Because she needed to know what happened. And her sister saw you gawking at her. You seem to have a serious problem, Eric."

His eyes jittered and then looked to the ground. "I know. I'm trying to fix it."

"I won't tell anyone, and neither will Hunter. We have plenty of our own issues to keep us busy."

Eric nodded and walked to the front door. Jazz grabbed her pack and shut the truck doors.

Once inside, Eric asked, "Where do I put this?"

Jazz and Hunter glanced at each other.

"Where do you want it, Hunter?" asked Jazz, lifting her brows and tilting her head slightly.

"Right there is fine," said Hunter. "I'll move it later. Let's go sit down." Eric dropped the bag and followed Hunter into the next room.

"I'll make some coffee," said Jazz. Once the boys were out of the kitchen, Jazz picked up the duffel and walked down the hall. She stopped at her room. Should she put it in there? What would he think? Where did she want him?

Her heart fluttered at that question. Next to her. Holding her. Maybe loving her.

She decided to put the bag in her room and then say she put it there because she thought he'd want to sleep on the sofa. She obviously couldn't lug it in there now. He could decide later.

She hoped Eric's memory—if Hunter could see it—was about him being victimized rather than him hurting a little girl. She didn't think she could take knowing that about him.

CHAPTER EIGHTEEN

Hunter sat in a chair with his computer on his lap. Eric leaned back on the sofa, staring at the ceiling. "What do I need to do?"

"I'm not sure. This is the first time I've tried to see someone's memory. Drew was still thinking about what had happened when she ran by us at lunch, so maybe try thinking about a memory. I know that's hard, but I don't know what else to tell you ."

Eric leaned over and put his head into his hands.

The rapid-fire beating of drums immediately filled Hunter's brain, Bonham's riff before Page's solo. He heard the ball slap against the wall then a basketball rim shake. He saw himself standing outside his old house, throwing the ball against the backboard. He heard his mother calling him. He walked inside the house then down the hallway to the door, slightly ajar. He pushed it open. "Mom?" he called. The room was empty. He heard a shower running and saw the bathroom door open. He watched as his mother stood in front of the mirror in panties and a tank top. She started to pull it off. He turned around and knocked on her door. "Mom? I'm here. You called me?"

"Just wanted to know where you were, Baby. I have something to show you. Turn around."

Hunter scrambled out and slammed the door. He heard her laughing. "You know you want to, Baby!" He ran toward the wall, which opened up into a bedroom.

Nearest to him was a twin bed occupied by a younger Eric, probably eleven or twelve years old. He was propped on a pillow against the wall, reading a book.

At the other end of the room, an older, much larger, teenager lay on his back with a laptop open on his chest, staring open-mouthed at the screen. His right hand bounced under the sheets as he moaned, "Jesus."

Eric heard the sound and turned his head. He watched, fascinated. He had seen Buddy do this on several nights but had never found the courage to confront him. "Hey, Buddy. What are you doing?"

Buddy jerked his head toward Eric. "Why are you still awake, asshole? Turn toward the wall and go to sleep!"

"Can't sleep now, especially with you moaning like that." Eric sat up. "What are you watching?" He figured it was some kind of pornography. He had never seen any and wondered what could make his brother moan like that.

Buddy shifted his gaze back toward the screen. He moved his hand more quickly under the covers.

"I'll show you, but get me that lotion on the dresser."

Excited, Eric flipped up the sheets and retrieved the bottle. He wore stretch brief underwear and no shirt. He went to the bed and held out the lotion.

"First of all, you will promise to tell no one about this, or I won't show you anything."

"OK. I promise."

"Plus, I will beat the crap out of you if you do."

"I won't tell!"

Buddy scooted to his right, making room for Eric. "Get in under the sheets next to me."

Eric climbed into the bed. Buddy pulled his hand out from the sheets and held it up to Eric.

"Give me a squirt."

Eric pushed the top down on the bottle, filling Buddy's palm with lotion, which then disappeared under the sheets. Buddy groaned.

"Show me," Eric pleaded.

Buddy turned the screen toward Eric whose eyes bulged, and his mouth opened. Eric saw two naked young girls jumping on a trampoline. They were twins, maybe ten or eleven years old. They laughed as they jumped around each other.

This was not what Eric had expected. "Buddy, where did you get this?"

"Do you like it?"

Not really, *he thought. "Yeah. Sure. But the girls are so young."*

"That's the point, little brother. That's the freakin' point. Watch this."

The girls lay down on their backs.

"Eric, put some lotion on your hands."

"What?"

"Do what I say or go back to your bed."

Eric squirted lotion into his hands.

"Now reach down and rub me."

"What?"

"Do it!"

Jazz entered the room with coffee cups then stopped when Hunter looked up from his computer.

He shook his head at her. They both looked at Eric who hid his face behind his hands, breathing heavily and crying. Hunter felt so sorry for Eric, but the girls? Who was filming them? Did they even know what they were doing?

Hunter looked back at his computer and continued to type.

* * * * *

Jazz knew Hunter was watching the memory, one he did not want to see. His face looked so pitiful, so pained. She backed away with the cups, watching tears drip down Hunter's face. She turned around and walked back to the kitchen.

Did she want to know Eric's memory? No. Why would she need more nightmares? Would she want Eric to see one of her memories? No.

She sat at the table and sipped her coffee. Her phone buzzed in her pocket. She pulled it out and saw a message from MawMaw.

How are you? How's your mother?

Jazz texted back. *Still in rehab. I might go visit her this weekend.*

Then a picture of her little sister appeared on the screen. Little Rosie, now five years old.

Jazz remembered a night of yelling between her mother and her grandparents. MawMaw said Jazz and Mom had to leave. They couldn't stay with them anymore. PawPaw held the baby. Mom screamed she would not leave Rosie.

"You are not taking this baby," said MawMaw. "You can't take care of her now. Leave her with us and see how things go."

"I don't want to leave!" Jazz shouted.

MawMaw hugged her. "You can't stay, Jazzy. Give it some time. Maybe in a year or two you can come back, but you have to leave now."

Jazz could not remember why MawMaw made her leave, but for some reason she understood. Maybe MawMaw knew that Mom couldn't make it by herself.

Jazz enlarged the picture of Rosie. She was so cute! Jazz had asked MawMaw about Face-Timing, but she had refused. Jazz knew they had not told Rosie anything about her mother . . . or even Jazz.

And why should she? The past five years were nightmares. The past few weeks were the longest Jazz had gone without some asshole man living there.

Jazz texted. *Mom said that maybe after she gets out we could see you.*

Jazz stared at the screen, hoping for a positive response, but nothing came back. She sighed and felt the familiar ache deep in her throat. She tried to swallow. Once again she felt like a little girl hoping for attention and affection. Once again she had to stifle her loss and pain and focus on something which made sense—science.

She flipped open her computer and went to Quora.com, posting the question, "Are memories stored outside the brain?" She scanned through answers, followed links to science journal articles, a process she had performed hundreds of times. Nothing in the literature would support what was happening to Hunter, yet his visions were real. He deleted memories. She had seen the evidence.

How did she know he had deleted one of her memories if she no longer had the memory? Because the memory was restored when she read his story. The bullet hole was real. She didn't remember making it when he first asked, then remembered when she read his story. Yet she had no idea which memory he had deleted at his father's. Did she feel different? Yes, but that difference was hard to define. Like a distant pressure, a weight, she had become used to was now gone. How did she know? She couldn't remember the exact feeling of that weight, but something felt different inside her, less burdened, like she could breathe more deeply.

She found a question posed by a skeptical scientist when considering whether memories could exist outside the brain: "Has anyone ever come across someone else's memory when wandering around the world?" Yes. Hunter had. Many times. Would it be easier to explain him diving inside a person's brain using telepathy than hijacking a memory during its recall outside the brain?

If memories existed in another dimension, they could interact. Dreams could be a subconscious journey through others' memories. The spark of creativity could be the result of many people's memories interacting with each other. And the idea of a collective unconscious might be easier to explain.

Her brain swirled with thoughts and possibilities until she heard talking in the living room. She closed her computer and rose from her seat. The boys walked into the kitchen.

Eric looked more relaxed, but Hunter dragged his feet. His shoulders hung, and he stared at nothing. He lifted his head when he stepped into the kitchen and peered at Jazz with haunted eyes. He pushed his wet hair back on his head.

"You can keep this," said Eric as he put Drew's story on the table. "I'm trying to fix it."

"I know. You told me. That's good, Eric." She reached out her hand. "No hard feelings?"

"OK." He shook her hand then backed up a step to look at them both. "I don't know what's going on with you two or how you're doing this. But I don't want you getting into my head unless I want you there. Is that clear?" He shook and breathed heavily. "Is that clear?"

Jazz saw the twitching in his eyes. "Hunter's not getting into your head, Eric."

"Then how's he doing it?" he pleaded. "I have to be the one to decide what he sees."

"I don't want to see what's in your head, Eric," said Hunter. "But I'll do it to help you."

"How? How are you seeing my memories?"

Jazz moved toward Eric. "I'll try to explain. Your long-term memories don't stay in your brain. At least, that's the theory I'm using. When you think about something from your past, your neurons light up like they did when the memory was formed which pulls it back into your mind. It's like downloading a photo from your cloud storage. The image on the phone is hazy and incomplete. It takes up less memory that way. When you want that photo, you tap it and after a few seconds, the full image is there. Hunter intercepts the memory before it forms in your mind. "

Eric squinted his eyes and shook his head. "Why does the memory leave in the first place? Isn't there enough room?"

"Theoretically, yes. But you're constantly making new memories. Like right now. Your brain's making a movie of everything we're doing and saying, using some of the same neurons that are needed for previous memories. It probably makes things run smoother if the old movies are stored elsewhere rather than gumming up the process of forming a new memory."

"How do you know this?"

"I don't *know* it. Scientists are still guessing. What they do know is if you suffer brain damage, you might not be able to speak or hear or balance, but you won't lose specific long-term memories. Why? Perhaps because those memories exist outside your brain, which is needed to communicate with that cloud we all have. Some scientists think the brain is a transmitter and receiver more than a storage device. When we get old, we lose the ability to send and receive signals. We don't suffer memory loss. We suffer signal loss—a communication breakdown."

"I still don't see why Hunter intercepts my memories."

"Because most of Hunter's memories were erased a year ago. His brain sends out a signal but nothing comes back. Except memories that are somehow related to the ones he lost."

Eric snapped his head toward Hunter. "Did you watch child pornography?"

"No," said Hunter. "But I was abused by someone in my family. At least, that's what I think happened."

Jazz nodded. "Hunter sees something from his past just before he sees another person's memory. And once that memory is in his mind, it can't be yours anymore. Like someone hacked your photo before it could fully download."

Eric shook his head. "So if I don't think about the memory, you won't see it?"

"That's what we believe," said Hunter.

"OK. Can I come by tomorrow after school? Can you take another one?"

Hunter rubbed his neck. "I'll try. Text me first."

"Sure." He held his hand out to Hunter. "Thanks, man."

Hunter shook hands then placed his closed computer on the table.

Eric looked at them both, gave a nod, and walked out. After another minute, Eric drove away.

"You look terrible," said Jazz. "You want coffee? Anything?"

"A hug."

Jazz pulled him to her. "Was that as bad as it seemed?"

"Worse. His brother abused him and introduced him to child pornography. There were twin little girls. Eric and his brother masturbated while watching several videos. Jazz, you wouldn't believe what the girls did. There are two girls out there being abused repeatedly, then videoed, so that people like Buddy and Eric can get off watching them, violating them again and again. It's sick."

He broke away from her and paced around the kitchen, his anger rising. "And what's worse is that nobody knows about it, except for the sickos who watch that stuff online, but they don't care about those girls. Nobody cared about you or me or whatever happened to Tatiana. Or any of the other thousands of kids who are abused.

"And why is that? Because most people don't know. Maybe they don't want to know. How would normal people react if all these stories were published and read?"

Jazz shook her head. "They'd think they're inappropriate for teens. The stories are too dark. Even adults wouldn't want to read them. Too much sex and violence."

"Tell that to the kids in these stories. One reason this stuff keeps happening is because it's kept secret. If Eric tried to explain to his classmates what happened to him, they'd call him a perv. If you or I showed our scars to everyone, they'd freak out and call us crazy. We hide our problems from everyone so the normal people can live in their fantasy worlds."

He began to pull off his shirts. "I'm not hiding these anymore." He tossed the clothes onto the table. "I guess I'll soon learn why and how I made these." He held out his arms to examine his cuts. He found one on each wrist with more pronounced scars than the others. "These must have been deeper cuts."

Jazz gently lifted each wrist to her lips, kissing his scars. "Your dad said he thought you'd bleed to death twice. Maybe that was after each of these."

"Would you be embarrassed to be seen with me if these scars were exposed?"

"No, Hunter. I'd be proud you were brave enough to show them."

He pulled her face to his chest. "Eric wants to keep seeing me until all his memories with the twins are gone. At first, I didn't think I could do it. But I have to. He was a victim. He needs a chance. And I need to find out whether those girls are still slaves."

She pushed her fingers through his hair. "You're amazing to try, Hunter. Who else would accept the worst memories of others?"

"You. If you could do it, I know you would."

"For you, yes. For Eric, I don't know."

"Even if Eric doesn't remember these events, they still happened to him. The fact that he doesn't remember this one incident of abuse will not cancel the impact it had on his life. Will it?"

"Who knows? But the haunting will be gone. I still see . . . so many scenes that I wish I could close my eyes to . . . forever."

He held her face in front of his. "I'll take all your bad memories. You'll forget why you made every cut. The scars will fade eventually, and you'll be whole again. I promise."

"Oh, Hunter." Could he?

"Show me. Please."

Jazz's heart thumped. She'd never shown anyone.

"Please."

She crossed her arms and reached for the hem of her shirt. Then pulled it off, clutching it against her breasts.

Hunter's eyes revealed no shock at seeing twice as many on her shoulders and arms than appeared on his body. Nor at the bruised red welts glaring against her pale skin. His chin trembled.

"Oh, Jazz. I'll fix every one." He kissed the scars on each shoulder until she wailed and pulled him to her, weeping into his chest.

"I know what I need to do," he said. "No matter how hard the visions will be, no matter how much suffering I have to live through, I will take away your pain and from anyone else who wants me to try."

She wanted him to take her memories. She would make the choice and always know she gave her nightmares to him. Unlike what happened to Hunter, who never consented, who had every memory, good and bad, shocked into oblivion.

Hunter stroked her hair. "I don't want a reset. I'll take what I can and write them down. Maybe someday others can read them and learn what you went through."

They stayed together for another minute, their breathing synchronized. Finally, Hunter removed his hands from her back and lifted her head away from his chest. "I like hugging you."

Jazz removed the shirt she held between them then pressed her skin against his. The warmth was so comforting, yet also enervating. She could feel her desire growing.

Then Hunter pulled away, breathing heavily. "I'm afraid."

"Why?"

"How can Eric ever have normal sex after what he's been through? How can you? Or me? I've seen so many people having sex during the past two months, all of it secret, most of it abusive or criminal. How can I touch you without thinking of all that? I keep seeing the little girls in Eric's memory . . . made to do horrible things. Seems like that part of our lives has been twisted so many times, it's broken. How can anyone heal from that?"

She moved toward him and touched his chest, her own heart fluttering. "By finding someone to kiss my scars and kiss your scars and then look beyond them."

Hunter swiped his forearm across his face, smearing away tears. "We're broken, Jazz. Look at us! Look . . ." Hunter raised the front of his shirt only to immediately drop it, as if in defeat.

She put a hand lightly to his chest over his heart. She stopped over an uneven ridge of flesh. "We are more than this, Hunter." Jazz leaned closer and moved her hand to press her lips where her fingers had been. She raised her eyes, then her head. They stood face to face. "I have to believe I can still love and be loved, that I can share my bed with someone real, not just a poster. We can't stay broken forever."

"I think the healing will hurt more than the original injury."

"Maybe. But we were alone then. We've got each other now."

"Before Eric's memory started in my head, I saw my mother . . . almost naked. I went into her room and saw her changing through the bathroom door. I turned away, and she laughed at me. She said I wanted to look at her."

Jazz saw such pain in his face.

"Maybe she didn't abuse me. Maybe I abused her." He grabbed his head with his hands and squeezed. "I wish I knew the truth."

"It will come to you eventually."

"Do you think we can ever be normal?"

"Maybe not normal, whatever that is, but able to love and be loved? Yes."

"What about your mother? Do you believe she can heal?"

"Maybe. If she can stay off the booze. If she can forget some things. Maybe if she can be with Rosie."

"Who?"

"My little sister." Jazz saw Hunter's brain working behind his eyes. "Is she in the memory you took?"

"No. Your mom was pregnant, though. And I saw the photo in your mom's room."

"We had to leave Rosie behind. MawMaw forced us to go. I don't remember why."

Hunter nodded and looked away.

Jazz touched his cheek. "Do I want to know why?"

"Not now."

"OK.

"So Rosie is a little Jazz without all the hurt?"

Jazz pulled out her phone and showed him. "Here's her picture."

"She does look like you."

"I'd like to see her." She hugged the phone to her chest.

"We'll go to MawMaw's after your mom gets back."

Jazz's eyes widened. "*We* will?"

"All of us."

"That would be very cool." She kissed his cheek. "I'm going to take a shower and change my clothes. I put your bag in my room—just temporarily. You can decide where you want to sleep. There's a quilt and some blankets in the hall closet. Make your bed wherever you want."

"I'd like my thermos."

She walked down the hall toward her room. "It's in here."

Hunter followed her.

"Are you tired?" she asked as she pulled some clothes out of her drawers.

Hunter sat down next to his duffel. "Yes, but my brain isn't." He unzipped the bag and pulled out his thermos. He flipped open the top and took a drink.

"You can stay in here if you want. Even lie down on my bed. And if you don't want Alessandro staring at you, just take him down. I don't think I need him anymore."

Hunter smiled at her. "Think I'll have to seriously work out to replace Alessandro."

"He's just a fake body to fantasize about, Hunter. Whatever pleasure he helped create kept the demons at bay only for a few minutes. You can eliminate the demons entirely. I'd choose you over Alessandro any day. Or night."

Jazz winked and left the room.

CHAPTER NINETEEN

unter took another sip from his thermos. Soon he heard the sound of a shower drifting into the room. He closed his eyes and the scent of Bombshell Seduction filled his nose—his mother's favorite perfume. He stood inside her bedroom, facing the door.

"I have something to show you. Turn around."

He felt dizzy, and the back of his throat ached. He knew what he would see if he turned around. Why did she do that to him? He stood outside her door hearing her laugh.

The sound of a basketball dribbling on the driveway snapped his thoughts away from her.

"Hey, Hunter!" his little brother yelled through the open front door. "Let's play HORSE."

Hunter walked down the hall and out the front door. Frankie was eight years old, a little chunky with a round face covered to his eyebrows in bangs. After a few games with his brother, Hunter heard his mother call him.

"I need you, Hunter."

Hunter tossed the ball to Frankie and walked inside. Where was she?

"In here, Baby."

He walked to her room and saw her standing in front of her dresser mirror, the back of her red dress open and her bra unclasped.

"Can you hook me up and zip? My nails aren't dry and I don't want to smear them."

Her dress plunged in the front. Just as he moved behind her, she bent over to pick something off her dress. Hunter saw her breasts swaying, barely covered by the bra. She looked up and saw his gaze through the mirror.

"Thought you weren't interested, Baby." She smiled as she pulled the front of her dress up. "It's nice that one man in this house likes my figure. Your father could care less. Hook my strap, please."

Hunter felt her warm skin against his fingers as he stretched the ends toward each other.

"OK," he said. "Done."

"Now zip. Go slow. This dress is tighter than the last time I wore it."

Hunter reached for the zipper and noticed the top edge of her panties. His heart pounded as the top of her butt crack disappeared. He zipped slowly until he reached the top.

"Can you see my bra strap?"

He wanted to avert his eyes, but he couldn't. "Yes."

"Well, that won't work. Guess I'll have to go braless. Unzip me and unhook it."

Hunter did as she asked. She looked at him through the mirror. "You can watch if you want to."

He turned around and looked at the wall. He heard the sounds of her dress being moved.

"You can turn around, Baby."

He turned and noticed the bra on the dresser. "Zip."

"Are you going somewhere?" he asked as he reached the top.

She turned around and put her hand on her hip. "How do I look?" He saw her tongue on her teeth.

"Pretty. Beautiful." She was. He had never seen another woman as beautiful.

"You are so sweet." She put her arms on either side of his neck. "You're such a handsome young man. Gonna be quite a catch for some lucky girl." She kissed his cheek and pulled his head against her chest.

Her perfume made him dizzy. "Where are you going?"

She pulled away. "I'm going out. I need a break, so I called a girlfriend and we're meeting for a girls' night out."

"Who is she?"

"Don't be so nosy. No one you know." She grabbed her purse off the chair and walked to the door. "C'mon. Out of here. I want to talk to you and Frankie."

They walked down the hall to the front door. "Frankie, come here."

Frankie and Hunter stood before their mother.

"You two will behave. I should be back around ten."

"Yes, Ma'am," the brothers said.

"Frankie, do what your brother says and get to bed by nine."

Frankie groaned.

She kissed each boy on his forehead and walked out to her car. She backed away waving at them.

At 11:30 that night, Hunter sat at the kitchen table, waiting for his mother to return home. He knew she wasn't meeting a girlfriend. She and Dad had argued before he left for Prudhoe Bay two days ago. Hunter remembered her yelling, "If you're not interested in me, I'll find someone who is." So he figured that's what she was doing.

What if she found another man? Would she leave him and Frankie with Dad? Was he worried about his mother or jealous? Maybe she was doing this to make him want her more.

Did he want her to stay because he would miss his mother, or because he wanted her to keep seducing him until he gave in? Then it wouldn't be his fault, would it? How despicable was that?

The idea of her leaving made him feel hollow inside. He bit his lip. What would people think if they knew his thoughts?

He saw lights coming toward the house—from two cars. Why two?

They pulled into the driveway. A man got out of his mother's car and ran over to the passenger door. Hunter walked onto the porch.

"Hey, kid. Come help your mother."

The man opened the car door to reveal his mother, slumped back in the seat, her legs spread apart. Hunter ran toward her. She flopped her head toward him and smiled. "Hunter, baby! You should've seen your mother dance. Every man in the bar couldn't keep his eyes off me." She laughed.

The man looked at Hunter and shook his head. "Jack and I brought her home because she was going to drive even though she's pretty drunk. Can you help her out? She's already got me in trouble with my wife."

Hunter leaned into the car. "Mom? Can you walk?"

"Sure, Baby." She put her right foot onto the driveway, hiking up her dress to mid-thigh. She laughed. "Not the most lady-like move I've ever made." She dragged her left leg out as Hunter held her up.

"Here are her keys." The man put them in Hunter's hand.

"Thanks for bringing her home," said Hunter.

"Do y'all want to come inside?" his mother called.

"No, Ma'am."

"Cowards!"

"C'mon, Mom." He helped her walk up the stairs to the porch.

"Not a pair of balls between them."

Hunter held one of her arms around his shoulders and held her waist with his other hand as she staggered up the porch stairs and into the house.

"Baby, you're so strong." She kissed his cheek long and hard. "And so handsome." She kissed again.

He couldn't help feeling pride from her praise. No one else paid any attention to him. "I'll take you to your bedroom."

"That's what I was trying to get a man to say to me all night. But they were all look and no touch."

Hunter opened her door and flipped on the light.

"Will you be all right?" asked Hunter as he sat her down on the bed.

"I'm not ready to go to bed, yet. The night's young!" She stood up and kicked off her heels. Then hiked up her dress and pulled down her fishnet hose. "Hang these on my chair, Baby." She tossed them to Hunter. She tried to reach her zipper but staggered too much.

"Baby, unzip me." She turned her back to him and held up her hair. Hunter pulled the zipper down. She pulled her arms out of the dress and dropped it to her waist. Turning around, she said, "Baby—"

"Mom!"

Savannah looked down then covered her breasts. "Woops! Forgot I didn't wear a bra tonight."

Hunter looked down and away.

"Please, Hunter. Don't look away. Please."

Hunter couldn't get enough air into his lungs. He slowly lifted his head and his eyes to her chest.

She dropped her arms. Hunter stared. "Come here, Baby." She hugged him to her. "You used to touch them every day. Now you're not supposed to, but I so yearn to be touched." She pulled back from him. "Will you touch me, Hunter?"

Hunter moved his hands from her back to her sides and then to her breasts.

"Yes, Baby. That's what I want." She kissed him on each cheek then pulled his hands up to her lips and kissed them. "Your mother is so lonely, so lonely.

I lay awake at night, crying. We all need to be touched, Hunter." She placed his hands on her breasts."

Hunter thought he would faint.

"Do you love me, Baby?"

"Yes."

"You're making me so happy. I haven't felt happy in a long, long time. Do you want to make your mother happy?"

"Yes."

She kissed his forehead and pulled him to her.

"I need a drink. Why don't you get the bottle and bring two glasses of ice and some tonic. I need to change. Go."

Hunter turned, and walked out of the room. He'd made drinks for his mother before, and he'd stolen shots off and on. He sliced a lemon and inhaled its aroma—tart and clean. Then squeezed lemon over the ice in each glass, hearing the crack of each cube. He added shots of vodka, pouring the drops at the bottom of the shot glass into his mouth, feeling the slight burn. The tonic water fizzed and bubbled onto the counter after he unscrewed the top. He poured another shot of vodka and downed it. After putting everything on a tray, he carried it back to her room. Just before he entered, "Whole Lotta Love" blared out from her speakers.

She had her back to him, juking her hip to the rhythm. She was dressed like the time she emerged from the mirror: braless, short shirt, yoga shorts. He handed her a glass, which she drank in three gulps. He drank his quickly and felt the mixture burn down his throat and into his chest.

Then they danced the same way as before, her hands raking across his crotch, moving under his shirt, all the time smiling at him, enjoying what she was doing to him, staring at his growing erection. He couldn't stop watching her body.

"Make us another drink, Baby."

He poured more shots and more tonic water. She went to the CD player and pushed a button until Hunter heard the opening guitar riff of "Stairway to Heaven." She turned on her dresser mirror lights then flipped the switch for the room. When he handed her the glass, she was swaying to the music, backlit by the lights, looking like a woman in a dream.

She drank then put her glass down, holding out her arms, summoning him to her. She pulled him close. Hunter could feel every part of her touching him. They didn't move their feet, just pressed as much of their bodies together as they could. She was so warm, so soft.

He melted into her. He loved his mother. She loved him. Most of him felt warm and comfortable. But another part felt desire. And that scared him.

She rubbed his back. He rubbed hers. She pulled his butt toward her. He could feel his erection against her as she moved her pelvis against his. After the guitar solo, she lifted her hands above her head, swaying her arms to the rhythm, still pressing her thighs and pelvis against him.

When the song ended, she whispered in his ear, "You're the most beautiful boy. I love you, Baby."

"I love you, too."

She kissed his forehead and pulled him toward the bed. "I don't want to sleep alone tonight. Will you snuggle with me? Like you used to?"

He nodded.

She pulled back the sheets and climbed in. He slipped in next to her. She faced him, smiled and kissed his nose, his cheeks, his neck. She put her hand underneath his shirt, rubbing his chest, then his stomach.

Hunter's heart pounded. He tried to swallow, but his mouth was so dry.

"I need you, Baby. So badly." Her hand moved to his stomach. "Do you want me, Baby?" Her hand moved lower. "Do you want me as much as I want you?"

She touched his erection.

"Yes, you do, Baby. Oh, God, Hunter, I love you!"

She pushed her hand into his underwear. Hunter felt a surge of panic. He pulled away.

"No, Baby. Give it to me." She grabbed him.

"Mom. No! Please!" He pulled away.

"You want it as much as I do." She grabbed.

Hunter was so conflicted. He could easily give in to her, but deep inside he knew this wasn't right. His mother was drunk. He was drunk. He had to leave.

"Mom, no. Please."

"Why?" she pleaded.

"No." He reached down and pulled her hand away.

"Dammit, Hunter!"

"Mom, this is wrong. Please."

"You fucking bastard. Just like your father. Get the hell out of my bedroom!"

Her anger stunned him. "Mom, please."

"Get the hell out. Now!"

Hunter scrambled out of the bed. She glared at him, breathing heavily, her lips curled back from her teeth.

"I'm sorry."

"Bring me my drink."

He hurried to her glass and brought it to her. She drank and held it to him. He filled it again and gave it to her.

She drank half of it. "I got to find somebody who wants me. I got to get out of here." She leaned back against the headboard.

Hunter didn't move. Had he done the right thing?

"Take the bottle with you. Otherwise I'll drink it all."

Hunter put his glass, the vodka bottle and the tonic water onto the tray and headed toward the door.

"Hunter."

Would she be angry? Or apologize? Or cry? "Yes."

Her voice froze him.

"We won't talk about this ever, you hear me?"

"Yes Ma'am."

"Ever."

Hunter staggered as he left the room. He closed the door and leaned against it. Did she hate him now? In a fog he walked to the kitchen and sat at the table. He drank three more glasses before he collapsed.

The next morning, his mother banged the table to wake him up. She said nothing and looked at him like he was a stranger. No smiles, no "Baby," no hugs.

Frankie ran into the kitchen and hugged her around the waist. He claimed he'd had a nightmare, that he'd been scared.

"Oh, no!" said Savannah. "If that happens again, come to my room and snuggle with me."

She wet his hair and brushed it down while glancing at Hunter blankly.

The message was clear: never speak about the incident, no more dancing, no more touching. No more anything. His brother was now preferred. Hunter was the pariah who wouldn't submit to his mother.

CHAPTER TWENTY

azz held the towel around her body as she stepped toward the full-length mirror hanging on the bathroom door, covered by a robe, which she always kept hanging to block the view. Her heart pounded as she lifted the robe and dropped it to the floor, shutting her eyes as she opened both hands.

After a few seconds of hesitation, she forced herself to look— so much skin covering her thick arms and legs, soft folds around her waist, and mounds of milky flesh perched over her ample torso. She remembered looking at herself at twelve, fascinated at how large her breasts were compared to the rest of her. Now after years of weight gain, she was large everywhere. But what overwhelmed her eyes were the welts and scabs marking her skin, most shriveled to white among the goosebumps forming as the shower steam dissipated, and the cold embraced her. Jagged zig-zags and cross-hatched lines stared back at her from shoulders to wrists and down her legs—the most recent along her hip, red and ridged, angry at the exposure.

She touched the lines on her hip lightly, wincing as the razor blade flashed into her mind, forcing her heart to race. Not from pain but memory of the steel opening her skin like mouths smiling with blood. She watched her finger trace the random lines along her upper thigh. Her breathing sped.

Before emerging from the bathroom, Jazz struggled with what to wear, whether to show all her scars and hope he still wanted to kiss them rather than turn away, or worse, run away. She pulled on a loose tank-top t-shirt with no bra. The welts on her shoulders and arms glared at her through the mirror. How could anyone stand to see them? In the end, she wavered about her legs, deciding to pull sweatpants up over her boxers.

Jazz took a deep breath and opened the door. She entered her room and saw Hunter curled up on her bed, his back toward her, hard sobs wracking his body and his eyes clenched shut. His arms were wrapped around himself, looking so small and vulnerable, tearing at her heart.

"I remembered, Jazz."

She sat next to him, touching him gently, feeling his body heave. "What happened?"

"My mother came home drunk after trying to seduce men at a bar. She exposed herself to me. She said I was the only man in the house who wanted to touch her or look at her. I drank with her, then we danced. She wanted me aroused and asked that I sleep with her. She tried to have scx with me, but I said no."

He sat up, staring at the far wall. "After that, everything changed between us. She invited my little brother to sleep with her. I don't know what happened after that."

"I'm sorry." She felt exposed and hugged herself.

He turned toward her. "She tried to seduce me, but I said no. Maybe that's all there is."

"Maybe." She hugged him.

"I drank with her. Vodka tonics. But I drank more after she rejected me." He stood up.

"She messed with your head, Hunter. She could've pretended the event never happened because she was embarrassed and decided to never seduce you again, but she chose to taunt you and make you feel jealous of your brother. She was still manipulating you. I don't think that was the last time she tried to have sex with you."

"Great. Something to look forward to." He moved toward her and touched the welts on her shoulders.

Jazz flinched slightly

"Thanks for trusting me to see these."

"I'm still afraid you'll turn away in disgust."

"I'll never do that."

He touched her shoulder again, but this time Jazz didn't flinch and felt the soft pads of his fingers move slowly along several scars.

"Can I see your legs?"

Jazz breathed deep a few times then slipped off her sweatpants. She saw the welts across her thighs, some thin, a little lighter in color than her skin. Others were dark red, some slashing across old scars.

Hunter dropped to his knees and slowly moved his fingertips down her thighs.

"When was the last time?" he asked.

She felt dizzy. "I think two weeks ago."

"Where?"

She swallowed then lifted up the bottom edge of her boxers on her left side near her hip. Hunter touched the two scab lines. He looked up to her face.

"Why?"

"Bad dreams." She raised her hands to her ears. "I kept hearing all of Mom's men taunting me, trying to get into the house." She paused to slow her breathing. "I couldn't sleep."

"Let's make these the last you ever do."

"I hope so."

He kissed them. She thought she would faint.

"Hunter, aren't you grossed out?"

"No. Just immensely sorry. And determined to keep you safe." He kissed her thighs.

Jazz couldn't suppress a whimper.

Hunter lifted his head to her. "In this house, we don't hide our scars. We don't hide anything."

She felt so light-headed. "Thank you, Hunter."

For the first time in her life, she felt comfortable in her own skin. She didn't need to hide herself from Hunter. Her clothes had always provided some protection against others who would ridicule her body, her skin. She had battled the world from behind the shield of secrecy, never allowing any sign of vulnerability. With Hunter she could expose both her appearance and her nightmares, knowing he would accept them, care for them, maybe even love them.

He stood. "I'm dead tired."

"Where do you want to sleep?"

"I'd love to sleep with you, but I think I should deal with my past first."

"I'm OK with that."

"I'll get the blankets from the closet. Can you bring me a drink?"

"Sure."

They both left the room. When Jazz returned with two glasses of vodka and Coke, she found Hunter sitting on the floor on top of blankets, leaning against the wall, holding the Mount Rainier knife he had found yesterday afternoon. She sat next to him as he held the bone-handled knife with a four-inch blade away from its leather sheath.

"Is it sharp?" she asked while handing him a glass.

He picked up the matchbook and pulled the blade across the cardboard cover, slicing it easily. "Seems to be."

"Can I see the sheath?" He handed it to her then took a drink.

The leather had been nicely worked to depict the famous mountain. Beadwork and leather fringe projected a Native American authenticity. She looked inside the sheath and saw what appeared to be darkened blood.

"Was this yours?" Jazz asked. She tilted the glass to her lips.

"I don't know."

"There's dried blood inside. Look."

She held it to the light so he could see inside.

"Maybe this was mine." He placed the blade against some of his scars. "Why would Dad keep this rather than burn it with everything else?"

"Ask him. Maybe he'll be more willing to give you answers over the phone without worrying about showing you his memories."

He returned the knife to the sheath and tossed it into his duffel. They both drank in silence until the glasses were empty.

"I hope I can sleep through the night," said Hunter.

"If you don't, I'll be close."

He smiled. "And I'm here for you."

She leaned toward him and gently kissed his lips. "I'd like something to think about as I try to fall asleep."

Hunter touched her lips with his fingers. "Your lips are so soft." He kissed them slowly and gently, barely pressing.

"Thank you." Jazz stood and smiled down at him on the floor.

"Good night, Jazz." Hunter lay on his side facing Jazz as she turned off the lights and climbed into bed.

"Good night, Hunter."

* * * * * *

Sometime during the night, Hunter opened his eyes and saw his old bedroom in his parents' house. He heard a noise coming from the hallway and sat up. He saw a twin bed on the other side of his room—empty. Where was Frankie? When did he sneak out of the room this time? The clock showed two o'clock in the morning.

Rising to his feet, he stretched, then heard a moaning. Mom?

He opened the door and stuck his head into the hallway. More moaning. What was his mother doing?

He stood outside her door and listened. He heard the bed shaking, his mother grunting, then his brother yelling, "Mom! What are you doing?"

She kept grunting.

"Mom! Stop it!"

Hunter opened the door and turned on the light. Frankie stood next to the bed, shielding his eyes.

Hunter saw his mother's body jerking under the covers, her jaw clinched. Her eyes flashed open.

"Frankie. What's wrong?" she asked.

"You woke me up," said Frankie. "You were having a nightmare or something."

She sat up and looked at Hunter, her eyes wide with shock.

"Frankie," said Hunter. "Go back to your own bed."

His brother stared at his mother, tightening his eyes like he was having trouble seeing her. "Mom?"

"It's OK, Frankie. Go back to your room. I'm sorry I woke you up."

Frankie walked out of the room, and Hunter closed the door.

Hunter tried to control his anger. "Tell me you were dreaming and didn't know what you were doing."

Savannah smiled. "I was dreaming and didn't know what I was doing. Which is the truth, Hunter. You know what else is the truth? I was dreaming about you." She licked her lips and smiled. "Want to know what we were doing?"

"You're drunk."

"Yes, I am. Or was." She flung back the covers. Hunter turned away, not knowing what she would be wearing. "I'm dressed, Baby. God, can any man in this house want to look at me?"

Rising out of the bed, she walked to her dresser. Hunter stole a glance to make sure she wore clothes. Seeing her panties and lace camisole top, he watched her grab the vodka bottle. She faced him, leaning against the dresser and took a swig from the bottle.

"Want some?" She offered him the bottle. He shook his head. "Do I disgust you?"

"A little."

"Only a little?" She walked toward him slowly. "I disgust myself more than that."

Hunter tried to keep his eyes on her face, but they kept drifting downward.

"Sometimes I think I should get in the car and drive into a tree." She stood so very close to him. He could smell her and feel the warmth radiating off her skin. "You think I'm that disgusting?"

"Not disgusting." Would she really kill herself? "I don't want you to die."

"Good. What do you want me to do, Baby?"

Hunter could not stop staring at her breasts through the lace. He was breathing so rapidly he felt dizzy. "I don't know."

She moved closer and gently hugged him to her, purring into his ear. "Would you want me to stop doing this?" She slowly rubbed his back. "I could stop touching you, Baby. Is that what you want?"

Warmth flooded his body, sending jolts to his fingers and toes. "No."

She backed up a little. "I could make sure you never see me dressed like this."

Again, he could not keep his eyes on her face. He could feel his penis pushing against his underwear.

Her eyes flashed and a sly smile crept onto her lips. "Your eyes don't lie, Baby. You do like looking at me." She put her fingers under the edge of her camisole. "Tell me when to stop."

She slowly pulled it up.

Hunter's heart pounded. He whimpered as he tried to turn his head.

"You haven't said stop, Baby." She continued to lift her shirt until the bottoms of her breasts were exposed.

He groaned. "S . . . stop."

"You sure?"

He could not move his eyes to her face.

"No."

"You want me to pull it down?"

He could not make his voice say, "Yes."

"Or off?" She slowly, teasingly, pulled her camisole completely off.

She pulled his face into her breasts. "I could make you so happy, Baby, just like you were in my dream. You want to be happy?" She pulled his pelvis against her and slipped both hands down his back inside his underwear.

"Yes."

"Like you were in my dream?"

"How?"

She sighed deeply and groaned. "Let me show you." She flipped the light switch and pulled him into the darkness.

Hunter groaned and squirmed on the blankets until the sound forced his eyes open. He was on his side in Jazz's room, naked, holding his erection. He felt a sudden coldness that struck at his core.

A small light clicked on behind him. "Hunter? What's wrong?"

He heard Jazz get out of her bed and move onto his blankets. His throat felt thick, and he could barely breathe. She touched his shoulder.

He flinched. Jazz pulled her hand away.

"Where are your clothes?"

"On the floor in my mother's bedroom," he spit out with disgust.

Jazz covered him with a blanket. "It's OK, Hunter. You were the victim. You were thirteen. What choice did you have?"

"I could have said 'No.' I could have walked out of her room, but I didn't. I couldn't keep from looking at her."

"And she knew that. She manipulated you, Hunter. She seduced you. I know how it feels."

He turned over and studied her face. "With Micah?"

She flinched. "Yes, and the guilt never goes away unless someone helps you forget. Like your father did. Have you remembered having sex with her yet?"

"No."

"When that happens, you'll wish you never wanted to remember."

He pulled a pillow to his chest. "I need to know what happened to her. Why she died."

"I'll be there to help you when you learn the truth. I'm going back to my bed. I'll lie down facing the wall. You put on your clothes and get in bed with me."

"I don't think—"

"If you don't, I'm going to stay here next to you all night, and I don't like sleeping on the floor."

She got up and slipped into her bed. Hunter put on his clothes, turned off her lamp, and climbed in next to her. He put his arm around her stomach. She grabbed his hand and pressed it to her.

"Despite everything?" he asked.

"Despite everything and more, Hunter. Good night."

CHAPTER TWENTY-ONE

The next morning, Hunter awoke and could not feel Jazz. He sat up, trying to breathe, his head pounding. Then he heard her singing from the kitchen, or maybe the bathroom.

He sighed deeply. After the visions of his mother, he'd slept soundly for the rest of the night.

Jazz entered the room. "Did you miss me?"

"Actually, I did."

"Good. I had to pry your arm off me, you were clutching so hard."

"Why'd you get up?"

"I had to call Patty and tell her I was sick, that I got whatever you had. I told her I puked my guts out all night. Not sure she believed me, 'cause she laughed a little, but so what? I'm hoping you can steal some of my memories today."

"I'll try. How did you sleep?"

"Like a baby." She kissed his forehead. "I woke up in the same position as I went to sleep in. I don't think either one of us moved. How about you?"

"It was perfect. I had no more visions."

"I think we should try it again tonight, if that's OK with you."

He watched her lips stretch across her face in a smile and forgot to breathe. "I'd like that."

"Cool. C'mon. Breakfast is ready." She pulled his hand and led him out of the room into the kitchen.

Jazz squirted syrup onto her cheesy eggs as Hunter watched with a grimace.

"Yuck," he said as he shoved a bite of sausage and waffles into his mouth.

"You have eggs on your plate which is covered in syrup. Every bite of eggs you take has syrup on it." She sucked a big bite of eggs off her fork.

"But that's by accident. I don't pour syrup onto my eggs. You always eat them like that?"

"Always. Try a bite." She held out her fork full of syrupy eggs.

"I'll try them for *you*." He opened his mouth and took the bite. What decadence! The thick syrup covered his tongue in creamy sweetness as his teeth pushed through the soft clumps of eggs.

Jazz raised her brows. "Yes?"

"Mmmm! That's good." He poured syrup onto his eggs then devoured them all while Jazz laughed. "Do you have any more eggs?"

"No. Sorry."

He lifted the syrup bottle and opened his mouth to receive the stream of liquid sugar he squeezed out.

Jazz laughed and covered her mouth.

"The syrup's the best part. Why use eggs and waffles as an excuse to taste it?" He held the bottle above her mouth.

She opened her lips and pushed out her tongue. Hunter squeezed the bottle.

"Yummm!" Jazz licked her lips. "Tomorrow, breakfast will be just a bottle of syrup." She waggled her brows and wiggled in her chair. "We can find creative ways to indulge our sweet tooths. Wait. You have a drop just beneath your lips."

She leaned over the table and kissed him. "Think I got it."

"You sure?" Hunter poured a little syrup on his finger and rubbed it on his lips. "I think you missed a spot."

She leaned across the table again, grabbed his face, and pressed her lips to his. "Double yummm!" She sucked his bottom lip and flicked her tongue along his top. "Definitely the best way to eat syrup. Did I get it all this time?"

"Yeah, but I see some on your chin." He kissed her chin. "And a spot on your nose." He kissed her nose. "And your lips." They kissed.

Finally they separated. Hunter smiled as he moved his fingertips around her face. "How many bottles of syrup do you have?"

"Plenty. Think we'll have breakfast in bed tomorrow." She walked around the table then hugged him to her. "We can do this, Hunter. We can break from our past."

"I hope so, Jazz. God, you feel good."

Jazz felt warm and weightless, floating in happiness. But she knew these feelings wouldn't last very long. She still had her memories. One nudged against her consciousness though she tried to ignore it.

Micah had pressed himself against her many times. How could she feel Hunter without feeling Micah?

They had work to do. She would have to relive her memories this morning so Hunter could take them away.

She squeezed Hunter again then released him. "Help me clean up?"

"Sure."

They gathered plates and utensils from the table and took them to the sink, now much cleaner than during Hunter's first visit.

Jazz scraped food into her trashcan. "I got an update on the shooting. The boy shot himself. Survivors said he had no expression on his face when he fired. He didn't say anything or even look angry. He came out of the bathroom with a Glock and an extended clip and started firing randomly. When his first clip emptied, he pulled another from his pants."

"Jesus. Why?"

"Lots of speculation, but apparently he'd been treated for PTSD during the past year."

"Caused by?" Hunter rinsed plates then put them in the dish rack.

"Something about his grandfather and the boy's dogs being killed by coyotes. But there were also rumors about him being beaten as a child."

"How does that lead to killing students?"

"I don't know. His parents are accusing the doctor of misleading them about their son's mental progress. And get this. The doctor's name is Ru."

"My doctor?"

"Could be. I haven't checked to see how many Dr. Ru's there are in Washington. But I did find a Hongyan Ru in Bremerton who specializes in child psychiatry and trauma therapy."

"Has he said anything?"

"So far no one's been able to find him." Jazz sprayed cleaner on her stovetop then wiped it down.

"I wonder if I should call Dad. He has the doctor's number."

"Could be a different doctor named Ru. Could be he's on vacation. Or decided to take one to avoid the press."

"Or he's guilty of something and disappeared on purpose." Hunter dropped utensils into the rack.

"That seems the least likely. I'm sure they'll find Facebook postings or something about the shooter's social life to give them clues as to why he killed his classmates. And doctors don't try to create mass murderers."

"Maybe this reset idea is bogus. I wonder if the shooter had an implant? Maybe we should contact the police in Bremerton."

"That wouldn't be a good idea. We already have three people who know about your ability. Do you want to risk more finding out?"

Hunter sighed. "No." He hung the towel on the stove handle.

"More coffee?"

"Yeah. I'll get my computer." Hunter walked out of the kitchen toward Jazz's bedroom.

Jazz put a pod in her coffee machine and rinsed Hunter's cup. She knew which memories she would start with, ones she did not want to relive. Micah was entirely to blame for what happened between them, but she wished she'd acted differently at the start. She was twelve, however, and had just discovered her sexuality.

*   *   *   *   *   *

Right when Hunter told Jazz how good she felt to him, he remembered dancing with his mother when she pulled him closer. He had tried to think only of Jazz's body and inhale her scent, but he could not shake the memory of his mother. When Jazz asked him to clean up, he felt relief.

How horrible was that? Would he always be haunted by his past? Would he never be able to hold Jazz without thinking of his mother?

He looked at the bed they had slept in and realized he hadn't thought of his mother while sleeping with Jazz. The difference was his arousal. Maybe that was his future—friendly contact was peaceful, but sexual contact brought back nightmares.

He wondered if Jazz had felt something similar. Possibly. But he could fix that by taking her bad memories. He was sure there were more about Micah.

He picked up his computer and went back to the kitchen. Jazz had set his cup of coffee on the table and moved into the living room. He took a sip and walked to a chair, facing Jazz. Her legs were crossed, and her arms covered her chest.

"You ready for this?" he asked as he sat down.

She shook her head. "No. Are you?"

"I'm afraid of how bad yours will be." His shoulders felt tight, and he shivered.

"I'm going to run through as many as I can. Hunter, you're the best thing that's ever happened to me, not just for taking bad memories, but for being you."

"Compared to what I've seen in your head so far, that's not much praise. But I know what you mean. I want to be."

She closed her eyes.

The pounding started immediately. He stood outside his mother's bedroom door and heard himself panting then "Ahhhh! Ahhhh!" Just like Plant during the middle section of "Whole Lotta Love." He heard his mother moan, then "Yes! Yes! Yes!" The hall turned pitch black. He wandered, disoriented toward the wall, seeing nothing.

A young, much thinner Jazz stood outside a bedroom door, listening, wide-eyed, her ear pressed against the door. She heard the bed moving and Micah grunting rhythmically.

"Oh, God, Micah! Don't stop! Don't stop!" Her mother yelled through gritted teeth.

"Uh! Uh! Uh! Goddammit!" yelled Micah.

Then silence.

Then laughter. Jazz smiled, lifting her head up.

"Whoa, Claire! That was special."

"Especially amazingly good!"

They laughed again. Jazz laughed and slipped, banging her knee against the wall.

"What's that?" asked Micah.

Jazz's eyes flashed open. She heard footsteps. She ran away from the door, through the kitchen, and down her hallway as silently and quickly as she could. She slid into her bed, turned her back to the door, and tried desperately to calm her breathing.

She heard his footsteps approach her room. Squinting her eyes open, she noticed the light change against her far wall and knew he was standing in her doorway.

"Jazz?" he whispered. "Are you awake?"

She did not move or breathe.

"Did you listen to us? It's OK if you did. I made your mother feel real good tonight. Remember that."

He walked away.

Jazz inhaled a slow breath. Why did he come to her room? What did he want?

She replayed the sounds of their lovemaking in her mind.

The next day appeared in flashes of moments. Micah paid special attention to Jazz's looks at him, trying to get her to smile when Claire wasn't looking. He rubbed his hand up and down the zipper on his jeans, caught her looking, and pointed at her with a wink. Finally after lunch, her mother went outside to smoke a cigarette. Micah moved very close to her and tried to get her to look into his eyes.

When she did, he smiled. "Did you?"

Jazz felt her face heat up and knew she was blushing.

"Did you?"

"Did I what?"

"Did you listen outside our door?"

She tried to turn away. He grabbed her arm gently. "I know you did. Was it fun? Did you enjoy it?"

She looked to the floor.

"C'mon, Jazzy. I'm not going to bite you. Do you even know what we were doing?"

Jazz looked at him like, "Do you think I'm an idiot?" but said nothing.

"You just admitted it without saying anything." He laughed. "You're pretty smart, Jazz. And you're pretty good-looking, too."

She glanced at him and couldn't keep the smile from stretching her lips.

"Did you rub yourself?"

Jazz felt her skin tingle. She couldn't keep her mouth closed. She looked away.

"Did you?"

Her heart raced as she turned and ran down the hall to her room.

How did he know? *She felt lightheaded as sweat beaded on her brow.*

She heard footsteps then the creak of her door.

"Tell you what. I'm going into town in a few minutes. Think I'll get you something special. Just between you and me. You'll love it."

He walked away.

Another scene flashed.

She'd just taken a bath and opened the door to peak outside. She had been trying to avoid him all evening. Every time their eyes met, he smiled and winked. She didn't see him in the hall, so she walked quickly to her bedroom and closed the door.

Later when she pulled back her covers, she found a magazine full of naked men and a computer tablet. Plus a note: Have fun, Jazz! Tell me in the morning whether you liked my gifts. *He'd also written out some website addresses.*

She wanted to put everything in her closet and have nothing to do with them. But she couldn't stop looking at the magazine, and she couldn't stop panting. Her heart felt like it would jump out of her chest. She slowly opened her door and peeked down the hallway. Empty.

She picked up the magazine and opened it. Oh, my God! *She stared. Turned the page. Stared some more.*

Her face burned as she climbed under the covers, every nerve on edge.

Other scenes flashed by quickly for most of the night, full of sounds and incredible sensations. She crashed sometime near dawn, her body slick with sweat, gasping for air under the sheets. Her head ached.

Hours later her door squeaked open.

"Jazzy," said Micah softly, almost singing. "Time to get up, girl."

Her eyes snapped open under her covers. She tried not to move.

"Lucky this is summertime and you can sleep late. And stay up late . . . doing whatever." He laughed. "I know you're awake. Either show me right now, or I'll rip off your covers. One, Two, Three . . ."

"I'm awake! What do you want?" She still hid under the covers.

"How was your night? Fun?"

"I slept."

"The magazine was on the floor, so I guess you looked through that."

Her stomach clenched.

"Don't worry. I picked it up. Wouldn't want Claire to find it."

Jazz tried to decide what to do. She bit her knuckle.

"I guess the tablet is under the covers with you? I spent some good money for those, Jazz. Thought you'd appreciate them."

Jazz slowly pulled the covers down to her neck, squinting in the light. He stood against her door, now closed, with no shirt, wearing boxers. And he had an obvious erection. She caught herself staring then snapped her eyes away.

"Can you say, 'Thank you, Micah?'"

Jazz felt her lips tremble and couldn't look at him. Her stomach felt like she'd swallowed a rock. What did he want? Why did he buy those things for her? Last night she felt excitement, but now she was embarrassed. And worried. What should she do? And say?

"Thanks, Micah," she said softly.

He smiled. "No problem, Jazzy. I aim to please. Just want you happy. If you think of anything else you'd like to have, let me know. By the way, Claire went to get her hair done. She'll be gone for a couple of hours. I told her I'd let you sleep in, but you're awake. So I'll make you something to eat. You want to get dressed? Or do you want to stay in your bed for a little longer."

"No, I'll get up."

Her heart raced thinking about being alone with him in his trailer for two hours. That hadn't happened before. Was she excited or scared?

He still stood by the door.

"So go make me some food while I get dressed."

He smiled. "Sure." He scratched his stomach then left the room.

Jazz got out of bed and dressed quickly. She hid the tablet under her mattress. She thought about showing the gifts to her mom. That's what she should do, but how embarrassing would that be? She'd had them all night.

And she'd listened to them having sex outside their door. How would she explain that? Still, she should talk to her mother.

But she didn't.

Would she do the same tonight if she had the opportunity? Maybe, but she knew she shouldn't. Especially not if he was going to walk into her room again, shirtless, and . . .

Would he keep asking her questions? Would he try to do more? Why? She was twelve. She didn't want to talk about it anymore with him. She'd just ignore him.

But what if he kept talking about it? And forcing her to talk?

Maybe he just wanted to embarrass her. Make fun of her. Watch her squirm. He'd keep doing it if she let on it bothered her. So she'd have to stop acting embarrassed. Just like with bullies at school. If they knew they were getting to you, they'd keep after you.

Hunter opened his eyes and watched Jazz. She was breathing heavily, like she'd been running laps for an hour. He wanted to scream at her to run from the house, to call her mom. He knew what would happen to her because he hadn't left his mother's room when he had the chance. They had made the same mistakes and paid for them with years of doubt and self-loathing.

CHAPTER TWENTY-TWO

She walked down the hallway into the kitchen. He'd set a plate with toast and a fried egg. A glass of orange juice stood next to it.

He sat on the other side of the table, his face hidden behind a magazine, still shirtless.

Oh, God! He was looking through the nude magazine he had given her.

She almost ran outside. She should run outside.

But she couldn't take her eyes off the nakedness. The men were gorgeous. She had to force herself to breathe.

She couldn't let him get to her.

With as much sass as she could muster, she asked, "Did you buy that for me or for yourself?" She sat down and jabbed her egg with a piece of toast.

He turned the magazine around. "I think you stared at this guy the most."

Jazz flinched and stared at her egg. Yes, that was the one. How did he know?

He laid the magazine on the table between them. "I see a smudge here and here. Think you kissed the page a few times." He chuckled.

She took a sip of orange juice and grimaced. "What'd you put in here?"

"You know what I put. You've snuck drinks out of the bottle several times. You've been doing it for weeks. I made you a Screwdriver. Since your mother

won't drink with me anymore, I thought we could share a toast." He lifted his glass, waiting for her to clink it.

"Mom's pregnant. She can't drink."

"So she tells me. But you can. Maybe we could share a drink before you go to bed tonight. Might make your evening more fun." They locked eyes, his glass held above the middle of the table. "Don't worry. I won't tell your mother. This will be our little secret." He smiled at her while moving his tongue across his teeth.

Her breaths were quick and shallow. She should leave the trailer, but she couldn't make her legs work. Just walk outside and wait for Mom to come home and then tell her what Micah did. Her chest ached.

But then, how would they eat? Where would they sleep? Go back to MawMaw and PawPaw's? Mom didn't want that. This was Micah's house. He bought everything for them. Mom was six months pregnant.

"Jazz, I really didn't buy you anything yesterday."

What? She scrunched her eyebrows and stared at him.

"This is your mother's magazine. She's had it for two months. You took it out of her nightstand."

Jazz felt her blood drain from her face as he sneered at her.

"And the pad is mine. You snuck it out of our room sometime yesterday. I found it on your bed when I got you up this morning."

She gasped. Her hand shook so she put down her fork and held her hands in her lap.

"You know that's a lie," she choked out. "You wrote me a note!"

He pulled the note out from the magazine. "Yes, I did. But now it's gone." He wadded it up. "So do we keep our little secret?" He wiggled the glass at her. "If we did, things would go much better for your mother. Don't think she wants a big fight right now."

Jazz's heart raced. What should she do? "What do you want from me?"

"Right now, I'd like you to share a drink with me. Will you do that?"

She tried to think of options, but they all ended in them leaving Micah. Maybe she could deal with Micah for the time being. If he tried anything, then she'd tell Mom. She picked up her glass and clinked his.

Micah nodded his head and smiled. "Drink up!" He poured the drink down his throat. Jazz sipped hers and winced. This was a strong drink.

"No baby sips in my house. Drink it!" His voice commanded while his smile twisted into a leer.

Jazz took bigger sips and felt dizzy. "Drink up, Jazzy!" He laughed. "It's good for you. Everyone needs vitamin C in the morning."

Jazz finished the drink and closed her eyes. Her head felt numb. She leaned back in her chair and tried to breathe. Heat flooded her neck and face. Her skin tingled.

She felt fingers raking through her hair then rubbing her neck. It felt so good. She leaned her head forward and felt the fingers go down her back and along her ribs, then up, then across her shoulders and down her arms. She felt so relaxed.

Her chair moved away from the table. Hands lifted her out of the chair and pressed her against . . .

She opened her eyes and saw Micah's chest. His hands moved around her back then down. She tried to push herself away, but she was too weak.

"What . . . what?" She tried to speak.

"You need to lie down, Jazzy. I think that drink was a little strong." He laughed then picked her up and carried her into her room. He laid her gently onto her bed.

Jazz's vision was blurred. What did he want?

Somewhere behind the humming and the tingling and the fog in her brain, she realized she had made the wrong choice.

Hunter wiped his eyes and looked at Jazz. Her cheeks were wet with tears. Her breathing was quick and shallow as she shook her head slowly.

Several scenes flashed by quickly, most in her bedroom. Hunter's fingers flew around his keyboard. Jazz was not recalling stories anymore, just events. And emotions.

Sometimes Jazz begged Micah to stop, sometimes she laughed. Often she groaned. Micah commanded, grunted, laughed. Sometimes he spoke tenderly while Jazz cried.

Jazz heard more and more fights between her mother and Micah—glasses breaking, fists pounding on furniture. Jazz covered her ears and sobbed. He screamed about her looks and her feeling bad all the time. He slapped her often then came for Jazz. The louder the fight, the more likely Micah came to her room.

Her mother felt horrible and rarely left her bed. She apologized to Jazz who tended to her whenever she could.

Her mother must have noticed how tired Jazz was, how dark her skin was under her eyes.

"Are you OK, Jazz?"

"Sure, Mom. I'm fine."

"Is Micah treating you OK?"

Jazz looked at her mother, trying to keep from crying, trying so hard to bite her tongue. Why did Mom ask her now? Did she suspect? Had Micah said something?

"Sure. Why wouldn't he?" Jazz fluffed up her pillow.

"You look so sad lately. And distracted. Are you sleeping OK?" Her mother touched her cheek.

No, I'm not sleeping. I do whatever Micah wants me to do, except screw him. He hasn't tried that yet, but I know it's coming. *That's what she wanted to say, but all she could muster was, "I'm OK. Looking forward to having a sister."*

Mom smiled and kissed her forehead. "Won't be long now."

One night after Micah left her room at three in the morning, she ran to the bathroom and puked her guts out. She stared at the slime that came out of her mouth as it drifted around the toilet bowl. Another spasm twisted her gut, but all that emerged was a groan from deep inside, a retching from her soul so dirtied, so corrupted.

She wailed and pulled her hair until some came out in her hands. But she felt no pain—just relief. She pulled out some more with a stifled scream then looked at the strands in her fist. For those few seconds when she pulled, she didn't feel dirty. She didn't feel Micah.

She saw the razor sitting on the edge of the tub. The tiny blades hypnotized her. Three of them. Shiny. Clean. Sharp.

Her hand reached for the handle. She wondered what it would feel like to drag the blades across her ankle.

In her mind she could not stop seeing Micah, smelling him, tasting him. But her eyes saw the blades as she set them on her skin then dragged slowly. The burning sting closed her mind so all she saw was the blood trickling onto the floor.

She gritted her teeth and released all the breath in her lungs.

She moved the blade up and pushed it harder this time. Deeper. Longer. Until the pain forced her fingers to drop the razor.

She watched the blood drip into tiny little puddles.

Her mind was a blank, numbed by the aching pain in her ankle. She sat there for several minutes finding comfort in the singular focus of her consciousness— her blood, the throbbing, and her mutilated skin.

Finally, she wiped her ankle with toilet paper then cleaned the floor with a washcloth. She watched the blood ooze from the sliced skin then remembered she had a half glass of vodka in her room. She hurriedly returned to get it and closed the door to the bathroom. Her heart racing, she sat on the edge of the tub and slowly poured the alcohol onto her cuts as she clenched her teeth.

The electric slap of pain shuddered her muscles and restored the emptiness in her head.

She walked slowly back to her room and slipped under her covers, her brain asleep before her head collapsed into her pillow.

Hunter pressed his fists into his eyes, trying to staunch his tears. He knew what scenes were coming, and he did not want to see them.

Jazz opened her eyes as if from a dream. The corners of her mouth quivered into a partial smile. "Just a little more, Hunter. Can you stand it?"

His voice was just a whisper. "Barely."

"Do you want me to stop?"

"I want you to feel whole again. Just hold me when you're done."

"I'll never let you go."

Jazz closed her eyes, and Hunter heard her mother screaming.

"Micah! Please don't."

Jazz was standing in the hall when she heard the slap and her mother crying.

"Micah. Please, that hurts!"

"Worthless bitch!" He slapped her again.

"I'm sorry, Micah. I can't do it. I'm sorry." She wept.

Jazz trembled. She knew what she would say to him, but he had to leave her mother's room. If he slapped her again, she would go to the door and tell him the faucet broke—or something.

She waited and heard nothing. She was about to approach their door when Micah burst out and stomped into the kitchen. He poured vodka and orange juice into a glass and chugged half of it.

Jazz took a few steps forward until she knew he could see her.

He leered when he saw her beckon him. His tongue dragging across his teeth, he slunk drunkenly toward her.

"What you want, Jazzy?"

"I'll give you what you want if you stopping hitting Mom."

His grin spread wide as he nodded his head and looked down her body.

"Is that the excuse you want to give knowing you've wanted me all along?"

He drained his glass.

"You have to promise not to hit her anymore. The only reason you're hitting her is because she won't screw you. The baby's due in a few days. Leave her alone. Let her have the baby. And you can . . ."

Jazz closed her eyes and breathed deeply.

Micah started unbuttoning her shirt. "And I can do what?"

"I'll lie down and let you do it." She grabbed his hands. "Deal?"

"Sure, Jazzy. Deal." She let go of his hands, which continued unbuttoning her shirt. "I've been looking forward to doing this for a long time."

He took off her shirt. Jazz turned around and went to her bedroom where she removed the rest of her clothes. She lay down and watched Micah leer at her as he removed his clothes.

Hunter grabbed his head and pulled. He felt like it would explode with all the pain inside. But his anger boiled in his gut. This shouldn't happen. Ever. Again.

Micah climbed on top of her.

"Please don't hurt me, Micah." Her insides seemed to drop into a hole, spiraling slowly.

"I would never hurt you, Jazzy."

A few seconds later, Jazz tried to stifle her screams.

Other scenes flashed into Hunter's brain. More cuts along her ankles, more late night visits from Micah, more drinking.

Three days after the first rape, Jazz remembered her PawPaw kept a pistol in a dresser drawer in his bedroom. She had found it two years ago when she went hunting for money in her grandparents' house. At the time, Mom had almost nothing left and wouldn't ask her parents for cash. Jazz found a few dollars here and there, but the pistol was her biggest find. She thought about stealing it and letting her mother pawn it, but decided to leave it. Soon after, Mom met Micah, and she and Jazz moved out.

Jazz took off on her bike to visit her grandparents with a small pack and a bottle of water. They were surprised to see her and begged for information about their daughter and the baby. Jazz slipped out of the kitchen while her grandparents prepared a late lunch and darted into their bedroom. She found the gun and stuffed it into her pack. In a panic, afraid of being discovered or delayed, she ran outside, jumped on her bike, and raced back home. She hid the gun under her mattress and swore to herself she'd kill him if he hurt Mom again.

More days passed and Claire still had not given birth to her daughter. Micah mumbled continually that their deal had not covered all this extra time. That Jazz needed to satisfy him again.

She didn't expect him to barge in that night, drunk, wearing nothing but boxers. He ripped off the covers and told her to remove her clothes.

She couldn't get the gun.

Her stomach rolled, and bile oozed up her throat.

She let him do it again while trying so hard to keep her screams behind her gritted teeth. He laughed at her and called her a drama queen.

She became a shell of herself, numb, with eyes that didn't see the world, just the loop of Micah grunting on top of her, ripping her insides.

Even repeated cuts to her legs wouldn't revive her.

Two nights later, she found herself staring at a butcher knife, blinking back at her as she rocked the edge on her wrist under the lamplight in her room.

Just a simple pull on the handle would do it.

She began to smile and count: one, two, three, four, five, slice. She dragged the blade lightly.

Blood came in a fast trickle. The edge was sharp. But the pain was nothing.

Harder next time. Deeper.

One, two, three, four . . .

Her mother screamed.

Jazz jerked her head up.

"Micah! Don't!"

She lurched off her bed and pulled the gun from under the mattress and put it under her pillow.

Her mother yelled again.

Jazz snuck down the hall.

The memory stopped. Hunter knew what happened next, but Jazz didn't remember.

His insides twisted and lurched, filling his throat with a suffocating wail. He grabbed his head as he fell to the floor, weeping.

"Hunter!" Jazz screamed.

His cries filled his head, his entire world, a guttural howl embodying all her pain. "Jazz! Jazz!" He pounded the floor until he felt hands grasping his arms.

"Hunter! I'm here. I'll hold you."

She pulled him into her, rocking him.

"I'll always hold you, Hunter. I'll never let you go."

Several minutes later he opened his eyes and felt her hand pushing through his wet hair. He buried his head into her chest, whimpering. "How could you survive that?"

"Survive what?" She held his face in front of hers. "I don't know what you're talking about, Hunter. You took it all away."

She kissed his forehead, then his eyes. "I'm free, Hunter." She kissed one cheek. "I can breathe because of you." She kissed the other.

"I can love because of you." She kissed his lips.

Hunter felt her tongue push into his mouth, felt the heat of her breath, and tasted the sweet elixir of her spirit. At that moment he disconnected from her memories screaming in his brain and relaxed in her arms.

He felt her fingers tracing every line and curve of his face as she gazed at him in wonder.

"Thank you, Hunter. I wish I could do the same for you."

After a few minutes of rest, Hunter stood. "How many other girls suffer like you did and continue to suffer? And how can no one know about it? Do the police ever catch the shits who do this? And if so, why don't we hear about it?"

"We don't because the kids are minors. Their names are protected, as well as the details of what happened to them."

"These stories need to get out somehow. Including mine. If people knew the truth, they'd do something. I can't believe they wouldn't."

He took a few steps and stopped. "Why was my mother able to get away with seducing me? Because she was the mother with total control over her kids. We were homeschooled, supposedly. Maybe we had no playmates, so who would we talk to? And even if we had friends, would we tell anyone else, or be too embarrassed to say anything?"

He paced around the room. "How many kids cut themselves without their parents knowing about it? Must be thousands. Who knows about Tatiana's purging?"

Jazz stood. "No one but us, as far as I know, though now it seems obvious." She gave him a hug. "Does getting angry help you cope with the memories?"

"Yes. Somehow, I need to find a way to fight back." He shook his head, every muscle taut. "Besides, every time I take a memory from someone else, I see more of my past. The only way I'll know the truth about my mother is if I do this."

Someone knocked on the front door.

CHAPTER TWENTY-THREE

Hunter looked at Jazz questioningly. Surely Eric wouldn't have returned so quickly. "Who?"

"It must be Tatiana. I told her to come by at lunch. You want me to ask her to come by after school?"

"No, let her in. I'll go put on my shirt."

Jazz touched the scars on his chest. "I remember doing most of my cuts, but I don't remember why I started. I think I'm more ashamed of them now."

Hunter kissed a few scars on her shoulders. "I saw you make your first cuts. No one had more reason. Most in your situation would have killed themselves or blanked out entirely. They signify your strength, not your weakness."

Jazz hugged him quickly. "Thank you. Maybe you should take a break?"

"No!" He knew he'd said this too loud. "I'm sorry, Jazz, but I can do this. You endured it. All I have to do is watch. I don't want to stop."

She held his head. "OK. I'll let her in."

Hunter went back to her bedroom and stood before her mirror examining his scars. They seemed larger, more obvious. How had he ever thought they came from a bike accident? Why had he cut himself? When? What was the pain so heavy in his mind that he had to cover it with a blade? His own guilt at succumbing to his mother's advances or something else?

He pulled on a t-shirt and went to the kitchen where he found Tatiana hugging Jazz.

"You always seemed so happy," Tatiana said through her tears.

"So did you." Jazz held Tatiana's shoulders. "Does anyone else know about your purging?"

"I don't know. I thought it would be obvious. When no one said anything, I thought they just didn't care." Tatiana looked at Hunter. "Jazz said you could help me."

"I'll try."

"Will either of you tell anyone?"

"We won't even tell you," said Hunter. "Once I see your memory, you won't remember you had it."

Tatiana lowered her large brown eyes. "Hunter . . . you're going to see . . . to see my body . . . I'm so sorry. I'm nervous."

"I understand. But when we're done, you won't remember that I saw it. Please don't worry."

Jazz held Tatiana's arm and led her into the living room. "Sit down here." Tatiana sat on the sofa. "You're going to have to relive the event. It will be painful at the beginning, but it should be the last time you'll have to think about it."

Hunter could have collapsed in Jazz's bed and curled into a ball, he felt so drained and spent, but his anger gave him strength. Why should this sweet girl suffer so much that she made herself puke every day? No one was trying to help her, so he would. He opened his computer lid then looked at Tatiana.

She stared back at him, wrinkling her brows. "So, let me get this straight. I'll think about what happened to me, and then what will happen?"

"I'll see what you're thinking," said Hunter.

"How?"

Jazz sat next to her. "We don't know how it works yet, but what you see in your head, he'll see in his."

Tatiana shook her head. "How's that even possible? Is it magic?"

"No magic," said Jazz. "Science. Your memories don't stay in your mind. They're like a halo around you, linked to your brain. When you recall an event, the memory floods your brain, stimulating all the neurons that were active when you formed the memory. Except this time Hunter hijacks the memory."

Her eyes widened at Hunter. "Then what?"

Jazz held her hand. "He writes what he sees, like he's living the memory."

"Like he's me?" She turned her face toward Jazz.

"Sort of."

"Will it hurt?"

"I felt a little dizzy when he took mine."

"Was it bad?"

Jazz smiled. "He says it was, but I have no idea because I don't remember a thing." Jazz touched her cheek. "Trust us, Tatiana. You'll feel so much better."

Tatiana lowered her head. "Will it hurt you, Hunter?"

"Not as much as the event hurt you. Don't worry about me. I want to do this."

Jazz smiled. "He sweats a lot afterward." Jazz squeezed her hand. "You ready?"

"Jazz, can you stay here with me?" Tatiana asked.

"Sure."

Tatiana pulled Jazz's hand to her chest and began breathing quickly.

Hunter heard pounding in the darkness. He felt hands all over him. He and his mother were naked, pressed together.

More pounding. "Mom! Where's Hunter?" Frankie's voice. He was knocking on the bedroom door.

Hunter whispered, "Mom. Frankie's at the door." He had to push her off of him before he ran into the bathroom.

"Mom!" Frankie pounded the door.

"What is it Frankie?"

From the bathroom, Hunter saw light shoot into the room.

"Where's Hunter?"

"Jesus, close the door. I don't know. Go back to sleep, Frankie. I'm sure Hunter will be back in bed in just a little while."

The light disappeared. Hunter crept back into the bedroom, trying to find his clothes.

"Come back to bed, Hunter."

"I should go."

"Five minutes. Just five minutes."

Hunter pulled on his clothes. "I'll come back later."

He put his ear to the door and listened. Hearing nothing, he opened the door slowly, peeking through the opening. The hall was empty. He slipped out of the room and saw light at the end of the hall. He moved toward it.

A younger Tatiana rode her bike in the park toward the river. She emerged from the trees and turned left where the road looped by some campsites. She was supposed to meet Molly, but her friend had been grounded. Tatiana was bored at home, so she took off by herself. She rode to the end of the loop, thinking it would be empty, then noticed a white van parked on the side of the road. She slowed and saw a man asleep in the driver's seat, so she decided to drive past him.

Just as she drew even with the front door, she heard the man groan. She looked over and saw him clutch his chest, which bucked up and down. He grunted then let out, "Ahhhh! Oh, God. It hurts!"

He stopped suddenly and slumped into his seat.

Tatiana braked. "Mister? Are you OK?"

The man moaned. "Help me."

She got off her bike and approached his door.

"What's wrong?"

"Think I'm having . . ."

His voice trailed off.

She got closer. "What'd you say?"

He clutched his chest and groaned. She moved closer. "Do you need help?"

She was three feet from his door when he pushed a pistol out his window and cocked the hammer.

Tatiana shuddered. She looked at the gun barrel then at his face. Her stomach turned cold, and she forgot to breathe.

"Don't move or scream or I'll shoot your pretty little face. Got it?"

Tatiana gasped and nodded her head. Her lips curled back from her teeth, and she felt sweat drip inside her clothes.

His hair was pulled into a ponytail. His face was grizzled, and his thick beard hung beneath his jaw hiding his neck. He sneered, revealing a silver tooth in his front teeth. He opened the door and climbed out of his seat, pointing the barrel at her face.

Tatiana gasped for air in spasms. "Please. Don't hurt me."

He moved closer. "Anyone else with you?"

"No." Maybe she should have said yes. "Yes. My family is just on the other side of the trees."

He leered at her. "Really?" He reached out his left hand and touched her breast.

She backed away and covered her chest with her arms.

He moved to her and pushed the barrel into her neck. "I didn't say you could move." He grabbed her wrist. "Get inside the van."

"Please!" Tears flooded out of her eyes. She didn't want to die.

He slapped her face. "Shut up! Get in the van."

She collapsed onto her knees. He grabbed her hair and yanked her up. She cried out.

He pulled her face close to his. "You fight me, and I'll cut you up. You'll have scars all over your face. Be nice, and I won't hurt you. Got it?"

She nodded. He pulled her toward the side door, holding her hair and jamming the gun into her ribs.

"Open the door."

Every muscle shook. She reached out for the handle but couldn't grab it.

"I said open it."

She pulled the handle with both hands. The door slid open, and he pushed her inside.

The area behind the front seats was open, the floor covered with a thin mattress. He slammed the door shut, plunging them into darkness.

The air inside was thick with the stench of cigarettes, sweat, and beer. He reached up and pulled a string, turning on a light.

Tatiana's eyes darted frantically around her. A curtain separated them from the front, and all the other windows were covered.

Tatiana couldn't breathe. Every nerve was on fire as she trembled. He would rape her and kill her. She couldn't stop trembling.

He pulled out a hunting knife and grabbed a roll of duct tape. After he cut off a six-inch piece, he said, "Lean forward."

"I can barely breathe. Please don't cover my mouth. Please. I won't yell. I won't yell."

He grinned. "OK, but if you make any sound at all, I'll cut your face." He moved the blade to her cheek. "Such a pretty face. Be a shame if it were covered in scars."

She stared at the blade, whimpering, then at his face. "I won't. I promise."

"Lie down," he growled.

Her eyes widened.

He moved the blade closer. "Lie down."

She scooted her legs toward him and then leaned back on her elbows.

"All the way down. And stretch out your arms."

Her chest heaved as she moved her arms away from her body. He moved up to each arm, lifting two heavy, round weights onto each forearm.

She couldn't move her arms, which started to tingle as her blood was cut off.

"Let's see what we got here."

He lifted her shirt away from her stomach and slipped the knife underneath, blade up, then cut the buttons.

She yelped. He laid the knife against her skin. "No sounds."

He moved the blade up the shirt and cut again.

Then again.

He spread the shirt away from her skin. "How old are you?"

"Four. . . fourteen."

He chuckled then pushed the knife tip under the middle of her bra. She flinched and gritted her teeth. "Oops. Nicked you a little." He chuckled again.

Tatiana felt blood drip down her side.

He pulled the blade sharply up and cut her bra.

She felt the flat side of the knife move up her left hip. She waited for the cut and flinched. But she felt no pain. He twisted the blade and cut the fabric.

She felt the blade slide along her right hip then rip away.

Tatiana felt her skin exposed when he pulled the shorts and underwear away from her.

"My, my, my. Think I'll take some pictures."

Tatiana tried to breathe evenly while she stared at the roof of the van, seeing the flashes and hearing the clicks.

Maybe that's all he wants, *she thought.* Pictures.

He started humming. She heard the rustle of clothes then saw him standing over her as he dropped his pants and kicked them away.

"You're gonna love this." He bent down and leaned his face over her stomach, dragging his tongue across her flesh.

Tatiana shuddered and tried not to squirm.

Hunter felt a hand on his arm. He looked up and saw Jazz with her phone. She whispered, "My Mom."

He nodded and looked at Tatiana who had leaned back in the sofa, holding a pillow against her face.

"Bad?" asked Jazz.

Hunter nodded once then looked back at his screen.

Jazz kissed the top of his head and walked out of the room

*　*　*　*　*　*

Jazz swiped to accept the call. "Hey, Mom. How are you?" She hoped she hadn't left rehab.

"I'm good, Jazz. I'm done!" Her voice sound cheerful and excited. "They're letting me out tomorrow. I finished six weeks."

Jazz sighed and shook her head. She was lying. "I thought the program was eight weeks."

"It depends on how you do. They said I've done great, so I can go."

Jazz sank onto her bed. "Isn't there a halfway house they want you to go to?"

"A what?"

"I looked at their website, Mom. You're supposed to spend a month at a halfway house once you leave rehab."

Jazz could hear her suck on a cigarette. "No one told me about that."

Jazz pinched her nose. "Did you get kicked out?"

She sounded so offended. "Why do you say that? Dammit, Jazz, can't you ever trust me?"

"Because there's nothing on the website that says anything about a six-week program." Jazz sighed and felt hope for something better disappear. "What happened?"

"Nothing happened—"

She jumped off the bed. "Don't lie to me! Did you drink?" Silence. "Did you drink?"

Her mother tried to fight back with her own anger. "Why aren't you in school?"

Jazz's throat tightened. "It's lunch! I'm at home for lunch. Did you drink?"

Jazz heard her blow smoke out of her mouth. "One of the advisors offered me one of those airplane bottles of vodka."

Jazz felt her skin heat up. "Let me guess. A male advisor."

"Yeah. He's in trouble, too."

"Why did he give it to you?"

"Because we were kissing—"

Jazz slammed her fist against the wall. "Oh, Jesus, Mom! Why were you hitting on one of the advisors?"

"He hit on me! Evidently, that's what he does. Trades bottles for sex. I wasn't the only one."

Her guts were churning. "You screwed him for a tiny bottle?"

"I didn't screw him. We were just kissing."

"And where's he now?"

"Out of a job."

Jazz kicked a pile of clothes on her floor. "He's not coming into this house!"

"Who said he was going to?"

"Goddammit, Mom. You were clean for six weeks. Why couldn't you do two more?"

"You try going eight weeks without drinking, Jazz! Could you do it?"

"I could now." She sat on her bed.

"Oh really."

"Yeah, I could." She thought of holding Hunter in bed. She'd never have to see those memories again. Yes, there were more, but the worst ones were gone. "When am I supposed to pick you up?"

"They want me out of here by ten tomorrow morning."

"All right. I'll be there."

There were a few moments of silence before Jazz heard her mother crying.

"Jazz, I'm sorry. I really tried."

Jazz slumped onto her bed. "I know, Mom. I know. I'll be there tomorrow morning." Should she tell her about Hunter? She'd have to because he would be with her. "I'll . . . I'll have a boy with me."

"A boy? Who?"

"His name is Hunter. We're good friends. He's helped me a lot."

"You have a boyfriend?"

Her mother's shock might have angered Jazz, but thinking of Hunter as her boyfriend tempered that response. Instead, warmth spread through her body. She felt her skin glowing. "He's more than a boyfriend. He's my savior. Maybe he can save you, too. I'll explain tomorrow. Good-bye, Mom."

"Good-bye, Jazz."

Her mother would be living with them tomorrow night. How would that change things? Hunter would see her memories. How much more crap could he take? Maybe they could leave town and be by themselves for a while. She could cradle him as he slept on her lap and protect him. But she knew he'd never agree. He was angry at the world for allowing these events to happen. He'd never accept hiding from them.

Jazz looked into the living room. Hunter typed a few more words then closed his computer. He leaned back and looked to the ceiling. Tatiana was asleep, curled against her pillow on the sofa. She seemed peaceful.

"Should I wake her?" whispered Jazz.

Hunter shook his head.

Jazz walked to him and cradled his head. Hunter clutched her, but this time he did not cry. Jazz could feel his body taut and coiled. She could feel the churning rage trying to find an escape.

He sat up and grasped his head, pressing furiously at his temples.

"Hunter, what's wrong?"

"My mother."

CHAPTER TWENTY-FOUR

Hunter's mind filled with drunken scenes of his mother, having sex, dancing naked to "Whole Lotta Love," afternoon sessions when they locked the house after forcing Frankie to play outside. The scenes flashing through his mind covered several weeks.

Hunter was no longer hesitant to Savannah's advances. They took more risks. They both drank more and more. On some mornings Hunter could not wake her. When she finally arose, she had two drinks before breakfast and sipped on vodka concoctions all day long.

She put on weight and spent less time fixing her face and hair.

The worst time was when Joe came home, and Hunter couldn't sneak into his mother's bed at night. Hunter heard his parents' arguments. She accused her husband of having an affair and demanded to look through his phone.

Hunter had threatened Frankie against saying anything to Dad about him catching Hunter in bed with Mom. The threats worked, but Hunter knew Frankie would eventually say something. He almost wished he would. Having to endure the pretense while his father was home was becoming more and more difficult. He counted the seconds before his father would return to Prudhoe.

After a particularly loud fight, Dad left two days early, which was good because Hunter had told his mother he'd planned to confront his Dad and ask him to move out. What good was he anyway? All he did was interfere with his relationship with his mother.

Savannah said that the next time he came home, she would demand a divorce.

They left Frankie by himself at the house while they supposedly drove to a nearby store. Actually, they found a quiet place in the woods and had sex in her car.

Hunter opened his eyes and tried to shut out the vision in his mind. Tatiana stared at him from the sofa, her shoulders slumped but eyes wide. She looked around like she didn't know where she was. "What happened?" her voice raspy and uncertain, like the first drowsy words of morning. She looked down at her arms, holding them out like she had never seen them before. "What time is it?"

"About two o'clock," said Jazz. "He thought you should sleep. Are you OK?"

She nodded slowly, not moving anything but her head. "I'm tingling all over, like my arms and legs had their circulation cut off."

Jazz grinned and reached over with her finger to touch her arm.

"No! Please don't," she giggled. She threw her head back, breathed slowly, and moved her fingers slowly. Then she shivered, squealed, and hugged herself. She looked at Hunter. "What'd you do?"

"I took your bad memory."

"What memory?" Tatiana's eyes showed confusion but not the terror or shame they had before.

Jazz sat beside her and hugged her. "Exactly. What memory?" She held Tatiana's face. "You feel good?"

"Amazing! But I'm hungry. Do you have anything to eat?"

"Sure," said Jazz. "I'll make some sandwiches." She rubbed Hunter's head then pulled her wet hand away. "God, Hunter. You're soaked. Your shirt is plastered to you."

He grinned. "Sorry."

"It's OK." She kissed his forehead. "Your sweat tastes good. Can I leave you alone for a few minutes?"

"Yeah, I'm hungry, too."

Jazz squeezed him one more time then walked toward the kitchen. Hunter stood up and stretched.

"Was it bad?" asked Tatiana.

Hunter looked at Tatiana and tried to ignore his memory of her trying to be silent and still while that man raped her twice. "Very. But you don't have to worry about it anymore."

"Will you . . . will you tell Jazz?"

"Not everything."

"Do you think less of me now?"

"No. I don't see how you lived through those events. You're an amazing girl."

A smile fluttered across her face. "Thank you."

As they both walked into the kitchen, Jazz tossed Hunter a fresh shirt. He stripped off his sopping t-shirt and saw Tatiana cover her mouth with her hands.

"You have scars, too?"

Hunter thrust his arms through the sleeves. "Yeah, but I don't remember how I got them." He pulled down his shirt. "Jazz thinks I see memories that are connected to my missing ones."

"But I never cut myself," said Tatiana.

"No." He almost said, "You purged," but he didn't want to remind her. "Bad things happened to you, and bad things happened to me. I'll remember everything soon."

"You want to remember?"

"I have to know the truth. Every time I see someone else's memory, I see something from my past."

"You're taking my bad memory and Jazz's so you can suffer your past again? I don't understand why you would do that."

"Because I see two young women who were hurt through no fault of their own smiling now, happy to be free from that pain. And that's pretty cool."

"Yes, that is," said Jazz, smiling at him, holding a knife covered in mayonnaise. "Tell me what you want on your sandwich."

While they ate, Tatiana asked, "Could I come over here sometimes? I like being with you guys."

Jazz smiled. "OK with me. Hunter?"

"Sure."

Tatiana smiled. "Would be nice to have friends who know the worst about me and still want to be friends."

"That would be nice," said Hunter. "Maybe next time I'll share everything in my past with you and see if you still want to visit."

"After what you've done for me and for Jazz," said Tatiana, "nothing would turn me away from you. You're willing to take other people's horrible memories. That's pretty special."

Jazz grabbed Hunter's hand. "Yes, it is."

"I better get back to school."

They all stood.

Tatiana reached out to hug Jazz. "Thank you, Jazz."

"You're welcome."

Tatiana held out her arms toward Hunter. "Can I?"

Hunter stepped toward her. "Sure." They hugged briefly.

"Bye!" Her eyes sparkled with happiness as she backed toward the door, smiling at both of them, then turned to leave.

Jazz watched from the kitchen window as Tatiana drove away. "Do you think she'll purge her lunch?"

"Maybe not. After the rape, she was afraid she was pregnant. She kept examining her stomach for any signs of swelling. She started throwing up to make sure she wouldn't get bigger. Plus she vomited to get him out of her. That man should be skinned alive." Hunter cleared the table and took the dishes to the sink.

"And she blamed herself?"

"Of course, she did. She thought she should have run away when he pulled the gun. She should never have fallen for a fake heart attack. She shouldn't have gone to the park by herself. All she's done since the rape is beat herself up."

"Did anyone else know?"

"Not sure, but I don't think so." He wet a towel and took it to the table, which he wiped down.

"Did you see more scenes with your mother?"

"Yeah, several." He threw the towel across the kitchen toward the sink. "I had sex with her every night and day at least once for several weeks except when my father came back from work. We were fucking hamsters!" He kicked a chair and shook his head. He laughed and pinched the bridge of his nose. "And my little brother knew some of it. I grew to hate Frankie, and I wanted my Dad out of the house. I think when he comes home the next time, the big secret will be revealed."

Jazz went to him and kissed his cheek. "Don't be so hard on yourself. When crap happens to us, we blame ourselves. Why? Because most people aren't raped or abused, so we must blame ourselves for getting into such bad situations. But none of this was our fault."

"I know, but it's still hard to accept that."

"On the other hand, my mother may have some blame. You'll get to find out."

"How?"

She ran her fingers through his hair. "My mother got kicked out of rehab. We're going to pick her up tomorrow in Fairbanks."

"What happened?"

"Another man offering booze for sex. The story of her life." She kissed his other cheek. "Maybe you can fix her, too."

"Remember what I said to you the first day we met?"

"Sex causes every problem in the world." Jazz kissed his lips.

He pulled his lips from hers. "Do you still disagree?"

She rubbed her fingers around the edge of his ears. "There's got to be good sex somewhere."

"Well, I haven't seen it yet."

"Tell me this isn't good." She kissed him again.

He felt her tongue and sucked it farther into his mouth. His mind emptied of thought, focusing entirely on her warmth and taste. Every nerve ending touching any part of her vibrated with heat, grasping for her. He wanted to melt into her.

"We could make amazing love to each other, Hunter. When I felt you against me this morning, I remember panicking. But you took that away. All I feel now is such deep want. No more hang-ups. I know your feelings are still complicated. Maybe when you learn the truth, you can just feel me. Or maybe you'll never be able to. But if we can share kisses like this every once in a while, that's enough for me."

He pulled her close to him. "Can we lie down for a while?"

"Yes." She pulled him toward her bedroom.

"When will Eric show up?"

"In an hour. Maybe two."

She kneeled by his duffle and pulled out his Tremarian folder. Then she climbed into her bed. "Spoon me and take a nap. I'm going to read through these stories. Did you start these while you were having sex with your mother or after?"

He shook his head.

She patted the bed. "Get in. I'll wake you up when he calls."

Hunter lay down behind her pressing his body tightly against hers. She was propped on her left side, the stories on the sheets in front of her. She pulled his arm to her stomach. Hunter slipped his hand under her shirt and fell asleep.

*　*　*　*　*

Jazz remembered the last story Hunter had shown her nine or ten weeks ago. She flipped through pages toward the end to find it. She wanted to know what he had written just before the visions started. She remembered his first memory story—a boy and girl Face-Timing while masturbating, caught in the act by the boy's mother. After she'd first read it, Jazz thought the boy and girl represented the illicit acts Hunter and his mother committed which were then judged and condemned by an adult figure. But maybe there was another interpretation.

The boy did not ejaculate until his mother entered the room. From what Jazz now knew, Hunter and his mother had frequent sex. It made sense that his first vision dealt, however obliquely, with a mother and son and sexuality. Those were at the core of Hunter's troubles, the memories that had to be erased.

What started their return?

She flipped to the last story in Hunter's Tremarian folder.

The woman and a teenage boy fled across the rocky plateau toward the cliff's edge, pursued by a squadron of Tremarian soldiers fighting for the Keen, the genderless ruler who started a war ten years ago against the only remaining country still committed to distinct genders. The Keen (a combination of king and queen) believed the Dumarians posed a threat to the demise of male and female sexuality, which had threatened the survival of the planet Marian years ago before most of society demanded gender neutrality.

Why? Because the increasing levels of murder, assault, abuse, oppression, and especially the destruction of fetuses through abortion and unhealthy living demanded change. Reproduction was now a lab procedure. Physical sexual differences and the act of sex were no longer necessary. Most leaders and citizens had acquiesced to genetic manipulation for them and future generations. Every Tremarian now had similar body parts. True equality had been achieved. They were no longer controlled by animalistic urges, which inevitably led to pornography, sex trafficking, prostitution, and beyond. They were no longer slaves to orgasm.

But the Dumarians had resisted. Their country provided a haven for those still intoxicated by sexuality. Some Tremarians had defected simply to engage in all sorts of hedonistic pleasures with Dumarian males and females.

The Keen knew that Dumaria's existence would eventually erode Tremarian dominance. Too many people could not resist engaging in sex if offered the opportunity.

After years of war, the Dumarian population had been decimated and isolated into vagabonds like this woman and boy.

But some believed sizable Dumarian groups still thrived in secret places, possibly underground or in caves.

"You cannot escape," shouted the Tre leader. "You must surrender or be killed." The squadron lifted their weapons, their tips glowing with a swirling white ball of energy, filling the air with an electric hum. Each soldier's head was shaved on one side, while the other side sported long hair tied in a braid.

The woman and son stopped and faced the soldiers, their backs to the abyss, long blonde hair whipping behind them in the wind.

Now that she stood still, her pregnancy was obvious.

"Open your robes!" commanded the Tre leader.

The woman smiled. "Certainly." She then untied the sash at her waist, revealing her nakedness.

Many in the squad gasped, having never seen a completely nude female body. Some lowered their weapons.

The Tre leader stood in front of his soldiers. "Focus on your duty!" Every soldier raised their weapons. "Today we kill three for the price of two. Such a bargain!"

The leader moved closer to the woman and boy. "Is sex so important to you that you would live on the run as animals? Where is the future in that?"

She held her womb. "He is my future, the Dumarian future."

"Where is the father? Or do you even know who he is?"

"You killed my husband." The woman reached out for the boy and pulled him to her. "My son is the father."

The leader spat in disgust as many of the soldiers yelled their objections.

The woman laughed. "Each of you would pay much to have taken my son's place. But none of you have the balls to do it."

The boy laughed.

The woman pulled her son closer. "You will always wonder about the pleasures you have been denied."

She laughed and kissed her son's lips. "We leave you now."

They jumped over the edge.

The leader shouted an order, and several soldiers raced toward the edge. After peering over the side, one looked back toward the leader. "They disappeared."

At that moment the air filled with high-pitched screams—wahoohoo, wahoohoo—as a hundred Dumarians ran at the Tremarian soldiers from behind, firing machine guns and automatic rifles. Soon all the Tremarians were killed.

They had indeed found a Dumarian stronghold.

Either Hunter's memories of his past had begun to push into his mind, influencing his Tremarian stories, or the events in his stories had inadvertently touched on his past reality. Or both.

The story revealed no revulsion toward incest by the mother and son, only by the genderless soldiers. Was that because this mother and son had been "forced" into this activity by the destruction of Dumarian men by the soldiers? Just like Hunter and his mother had been "forced" by his father's homosexuality and Hunter's isolation from others his age?

The first stories Jazz had read presented the Tremarians more favorably, while the Dumarians were the villains, the cause of abuse of women and children, the evil that must be tamed for the world to be more livable. This story confused the issue. The author's sympathies seemed to lay with the mother and son. They were hunted, they escaped, and their friends killed the enemy.

And why the pregnancy?

Did Hunter make his mother pregnant?

Hunter's phone vibrated. Jazz pulled it from his back pocket. Eric wanted to know if he could come over.

"Hey, Hunter." She turned over and kissed his forehead. "Wake up, sleepyhead. Eric wants you."

Hunter moaned and stretched. He sat up. "I am not looking forward to this."

CHAPTER TWENTY-FIVE

Hunter took his computer into the living room, dreading what he knew would come from Eric's mind. He'd see the two girls again, maybe others. Hunter heard the front door open and saw Jazz leading Eric into the room.

"Do either of you want something to drink?" asked Jazz.

Eric stared at Jazz, obviously looking at her scars. His face paled. "What happened to you?"

"I used to cut myself, Eric. Most of these are years old. I don't remember why I did most of them, thanks to Hunter. Do they bother you?"

He raised his eyes to hers. "Yeah. Who wouldn't be?"

"Do you still want me to change clothes at PE? Will you still insult me for sitting in my own sweat during afternoon classes?"

"No. I'm sorry." He sat down.

Jazz folded her arms across her chest. "People look a little different when you know something about their past, don't they?"

"Yeah."

"Like how hard it was for you to live with your brother."

Eric flinched. "You know?" He looked at Hunter, wrinkling his brows.

"Just a little bit. Enough to know I was wrong about you. Do you still live with him?"

He shook his head. "No. He's in jail. Possession of child pornography. His boss caught him at work."

"How long ago?"

He looked to the floor. "About six months."

"Are you in possession?" Hunter asked.

Hesitantly, Eric met Hunter's eyes. "Not anymore. I got rid of everything last night."

"Last night?" asked Jazz.

Eric's face turned red. "Yeah. You'd think I'd have done it when Buddy was arrested. But I just couldn't."

"I'm glad you're trying, Eric." She squeezed his shoulder when she walked past him.

"You know what to do," said Hunter.

Eric closed his eyes. Like the last time, the pounding started immediately.

Hunter heard a shower running through his mother's partially opened door. He opened it and stepped inside. His mother was crying in the bathroom.

"Mom?"

"Not now, Hunter!"

"What's wrong?"

"I said not now! Please leave." She cried some more, then the bathroom door slammed shut.

Hunter went into the hallway and saw a gravel road outside the wall. He walked toward it.

"Where are we going?" asked Eric from the front seat of Buddy's truck.

"To see the two girls you beat off to." Buddy flicked ash from his cigarette outside the window.

Eric half smiled. He didn't remember it quite that way. The image he couldn't get out of his head was his brother's face between his legs, and then he had to do the same to Buddy.

"We're just going to see them?" asked Eric.

"And do things with them. I told Wesley about you. You're their age. He's gonna make some videos of you and the girls." Buddy sucked his cigarette then leered at his brother.

Eric smiled and tried to figure out what his brother was saying. He was sure he was going to be called stupid again. "Doing what?"

"Whatever Wesley decides. You're gonna love it." Buddy chuckled.

Eric watched as Buddy turned off the Parks Highway onto a gravel road that wound through the trees before dropping down closer to the Nenana River flowing north toward the Tanana. Open areas were covered with tall fireweed, just the top hot pink petals remaining in early-August.

"They live out here?" asked Eric.

"Hidden in the trees. Wesley doesn't want anyone around him. Runs his business from here."

"What business?"

"Pornography. Photos and videos. Plus prostitution for special clients."

"Like who?"

"Like me."

Eric's eyes widened. "For sex with who?"

"The girls. With either Danielle or Destiny or both." He laughed. "I like Danielle the best. You can tell me if I'm right after you're done."

Eric felt his stomach quiver. "Done with what?"

"God, are you that stupid? You're getting laid, little brother. Several times. And you'll have a video you can keep forever. You are so lucky. My first was Emily in 8th grade. What a pig!"

Eric scratched his head to get rid of the tingles on his scalp. He saw the girls in his mind—slender with curly brown hair and pale skin. And so young. How could they have sex with him?

"Who are the girls?"

"What d'ya mean, who are they?"

"Are they Wesley's kids?"

"Hell no!" He shot Eric his special look that always meant the same—How can you be that stupid?

"Then where'd he get them? And why do they want to do . . . all those things?"

"He bought them two years ago."

"Bought?"

"Yeah. Went to Anchorage. Lots of homeless down there. Found a family with several kids. He told them he'd take care of the girls, that his church would find a good family for them." He scoffed. "He gave the parents some money to feed themselves and their other kids, then took the girls. People are so stupid."

After another hundred yards of potholes and ruts, Buddy pulled up to a gate with a thicket of trees on either side. He reached out to a keypad and pushed a button.

"Is that you, Buddy?"

Hunter stopped and looked at Eric who held his face in his hands, his elbows on his knees. He knew that voice. Kind of high pitched for such a mean looking face.

The memory continued in his mind.

"Hey, Wesley. I brought my brother."

"Great! The girls are cleaning up. Punch in 673."

Buddy punched the numbers and heard the lock click on the gate. "Eric, open the gate and shut it after I'm through."

Eric did and jumped back into the truck.

"Crazy coot! He always uses the same three numbers. 673. 376. 736." Buddy laughed. "Guess he's not that worried about unexpected intruders. Plus, he's got video cameras everywhere."

The driveway wound through trees for fifty yards then broke into a clearing with a small house covered in weathered plywood on the left, a trampoline in the center, and a metal building on the right.

A short man with a ponytail, grizzled face, and thick beard hanging below his jaw came out onto the porch. He waved Buddy over.

"Park behind the metal building. We're going to shoot outside first."

Eric noticed that one of his top front teeth was silver. The man's body was large above his waist. Below his belt were skinny legs. When he turned around to go back inside, Eric noticed Wesley had no butt.

Hunter saw Tatiana's rapist.

The two brothers left the truck and walked toward the house. Eric noticed a ladder leading up to a two-level platform on the far side of the trampoline.

"Think they're going to screw you right there."

"On the ladder?"

"No, stupid. On the trampoline."

Eric tried to slow his breathing. He was going to be outside, naked, being filmed with two naked girls? He felt nauseous and had to fight an urge to run back to the truck.

Buddy opened the door to the house, and they walked inside.

The first thing Eric noticed was a metal picket cage on the right side of the room. It was 10 x 10 feet, maybe 6 feet tall. Inside the cage he saw the two girls standing naked on a towel spread beneath a five-gallon bucket. They dipped rags into the water then wiped themselves. They took turns washing each other's backs.

Eric stared at the girls, unable to close his mouth. They paid no attention to him.

"Don't wash your hair," said Wesley to the girls. "I don't want it wet during the video."

"This here is Eric." Buddy pushed his brother toward Wesley. Eric reached out his hand to shake.

"Take off your shirt," barked Wesley.

Eric looked back at his brother. "Do what he says."

Eric unbuttoned his shirt and took it off. He felt cold and shivered.

"Now your pants," growled Wesley. "And your underwear. Want to make sure you don't look too old."

Eric pulled down his underwear, trying not to cry.

"Shit! Too much hair." Wesley stomped over to a table, grabbed a pair of scissors, and approached Eric whose eyes nearly popped out of his head when he saw the blades open. He covered his genitals.

"Move your hands boy. I'm just gonna trim your pubes."

Eric stared at his brother, his mouth open, ready to scream. Buddy lit a cigarette and chuckled.

Wesley brushed clippings off Eric's skin with a few hard whacks then gazed at his handiwork. "That'll do for now."

Eric picked up his underwear and lifted a foot. "No need, boy. Just stay like you are."

Eric looked toward the cage and saw one of the girls sitting on a portable potty—a toilet lid on top of a five-gallon bucket. She wiped herself with toilet paper then stood.

"Destiny," barked Wesley, "you need to do that before you bathe. Wash yourself again. Maybe missing dinner will help you remember."

She hurried to the water bucket and wiped herself with the rag.

Eric noticed the pistol Wesley had shoved into his belt against his tailbone.

Wesley turned toward Buddy. "She's got no sense at all."

Buddy chuckled.

"Come here, Eric," commanded Wesley.

Eric slowly walked to Wesley, holding his hands in front of his genitals.

"Girls, come see Eric. You're gonna have a lot of fun with him on the trampoline."

They both walked toward the bars. Though they were twins, Danielle was slightly taller and more developed than Destiny. Neither looked well-fed.

They certainly didn't look like the happy girls in Buddy's video. Eric tried to keep his eyes on their faces.

"Move your hands," barked Wesley. "Show them what you got."

Eric moved his shaking hands away from his genitals.

"What do you think of the girls, Eric? Turn around girls. Let him see you."

With slumped shoulders and dull eyes they turned around.

"Well?" barked Wesley.

Eric swallowed. "They look good."

"Buddy, are you sure he wants to do this? He don't seem interested in them at all."

Buddy stomped toward his brother and pulled him to the other side of the room.

"You'd better change your attitude, Eric," spit Buddy. "Right now. He's giving me free videos forever if you do this right. You hear me?"

Eric nodded sharply, his heart racing.

"If you're not going to use it," pointing at his crotch, "I'll cut it off."

"OK. OK." Eric strode toward the cage and locked eyes with the girls. "You both are real hot. Can't wait to fuck you."

Danielle rolled her eyes and Destiny sneered.

Wesley pulled a marijuana joint out of his pocket. "Think this funeral needs a little lightening up." He lit the joint and gave it to Eric. "Take a toke, boy."

Eric took the joint and looked at Buddy.

"It's like a cigarette, Eric. Suck in the smoke and hold it in your lungs," said Buddy. "Such a dumb shit."

Eric inhaled and felt the smoke trickle down his throat until he coughed it out.

Danielle reached through the bars. "Give it."

Eric handed her the joint. She sucked on it then gave it to her sister. After a few more rounds, Eric felt dizzy and light-headed.

"Girls, you need to welcome the young man."

They stared at Eric with the most forlorn faces he'd ever seen.

"Now!" growled Wesley.

The girls instantly became coy and seductive, puckering their lips. They now looked lewd and vulgar. The change rattled him. Danielle stuck a finger through the bars and slowly curled it back toward her.

Eric forgot to breathe as he walked toward them in a daze until he felt the cold metal pickets against his skin. Danielle pulled his face toward her and kissed him on the lips. He felt Destiny's hands rubbing him. His heart pounded as Danielle groaned and kissed him again.

"Think we're ready now," chuckled Wesley. "Let go of him, girls."

Danielle and Destiny instantly resumed their sad, tired demeanor.

Eric backed away from the cage and looked down at his erection.

Wesley grabbed a key out of a drawer near the sink and a short-barreled rifle from the counter. He shoved the key into the lock on the cage door and opened it. "Let's go outside," Wesley ordered.

Buddy opened the door and waved Eric outside.

Wesley grabbed his camera off a table by the door and shuffled out toward the trampoline, the girls walking together in front of him.

"Eric, get up on the trampoline." Eric walked up the steps and stood on the edge.

Wesley gave the rifle to Buddy. "This fires bean bags. Use it on the girls if they decide to run."

Buddy nodded.

The girls stood at the bottom of the steps while Wesley climbed up the ladder to the platform and readied his camera.

"Eric, I want you jumping by yourself, smiling and having fun. Then on my signal you girls run up to the edge, giggling and leering. You are so eager to get to him. Then you get up there with him, jump with him, then have fun with him. Got it? OK. Eric start jumping."

Eric jumped in circles.

"Hey, Eric!" cried Wesley. "People want to see your dick, not your ass. Face the camera for God's sake."

Eric turned and jumped.

"Now, girls," growled Wesley.

The girls giggled and leered. Then ran up the stairs to Eric, jumping with him for a few seconds before they pushed him down.

Hunter felt his phone vibrate. He pulled it out of his pocket and saw the call was from his father. He pressed the home button and sent Jazz a text. *I need you in here.* After a few seconds, Jazz entered the room, and Hunter held out the phone to her. She walked over. "Talk to him. I can't stop now."

CHAPTER TWENTY-SIX

Jazz took the phone and walked into the kitchen, swiping the slider to accept the call. "Hello, Joe. This is Jazz. Hunter is busy right now. Can I help you?"

"Hello, Jazz. Has Hunter written more stories since he left last night?"

She moved into her bedroom and shut the door. "Yes. And he's had more memories of his mother."

Joe paused. "Such as?"

"Having sex with her. She tried to seduce him, he resisted, she used his brother to make him jealous, then he finally gave in to her."

"Then what?"

"Nothing beyond having repeated sex with her. In the last scene, you were scheduled to return home, and he thought a major argument was coming."

"He's right about that." Joe sighed.

Jazz sat on her bed and spoke gently. "Joe, why don't you tell him what happened and get this over with?"

"Because I saw how he reacted the last time. It nearly killed him."

"He's older now. He's already seen so many other kids being abused that the stories don't affect him the same way they did before. He's more angry than destroyed by them. He wants to help others like him. He wants the world to know what happens to kids while everybody is looking the other way."

"What other kids?" Joe barked. "Who's he talking to? And how does he plan to tell the world? What kind of nonsense is he planning?"

Jazz tried to check her anger and keep her voice calm and persuasive. "He's trying to save others, just like he saved me. He took many of my memories this morning, and I feel so much better. I'm not ashamed of my scars. You have no idea what that feels like."

"He's going to get himself hurt unless he resets his chip!"

She took several deep breaths. Why was this man so stubborn? "He's saving kids, Joe. One of our friends was raped at fourteen. Now she doesn't remember that. How can helping her be bad?"

"Because she'll tell others, and eventually the government will kidnap him and have him interview terrorists. Or another country will take him and make him identify traitors. Lots of people with bad intentions will want him. He'd lose whatever freedom he has."

Jazz's suspicions rose with the blood rushing into her head. He seemed to be trying too hard to convince her of an impending calamity. "Are you really concerned about him or about protecting the secret you're hiding from him?"

"His doctor agrees with me! He called me a little while ago and asked me to do the reset."

"Really?" Jazz's nerves tingled. She had just read an update about Ru and the shooting while Hunter was with Eric. The shooter's parents blamed Ru for their son's mental breakdown and planned to sue him. "Why did he call?"

"He wanted to know if Hunter had shown any signs of violent behavior."

Jazz's mind whirled. There must be something in common between the shooter and Hunter. The parents claimed Ru wanted to talk to their son and when they denied access to him, Ru told them about an implant that should be reset. They'd never been told about an implant, they claimed. Then Ru supposedly denied telling them anything about an implant.

Jazz flipped open her computer. "Have you heard about the school shooting near Bremerton, Washington?"

"Yes. Why?"

"The shooter was Ru's patient. Is Ru worried that Hunter will kill someone?" The article was still open on her screen.

"He mentioned that one of his other patients started hearing voices and seeing visions in his head. That this patient had received treatment similar to Hunter's. Ru said nothing about who the boy was."

"What did you tell the doctor?" Jazz scrolled through the article until she found quotes from the parents.

"I told him I'd get back to him. Then I called Hunter."

"Ru's lying about the chip. The parents claimed they were never told about an implant. Did Ru tell you that Hunter was given an implant?"

Joe paused. "Only yesterday. But he claimed he'd told me years ago. Maybe I forgot."

"Or maybe he never told you or never put one in. Ru had told the parents the boy was improving, then suddenly he had anger episodes, breaking things in his room. They called Ru about the sudden change. He wanted to speak to the boy, but they said no because they had been misled and decided to find another doctor. Then he told them about the chip and reset."

Joe spit out his words. "And they ignored him then the kid murdered a bunch of students and teachers!"

"Hunter's trying to help kids. There's no possibility he'd murder anyone. Why should we listen to anything Ru says?"

"Because Hunter was suicidal and catatonic before Ru treated him. And for almost a year since his treatment, Hunter was fine."

Jazz leaped off her bed, her muscles tense. "Fine? You and Ru ripped everything away from him, all of his good memories as well as the bad."

"Because the bad was more than he could take."

"He's already seen a lot of what his mother did to him. Plus other kids' memories of rape and horrible abuse. He's not suicidal at all. In fact, he's determined to help others who've experienced the kind of suffering he lived through."

Jazz heard the exasperation in Joe's voice. "No matter what he thinks he knows about his past now, the full story will put him back to where he was—cutting himself, screaming and crying all the time. Please, take my word for it. We need to try the reset."

"Did Ru ask to speak to Hunter?"

"Yes. I said no because I was afraid his voice would trigger his memories."

'Then he mentioned the chip. Right?

"Yes."

"That's the same pattern that happened with the shooter's parents. Why don't you give me his number so Hunter can call him?"

"Not a chance in hell! Hunter needs the reset!"

Jazz remembered the Tremarian story she'd read earlier. "Tell me this, Joe. Did Hunter get his mother pregnant?"

Joe gasped then said nothing for several seconds. "Has he told you that?"

"No. I read it in one of the stories he used to write before all the memories invaded his mind. But you just told me that he did by your reaction. How did his mother die, Joe?"

Almost robotically, Joe said, "In a car wreck on an icy—"

"That's bullshit. Did you kill her? Did Hunter?"

She heard him breathe a few times then very quietly say, "No."

Jazz could not stifle her anger any more. "If I were Hunter's parent, I know I'd come over here to be with my son and try to comfort him. But you won't because it's more important for you to protect your secret than to help Hunter. You'd rather wipe his mind clean again no matter the cost to him. Are you worried he'll hate you if he learns the truth? Do you really care that much about his opinion of you?"

"No. My opinion of me. I'm sorry, Jazz."

She pleaded with him. "He can help you forget, Joe. Your mind will be clear. The weight will be gone. I know what I'm talking about. You can't believe how good it feels to remove that burden. Let Hunter help you."

"I'm sorry." He disconnected.

She threw her phone onto the bed. *What is this man so scared of?* Did he really want Hunter to lose his memory again? Why wouldn't he want his son to face his past and try to cope with it? And how could he not appreciate what Hunter was doing for others?

But she realized she hadn't had to deal with a suicidal Hunter, slashing his wrists. And soon, Hunter would relive those days. She was determined to help him as much as she could because she knew that the worst part of cutting was its isolation, the feeling that you're entirely alone, your only friend—the knife. And the fear of being caught made the isolation worse. She'd needed someone to kiss her scars, not be repulsed by them, not flee from such craziness like it was the plague.

And what was the truth about Ru? Was there an implant or not? She'd researched that topic and knew that an implant needed power from a sizable battery pack. Where had Ru implanted that? It made no sense.

Had the shooter started seeing visions, too? Maybe he didn't know what they were and freaked. She tried to swallow, but acid burned her chest. Ru had called Joe because he was worried Hunter would turn violent. Could he?

She opened her bedroom door and walked into the kitchen where she heard Hunter's raised voice.

"Are the girls still with Wesley?"

She moved toward the living room.

"Yes." Eric looked at the floor, breathing heavily.

"All this time? They're still in a cage?"

"Yes."

Hunter stood. "What do they look like?" His face looked haunted with dark shadows under his eyes and deep lines across his forehead.

"A little taller. Skinny. He doesn't feed them much because he wants them to look like kids, not teenagers. He makes more money off them if they look twelve, not sixteen.

Jazz went to Hunter. "How do you know this, Eric?"

Hunter glared at Eric. "When's the last time you were out there?"

Eric raked his fingers up his hairline. "Two weeks ago," he wailed.

"You're still fucking them?" Hunter charged toward him and shoved him back onto the couch.

Eric's face turned red as tears streamed down his cheeks. "I'm sorry."

The cords in Hunter's neck bulged as he leaned over Eric. "All these years you cared more about your dick than the lives of two girls who've been living in a cage for . . . what? Four years, five? Did you ever feel any pity for them?"

Eric stared at them, his eyes glazed, panting his breaths. "No. They liked having sex with me. They told me."

Hunter spit his words. "You piece of crap! They acted like they did because Wesley wouldn't feed them if they didn't. I saw it in your goddamn memory. How would you like being them, Eric?"

"You need to take away all those memories," he begged. "I keep thinking about them. I keep having sick thoughts. I can't help myself."

"I'm not taking another memory from you until we figure out a way to save those girls. You need to talk to the police."

Eric stood. "I can't do that, Hunter. Wesley films everything. He's got cameras everywhere." He waved his arms while his face reddened. "If I send the police, they'll find all kinds of files with me committing crimes. I can't go to jail. Buddy gets raped all the time. Prisoners hate pedophiles. I'm not going to jail!"

"Then you'd better think of another way to get those girls out. If I have to drive up and down the highway and try every gravel road leading through the woods to find Wesley's house, I'll do it. And I'm sure the troopers would help me."

"Please don't. I'll think of something."

"You need to leave, Eric. Get back with me tomorrow."

Eric turned and looked at Jazz. She thought he wanted her to reassure him and tell him, again, that he was trying to make amends, but Jazz could barely stand to look at him. "Go home, Eric," she said. "Think of a way to help those girls."

He nodded and left.

Jazz pulled Hunter into her chest. "I'm so proud of you."

He pulled back his head until his eyes met hers. "The man who keeps the girls is Tatiana's rapist."

Jazz felt a cold chill flood her stomach.

CHAPTER TWENTY-SEVEN

The only thing that kept Hunter from puking in disgust at what he'd seen in Eric's memories was his anger at Wesley, Buddy, and Eric and his determination to free the girls. If every client were filmed during their sex with the girls, the client would be reluctant to report Wesley—unless he could reach a deal with the police beforehand. Would Eric agree to try? Probably not because he had been involved with the girls for years, even after his brother had been imprisoned.

What about Buddy? Maybe he would provide evidence against Wesley for a reduced sentence? Maybe Eric would ask him.

What could Hunter do? Find a trooper and tell him . . . what? *I read memories and saw two girls being abused, but I'm not sure where the house is?*

"What's going on in your head?" asked Jazz, still holding Hunter.

"I can't get those girls out of my mind. How can people want to have sex with twelve-year-olds? How can they risk their jobs, their families, and their freedom for that?"

"Because it's like taking drugs. The high has to be stronger each time or it's not fun. If all you care about is the orgasm, then the sex has to be wilder or kinkier or nastier each time or else it gets boring. Bondage, pornography, fetishes, multiple partners—all are more popular now than ever. Every one of

Mom's boyfriends pushed her into more extreme types of sex. Leon's sadism wasn't even the worst example. How much kinkier and nastier can you get than having sex with little girls—or boys?"

"How do those girls ever recover? I could steal their memories for months and still not make a dent."

"Would you try if you had the chance?"

"Yes. But how do I get the chance?"

"We'll figure it out."

"I want to take a shower. I feel so dirty."

"OK. I'll make you something to eat when you're through."

Hunter opened his computer and sent Eric and Tatiana's stories to his printer. "You should read these stories." He pulled them out of the printer he had set up on the table. "Maybe you can see something I'm missing." He handed the papers to Jazz. "Oh. What did my father want?"

"He's desperate to reset your chip."

"That's for his benefit, not for me."

"Ru called him."

Hunter froze. "Why?"

"He wanted to talk with you. Somehow there's a connection between you and the school shooter."

"How?"

"I'm not sure. He told the parents about an implant then denied it. The boy complained of hearing voices. Maybe Ru deleted his memories the same way he did yours."

"OK, but how would that turn him into a mass murderer?"

"I don't know. I need to do more research. You go take a shower. You'll feel better."

"Yeah. So much to think about." He felt dizzy.

Hunter went to Jazz's bedroom and pulled some clothes out of his duffel bag. He also picked up the Mount Rainier knife. *Who did this belong to? Is that my blood inside the sheath?*

He left the knife on the floor then walked to the bathroom where he shut the door and stripped off his clothes. He turned on the bath to get the water at the right temperature before flipping the lever to start the shower. While the water poured into the tub, he looked at himself in the mirror, noting his scars. Had he used razors like Jazz did or a knife?

His mind wandered back to walking into his mother's bedroom while she sat crying in the bathroom.

"Mom, what's wrong."

"Hunter. Not now. Please leave."

He heard her grunt in pain through clenched teeth. Then cry.

He rushed toward the bathroom door. "Mom?" He pushed the door open and saw her sitting on the toilet in her underwear while the bath ran. She held the Rainier knife in her right hand, the blade just above a bleeding cut on her left forearm. Hunter sank to his knees, his mouth open, his stomach swirling, unable to comprehend the scene.

Breathing heavily, she turned her face to him, a few tears running down her cheeks. "It didn't hurt as much as I thought it would." She gritted her teeth and quickly pulled the blade against her arm again, slightly lower on her arm. This time her grunt was coupled with a yelp, and she dropped the knife. More blood ran down her arm. Her breathing quivered. "That was deeper." She shut her eyes and rocked her body.

Hunter's head spun as he stared dumbly at the cuts. After a few seconds he lunged toward a towel and pressed it on Savannah's arm. He noticed the vodka bottle and a glass on the counter. "Mom, why are you doing this?"

She looked at him through a fog of awareness. He could smell the alcohol on her breath. "Because that's a pain I can deal with. I can bandage my arm and it will heal. I can't fix what's wrong inside me."

"What's wrong inside?" Hunter wanted to scream. What the hell was going on?

They both heard the honking horn outside.

Her lips curled into a half smile. "Your father's home. You should run outside and greet him."

"I don't want him here. You said you were going to divorce him. He can't stay here anymore. I don't want him sleeping with you."

She snorted trying to laugh. "I don't think you'll have to worry about that happening. Get me the gauze and tape out of the cabinet."

Hunter stood, fumbled through the shelves, and nervously handed her the items.

"And some scissors. No, the knife. I should use the knife. Give it to me, Hunter."

He reached for the blade. "I should keep this."

"Don't be silly. I just want to cut the tape."

She wrapped gauze around her cuts then peeled off several inches of tape. "You cut it, then."

He sliced through the tape with the knife.

"Now go outside. You and Frankie have to be outside while I talk to your father."

"Are you going to tell him to leave?"

"Sure, Hunter. That's what we need to talk about."

Hunter got up.

"Take the boom box and play some music. I don't want you two to hear what we're saying."

Hunter backed out of the bathroom, still nervous about leaving her alone.

She smiled at him. "Go on. I've got to get dressed."

Hunter turned around, grabbed the CD player off her dresser, and left her room. Frankie and Joe were just entering the house when Hunter walked into the kitchen.

"Hunter slept with Mom a lot," said Frankie. "Probably every night."

Frankie saw Hunter's glare and froze.

Joe squinted at Hunter as he walked through the front door. "Is that true?"

Hunter directed his gaze firmly at his father. "Had a few nightmares. So did Frankie. We watched a bunch of scary movies."

"Uh huh! Liar!" yelled Frankie.

Hunter moved toward his brother. "We need to go outside, Frankie."

"Why?"

"Because Mom and Dad need to talk."

"We do?" asked Joe.

"Take it up with her," said Hunter. "She told me to take Frankie outside."

"Go outside, boys," said Savannah from the hallway.

They all looked at her, trying to tie her robe sash as she carried a glass of vodka in one hand, her hair a mess, moving slowly and unsteadily toward the kitchen. Hunter could see a little blood oozing into her left sleeve. He started to move toward her, but she shooed him away. "Go. Out. Side."

Hunter turned, grabbed Frankie's arm, and pulled him toward the front door.

"You don't need to pull me!" He jerked his arm away from his brother.

The door slammed shut behind them as they walked to the driveway.

Hunter pushed his brother's back. "What the fuck is wrong with you, Frankie? I told you to keep your mouth shut."

"Dad asked me if anything strange happened while he was gone, anything unusual between you and Mom, so I told him. What the hell you doing in her room all the time, anyway?"

"I'll kick your ass later. Get the ball." Hunter set the player on the edge of the fake water well in the front yard and punched the play button. "Whole Lotta Love" roared from the speakers as Hunter turned the volume all the way up. Frankie shot three free throws, making one. Hunter shot two in a row, so he was the first shooter in their game of HORSE.

He kept staring at the front door, wondering what was going on inside. He launched a long shot from straight on which hit the backboard hard, bounced off the rim and rolled down the driveway toward the road. Their house sat fifty yards back from a two-lane state highway on a little rise a quarter mile from the nearest house. Frankie took off after the ball as it bounced and rolled, stopping against the chain link fence pole on one side of the driveway . Frankie picked it up as a car sped by about thirty feet away.

Frankie trotted back. "Pretty crappy shot." He launched one from the corner of the key and made it. Hunter matched him.

Hunter wondered what they were saying inside, whether he would soon see his dad leave the house, never to return. He couldn't stand to think of the alternative—his father sleeping with his mother that night.

"Shoot or give up your turn," shouted Frankie.

Even if Dad left, Hunter would still have Frankie spying on him. Such a little shit. Hunter would still have to sneak into her room. He and Mom could have so much more fun if Frankie were gone. Maybe Dad could take Frankie when they divorced.

Hunter spun the ball in his hands. "Why'd you have to say anything to Dad? It's none of your business where I sleep. Dad doesn't care about Mom at all. She's the prettiest woman I've ever seen, and he won't even look at her."

He threw the ball as hard as could at the backboard. The ball bounced back to his hands. He threw it again, smacking against the wall above the garage door. Hunter caught it.

"Hey, you already took your turn!" yelled Frankie.

Hunter slammed it harder against the house. Then again. Frankie tried to intercept the return, but Hunter grabbed it.

"You want it?" taunted Hunter as he threw the ball again then caught it.

"It's my turn!"

Hunter threw it again then moved away so the ball bounded down the driveway. Frankie took off after it.

Joe barged out the front door. "Stop hitting the house! Hunter! What's going on?"

Hunter pointed at Frankie chasing the ball, which would not stop before rolling onto the road. Hunter laughed.

"Frankie!" shouted Joe as he raced down the stairs off the porch. He caught his heel on a step and fell onto the ground. "Frankie! Hunter, stop Frankie!"

"You stop him!"

Joe tried to stand, but his knee gave way. He grimaced and sat on the step. "Hunter, run down there and stop him!"

Hunter saw Frankie racing after the ball as a truck rolled around the corner, about to cross in front of their house. Another car was approaching from the other direction.

"Hunter!" screamed Joe.

"He's not an idiot!" screamed Hunter at his father.

The ball rolled into the highway. The truck blew its horn and raced by. Frankie stopped on the shoulder about ten feet from the road. The ball rolled into the far lane and was hit by the car.

The ball rose into the air flying across the lane diagonally toward the house when it hit the driver's-side windshield of the car following the truck. The driver slammed on his brakes and swerved off the road, heading straight for Frankie.

The boy screamed and tried to run back up the driveway, but the car plowed into Frankie's ribcage and drove him into and through the chain link fence before he disappeared under the car, its horn blaring continuously. Other cars slowed down and pulled off the side.

"No!" shouted Joe as he tried to hobble toward the road.

Hunter stared at the scene, his muscles locking tight. He couldn't breathe as his insides froze. He didn't expect this. Surely, he didn't.

His head felt so heavy he couldn't hold it up.

Joe stumbled past him, crying Frankie's name.

Hunter tried to follow, but he couldn't feel his feet touch the ground.

He gasped, bent over, and puked on his shoes.

Joe stopped, turned, and yelled at Hunter. "Go check on your mother."

Hunter tried to straighten up, swallowing bile. He held his ears. The horn plus the looping song assaulted his brain. He turned and stumbled back toward the house.

Just as he reached the steps, his adrenaline kicked in, and he bounded up onto the porch.

"Mom!" he yelled as he opened the door. Seeing no one in the kitchen he raced back toward her bedroom. "Mom!"

He opened her door. The room was empty. "Mom?"

He heard a moan from inside the bathroom. He walked toward the door and opened it. He didn't see her, but he heard a small splash."

"Mom?"

"Hunter." The sound barely separated from her mouth.

He saw her nude body lying in blood-red water, her head leaned back against the wall. The bloody Mount Rainier knife had fallen to the tile floor underneath her right wrist, gashed and bleeding.

He collapsed onto his knees, sobbing.

Her eyes stared blankly from her pale face, barely moving her mouth as she struggled to speak. "Why didn't you come? I . . . c-called for you." She shivered.

"Mom. Why? Why did you do this?"

"Because . . . you got me p-pregnant, Hunter."

"You're pregnant?"

"You shouldn't have, Baby. You shouldn't have . . ."

Her head slowly turned toward him, her eyes fixed on nothing.

"Mom?" He clutched his legs to his chest and rocked. "Mom?"

His lips curled back from his teeth as the pain in his heart forced his mouth open. The screams that pierced his brain would echo in his head for the next three years until Dr. Ru shocked his memories into oblivion.

"Hunter?" The bathroom door burst open. "Hunter!" shouted Jazz as she pulled him to her. "I'm here. Come out of the nightmare, Hunter. I'm with you."

Hunter opened his eyes. He was naked on the floor, hugging his legs, facing the bathtub as the water ran into the drain.

He still saw the bloody water and her lifeless eyes. "She killed herself because I got her pregnant. She sliced her wrists in the bathtub. She told me I shouldn't have, like I had raped her."

"No, Hunter. She didn't know what she was saying. Her body was shutting down."

"I caused Frankie's death. He told Dad I had slept with Mom, and I didn't want him bothering us anymore. We were outside while Mom and Dad talked. I rolled the ball into the road. They're both dead because of me."

"No, Hunter. Your father's hiding something he did. You still don't know the full story."

"I killed them." He wept and buried his head beneath his arms. "They'd both be alive if I hadn't raped Mom. I'm no better than Wesley."

"Hunter, look at me. You were thirteen. You didn't decide on your own to have sex with your mother. Getting mad at your little brother doesn't mean you killed him. We need to see your dad. You need to find out what Joe said to your mom." She stood and turned off the bath.

She bent down and helped him stand then held his face in her hands. "Hunter, you are not to blame for any of this. Your parents made mistakes. Your mother took advantage of you. Now you're saving others. You can't save Danielle and Destiny if you're beating yourself up."

"You read the stories?"

"Yeah. I will personally shoot Wesley if I have the opportunity."

CHAPTER TWENTY-EIGHT

Joe sat outside drinking a beer, thinking about his conversation with Jazz. Should he trust Ru? Was there a chip he could reset, or was that a lie? He wanted to believe in Ru because he had saved Hunter's life a year ago. But the shooter in Washington made him replay all his conversations with Ru. Joe knew he wouldn't have forgotten an implant in Hunter's brain. If reset weren't an option, then what? Hope that Hunter stayed with Jazz, away from Joe's memories?

There were many times he'd almost abandoned Hunter, leaving him trapped inside one of the psychiatric hospitals they'd tried. But he couldn't. Just like he couldn't abandon Savannah when she told him she was pregnant. He would never have married that girl otherwise.

He met her during a Friday night happy hour at Hooters' where she waitressed. The guys dared him to hit on her. After several drinks he did, and she took him to her apartment after work. She liked having sex. A lot. He'd always been a little shy around girls and never impressed the few he'd dated with his lovemaking skills. But Savannah took charge and created her perfect lover, one who always said yes to whatever crazy scenario she imagined. For a time, he thought his life was a blast. None of his friends could match Joe's stories of his sex life with Savannah.

During one of the few times they actually talked to each other, he'd learned that she'd left her family in California. Her parents had laughed at her when she accused her brothers of raping her multiple times. So she ran away at seventeen, lied about her age, found work as a stripper and never looked back. She made porn videos on the side, bragging that she came up with many of the plot lines herself. She claimed she'd acted nearly every role—sister, mother, daughter, lesbian, master, slave—in every combination imaginable. Plus live chats, which was what Joe caught her doing the day he came home from the factory with his pink slip.

He'd planned to break up with her the day she told him about being pregnant. But he couldn't. They'd made a baby, and she wanted to keep it. Maybe she'd hoped having a baby would give her something else to obsess over than sex and her body and making men horny. She'd told him once that knowing hundreds or thousands of men beat off watching her in a film gave her more pleasure than an orgasm.

For a while, caring for Hunter changed her life for the better. Then Frankie's entrance recharged her batteries and filled her days, and nights, with purpose. But the thrill of motherhood waned as she worried she was getting old and fat, and Joe didn't show the same interest in her as before. She secretly got back into porn until Joe lost his job.

They moved to the middle of nowhere where Joe could do odd jobs for cash and Savannah had to raise the boys full time. Money was tight until he found work at Prudhoe Bay. Then his lengthy absences began to erode their relationship even more.

He'd thought many times about his decision to marry her. He should have walked away, but he felt guilty about leaving his baby. He'd worried about the kind of life Hunter would've had without a father. The irony of that concern now punched him in the gut. How could Hunter's life have been any worse than it'd turned out to be? And Frankie wouldn't have lived just to be killed by a car.

He'd pretended to be straight, he'd pretended to be in love with his wife, and now he was pretending to worry about Hunter's memories returning, when he was really worried about Hunter acquiring new ones.

He desperately wanted to stop pretending—to be honest and open for once in his life.

He sipped his beer, gazing down the road, waiting for Stanley to arrive. They hadn't actually been together since the morning he drove home four years ago. He'd spent the night at Stanley's house in Fairbanks then caught a morning flight to Seattle. Joe had known there would be an argument with Savannah when he came home. He'd already consulted with an attorney about gaining custody of the boys, had already checked job options in Fairbanks. But he hadn't been ready for what met him that day.

Once the boys were outside in the driveway, Savannah pulled a piece of paper out of her robe pocket. "Stanley Collins. Detective with the Fairbanks Police Department. Thirty-eight years old. I also have his picture. Nice looking man. According to the private investigator I hired, you've spent the night several times with him."

Joe didn't expect that. His face burned as a tingle swept up his neck.

"Which explains why you lost interest in me months ago. You're a fag." She sneered. "Wait until the boys find out."

Joe tightened his stomach, trying to keep fear from drowning him. He couldn't let her shame him in front of the boys. "There is no law against homosexuality. There are, however, laws against incest and sexual abuse. You're going to jail, Savannah."

She pulled her robe tighter and lifted her chin higher. She shook her head and moaned.

Joe flinched when the ball hit the house.

"Oh, really?" She moved toward the front door. "Boys! Come inside. I have something to tell you."

Joe walked in front of her and pushed her shoulders. "How long have you been screwing Hunter?"

Savannah winced and grabbed her left forearm. "What are you talking about, you pervert."

"The first thing Frankie told me when I drove up is that Hunter has been sleeping with you. He also said he's heard lots of sounds coming from your room when Hunter is in there. He told me some of the words he's heard—'Oh yes, Hunter.' And 'Fuck me, Hunter.'"

She'd waved her right hand in dismissal. "What an imagination he has." She then noticed blood on her palm and brought it closer to her eyes.

"Frankie's too young to make that stuff up . . . " Joe too noticed the blood seeping through her sleeve.

Savannah stared at her bloodied hand, breathing heavily.

Joe pointed at her arm "Why are you bleeding?"

The ball slammed into the house again.

She staggered to the table and plopped into a chair. "I had an accident in the bathroom." She pulled back her sleeve to reveal the bloody gauze then chugged the rest of her drink. "Actually, I cut myself on purpose." She pulled out the Rainier knife from her robe pocket. "Remember this knife? You bought it for me on our first camping trip together." She removed the blade from the scabbard. "You screwed me at least six times on that trip. I was impressed."

She pulled the blade slowly against her skin above the other cuts, hardly changing expression. The blood dripped off both sides of her arm onto the floor. "Now you screw Stanley instead." She sliced her skin again, whimpering a little. "It's your fault I'm pregnant."

Joe's stomach locked as his head spun. Bile burned in his throat. "You're pregnant? From Hunter?"

The ball hit the house.

She sneered. "I think Hunter's mad I'm talking to you alone. He's jealous." She laughed. "Haven't had anyone jealous of me in a long time."

Joe had suspected for weeks that she was acting inappropriately with Hunter, but he had never thought they were actually screwing each other until Frankie told him what he had heard. He placed his hands on the table across from her, his muscles tight with anger. "Do you realize what you've done to that boy?"

"Yeah, I made him happy. He made me happy."

"So happy you're cutting yourself. You're nothing but a drunken pedophile. A child abuser! Look at you! Drunk. Bloody. And pregnant with you son's child!"

Her tears brimmed over her eyelashes and ran down her cheeks. "I was so lonely. You wouldn't touch me."

"Don't justify your disgusting behavior by blaming me. Hunter is thirteen, barely old enough to know what sex is. And you've ruined him! Forever!"

Savannah wailed. "I want to die!"

The ball pounded against the house.

He threw up his hands and barked, "Then die! That would be the best thing for you and the boys."

The ball slammed against the wall again.

"Dammit! What's wrong with them?" He looked out the window.

Savannah stood up, gripping her knife.

"You want me to die? You don't care?"

Joe turned toward her, stabbing at her with his finger as he moved closer. "You're either going to jail or to a psychiatric ward. Or to both. And then straight to hell. Either way you'll be out of my life and the boys' lives forever. So if you'd rather kill yourself, then by all means, kill yourself."

Savannah stood, her eyes wide open and quivering as she clutched the knife. She removed her robe, standing naked in front of him. "Look at me! Please look at me!"

Joe's eyes widened as he stared at her. He hadn't seen her body for months. Blood dripped down her left arm, which she held out to him. She wiped her bloody hand across her stomach, as if to clean it, then held it to him again. "Please, Joe."

"No one wants to look at you, Savannah. No one."

She shuddered and pulled her hand to her mouth, her eyes pleading with him. She shook her head as Joe made no effort to hide his disgust with her.

She whimpered, "Goodbye," then ran down the hall.

The ball pounded again.

"Shit!" Joe ran toward the front door, ripped it open, and yelled. "Stop hitting the house!" He ran down the stairs and fell.

Later he found Hunter in the bathroom, shivering on the floor, covered in his own blood. He had slashed his arms with the same knife Savannah had used to slit her wrists.

For weeks afterward, Joe had blamed himself for caring more about being with Stanley than tending to his family and trying to get help for Savannah. He never told anyone the real topic of his last conversation with Savannah. Or about his relationship with Stanley. Or that he hated Hunter and blamed him for Savannah and Frankie's deaths and condemning him to years of having to deal with a crazed son, screaming and cutting himself repeatedly.

But that wasn't the worst thing Joe had done. The rest is what he never wanted Hunter to know under any circumstances.

A black Ford Explorer pulled up into Joe's driveway—Stanley's. Joe stood and tried to clear his mind of Hunter and Savannah. He wanted to enjoy this reunion. He hoped Stanley had brought a suitcase.

* * * * * *

Hunter stared out the windshield as Jazz drove south along the highway. He kept replaying his final memories with his mother in his mind, searching for something he may have missed, some detail that might explain why she killed herself. He held the sheathed knife in his hand.

Why would Dad keep this knife? Was it his or hers, or maybe Hunter's?

And why would his mother use it to kill herself? Had she already decided to commit suicide before his father returned? Had she slashed her arm to see if she could slit her wrists? She had told him that the pain was something she could deal with rather than what was wrong inside. The same reason Jazz had given him to explain her cuts. If so, the cuts wouldn't be a prelude. They would be preventative.

What had she and Dad talked about when he was outside? Obviously, Dad hadn't comforted her. As soon as he ran outside, she must've gone back to the bathroom. How much time had elapsed between when Dad fell down the stairs and when Hunter went inside?

Mom said she called him, but he hadn't come. What had she wanted? If he had come sooner, would she have died?

And then he remembered that his dad had told him to check on his mother rather than go down to the road. Why? Because he knew she was suicidal? What other reason would there be? Why hadn't he expected her to come outside?

His whole body tingled in realization—he knew she was killing herself. He had to know! And he'd let her do it.

He opened his computer and started typing.

"What's going on in your head?" asked Jazz.

"Dad knew Mom was suicidal, yet he left the house anyway. He told me to check on her after Frankie was killed. He knew."

"Why wouldn't he stop her?"

"Because he wanted her dead."

"Why?"

"She was pregnant with my child. He didn't want to deal with that."

"She could've aborted it."

"He didn't want her."

"Was there someone else?"

They both saw the second car in front of Joe's house as Jazz drove down the road toward his driveway.

"Maybe," said Hunter. His heart pounded as Jazz parked her truck. He knew he would soon learn the truth.

Joe opened his front door and walked outside. "Couldn't you have texted you were coming over?"

"Why? Got something or someone to hide?" sneered Hunter as he moved toward the door.

Joe threw his arm across the jamb. "Not now, Hunter."

Hunter held the sheathed knife in front of his father's face. "Recognize the knife?"

Joe's eyes bulged, and his mouth dropped open.

"I'm curious why you kept this. Out of all the triggers you burned, this is the one you kept. Why?"

Joe stared at the knife, his breathing quickening.

"We need to talk," said Hunter.

Joe's eyes darted from Hunter to Jazz then back to Hunter.

"Joe," said Jazz. "You knew Savannah was going to kill herself. Hunter can help you."

Joe slowly moved his arm away. Hunter jerked the door open and walked inside where he saw a man standing by the sink, drinking a beer.

Joe closed the door after Jazz entered. "This is Detective Stanley Collins, a friend of mine. Stanley, this is my son, Hunter, and his girlfriend, Jazz."

Stanley smiled and offered his hand to Hunter, who made no attempt to shake it. "How long have you and Dad known each other?"

Stanley looked to Joe.

Hunter pulled the knife from the sheath. "Don't lie to me because I'm going to see your memories, Dad." He held the sheath with the open end toward his father. "Did you know there's blood inside? Is it Mom's? Or mine? Or both?"

Joe moved toward his son. "Hunter, you need to leave. This is not a good time for this."

Hunter held the knife toward his father. "Back off! I'm going to tell what I know, Dad, until you can't help thinking about that day. Then I'll know the truth. Stanley, did he tell you how his wife died?"

Stanley cleared his throat. "She committed suicide."

"Yes! With this knife. And when did he tell you this? Recently, or four years ago?"

This time Stanley locked his gaze onto Hunter's eyes. "Years ago."

Joe pulled out a chair and slumped into it.

"But did he tell you he knew she would do it and didn't try to stop her?"

Joe grabbed his head. "How do you know . . . ?"

This time, Hunter did not hear pounding. Just the voices of his parents yelling at each other while a ball slammed against the house. He saw his father jabbing his finger at her, then his mother drop her robe, cry, and stagger out of the room.

Through Joe's eyes, Hunter saw himself slumped onto the bathroom floor, his arms bleeding. His mother lay dead in the bathtub.

His father didn't scream at seeing Savannah. He glanced at her once. Joe kneeled and reached for Hunter's neck, placing his fingers against his carotid artery. When he felt a faint heartbeat, he said, "Shit!"

He stood and wiped his hand on a towel. His father debated with himself about leaving the house so Hunter would bleed out. Who would know? Just when he was about to exit the bathroom, Hunter moaned and moved his head. His eyes opened and saw Joe.

"Jesus. Were you trying to kill yourself, or just make a mess?"

"Mr. Williams? Hello, Mr. Williams?" The voice came from the living room. "I'm Trooper Lawrence. I'd like to speak with you."

Shit, thought Joe. "I'm in here!" He yelled, cracking his voice. "I have an emergency!" He threw towels on the floor, saw the gauze and tape on the counter, grabbed them and kneeled to cover Hunter's wounds.

Joe heard footsteps. "Where are you?"

"In the bathroom. Go through the bedroom."

After a few seconds, the trooper appeared at the bathroom door. "Oh, my God." He radioed for an ambulance.

Joe wiped his eyes with his arm. "She slit her wrists, probably forty-five minutes ago. The boy found her twenty minutes ago, and I just came inside to find them both."

After a few more minutes, Joe and the trooper had bandaged all the cuts. He helped Hunter sit up and gave him some water.

"Can you walk?" asked Joe. "I'd really like to get out of this room."

Hunter nodded. Both men helped him stand and walk to the kitchen where they sat him in a chair.

"What happened?" asked the trooper.

Joe, breathing heavily, took the man outside on the porch. "I just got home an hour ago. The boys were playing outside, and my wife told me what Hunter had been doing to her for the past several weeks. She was very drunk. Hunter has had a porn problem. We thought it was licked, but he never stopped, evidently. He told her he would complain to child protective services about her abusing him if she wouldn't have sex with him. He raped her and threatened to do it again. She always drank, but she hit the bottle really hard when all this started happening. He forced her to have sex with him until he got her pregnant. I think that's why she killed herself.

"She'd begun to cut herself. She'd just shown me a couple of cuts on her arm when I heard a crash outside. So I ran out of the house and found Frankie had been killed." He dug the heels of his hands into his eyes and whimpered. "Hunter never even walked down the driveway to see his brother. Hunter must've disappeared into the house. I found him on the floor, bloody and barely conscious.

"The boy is sick. I think he purposely rolled the basketball into the road so Frankie would try to get it. He just destroyed my entire family." Joe broke down sobbing.

The trooper squeezed his shoulder and said, "I'm so sorry."

Hunter opened his eyes and found himself slumped on the floor being held by Jazz. He raised his head and saw his father. Rage surged through his veins, released by a scream. He leapt up, held the knife above his head, and charged after Joe.

"I'll kill you!" Hunter yelled.

"Hunter!" Jazz screamed.

Stanley moved quickly and grabbed Hunter's arm, twisting it behind his back until he could take the knife from his hand. Hunter lunged after Joe again.

Jazz raced toward Hunter, trying to pull him away from Joe. Both Stanley and Jazz held Hunter.

"Hunter. Please. Calm down," begged Jazz.

Joe removed his phone from his back pocket, punched the home button and swiped, then moved toward Hunter holding the phone away from him.

"Hold him, Stanley."

"What are you doing?" yelled Jazz.

"What I should have done yesterday."

Hunter struggled against Stanley's arms.

"Nooo!" Jazz flew toward Joe, pushing him and shoving him.

Joe slung her to the ground then gave the phone to Stanley who had a tight grip on Hunter. "Hold that to his right ear."

Stanley took the phone and held it against the side of his head. Jazz jumped up, screaming, trying to get to Hunter, but Joe held her off.

Hunter heard a strange rhythmic beat repeated several times. After a few seconds, he felt calm. His muscles felt heavy, and his breathing slowed. He slumped into Stanley's arms.

"What did you do?" cried Jazz.

"What Dr. Ru told me to do. I reset his chip."

Stanley sat Hunter in a chair.

Deep in his mind, Hunter heard a voice telling him what to do.

CHAPTER TWENTY-NINE

Hunter gazed at Jazz as he reached into his back pocket for his phone. He punched in the numbers he heard in his mind and waited.

"Who is this?" asked a very nervous Dr. Ru.

Hunter recognized the friendly voice. "Hello, Dr. Ru. This is Hunter Williams."

Joe's face turned pale as he leaned against the wall.

"Thank you for calling, Hunter. How are you? And where are you?"

Hunter stood and moved across the room, farther away from Joe and Stanley. Jazz followed him.

"I'm in Alaska. I think my father thought he was resetting my chip that would wipe out all my memories again. He didn't want me to see what really happened four years ago."

"I lied to your father about the chip. I'm sorry. At the end of your treatment, I used hypnosis and planted a deep suggestion in your mind to calm down and call me if you heard a specific musical sequence. You don't have a chip in your brain, Hunter."

"Dr. Ru, I'm going to put you on speaker now." He pushed the button. "I never had an implant?"

Joe sat up in his chair, his face slack and his mouth open.

"No. And I never mentioned the chip to your father until he called me yesterday. I wanted to speak with you, but I think he was afraid your memories would return if you heard my voice."

"And now I know why he was so worried about that happening. Did he tell you I had raped my mother?"

Ru hesitated. "Yes, he did, Hunter."

Stanley looked at Joe with a quizzical expression. Joe stared back and shook his head slowly.

"Did you believe him?"

"At first, but that's not what you described to me during our sessions."

"Did he tell you I was addicted to pornography and forced my mother to have sex by threatening to call Child Protective Services?"

Resignedly, he answered, "Yes."

"Did he tell you he told my mother to kill herself and left the house when he knew that's what she intended to do? And that when he found me bleeding on the floor in the bathroom, he wanted me to die?"

Everyone stared at Joe who looked confused.

"No, Hunter. How do you know this?"

"Because I saw his memories. And now he doesn't remember what he said or thought during those moments."

Ru's voice turned more urgent. "Explain please. Joe told me you saw memories, but he said nothing about deleting them."

"When I see a memory, the person thinking about that memory forgets it. Always. I've taken bad memories away from my girlfriend, Jazz. And from two students at school."

"Did they know you were doing this?"

"Yes, they wanted me to. They think about the event, I write it down as I see it, and afterward they don't remember the rape or the abuse or whatever the event was."

"I've never heard of anything like this, Hunter. There was another boy who had a treatment similar to yours. His parents told me that he started hearing voices. Maybe he was seeing memories, too."

Jazz took the phone from Hunter. "Dr. Ru, my name is Jazz. Hunter took many of my memories. He saved me, and I can never thank him enough. I want to ask you about the shooter in Washington, if that's OK? The news reports have made you out to be a villain."

"Yes, they have. The parents are suing me. The press is after me. Some are trying to blame the boy's murders on me."

Jazz glanced at Hunter. "Did you tell his parents you'd given him an implant?"

"Yes. I was desperate to speak to the boy. But the parents wouldn't allow it. I had implanted a hypnotic suggestion, similar to Hunter's." He paused, breathing deeply and rapidly. "I'm sorry. I keep thinking about that poor kid shooting his friends. I know if I had been able to speak to him, I could've stopped it."

Jazz looked at Hunter then lifted the phone closer to her mouth. "The media said he was traumatized by an incident at his grandfather's. They mentioned a coyote attack. Is that what happened, or was he abused?"

Ru cleared his throat. "I shouldn't speak about another patient. If Hunter had talked to the boy, I'm sure he would still be alive, as well as so many other children."

Stanley moved toward Jazz and directed his words to the phone. "Dr. Ru, my name is Stanley Collins. I'm a detective with the Fairbanks Police Department. Are you withholding information from the police in Bremerton?"

Hunter felt his muscles tense. He shared a grimace with Jazz. "I'm sorry, Dr. Ru. I should have told you there was a detective in the room."

"That's OK, Hunter. No, Detective Collins, but I needed to hire a lawyer before speaking with them. Since you've evidently witnessed Hunter's abilities, you can help me. The shooter's memories were erased using electroconvulsive therapy, similar to what I did for Hunter. The boy's memories must have started to come back, but unlike Hunter's, they were of physical violence to him and his pets. He may not have recognized them as his own memories and thought he was going crazy. Or perhaps he saw memories of violence from others. I wish I could've spoken with the boy. I have no idea why or how Hunter or that boy would tap into other people's memories."

Hunter took the phone from Jazz. "Jazz has a theory, Dr. Ru. She can text you or call you later if you want."

"Yes, please," said Ru. "Hunter, do you want to keep deleting memories?"

"Yes," answered Hunter. "At first I wanted them to stop, but now that I know how much others have suffered, like Jazz, I want to help as many as I can. There are two girls nearby who have been sex slaves for several years, forced to live in a cage since they were twelve or younger. I haven't met them yet, but I want to save them then delete all they've experienced."

"Sex slaves?" asked Stanley.

"Yes. I've seen them twice in a friend's memories, but I don't know where they are."

"Hunter," said Ru, "you have a very good heart, despite all that's happened to you. Your mother abused you, Hunter. You did nothing wrong, despite what your father wanted you to believe. And all the others that you've helped and plan to help did nothing wrong, either. They are children who've been forced to live in their own hell, most often by selfish adults. Sometimes I can barely get to sleep thinking about all the stories I've heard."

"Hunter and I know how that feels," said Jazz, holding Hunter's arm, "but we do better together."

"Yes, I don't know how I could cope without my husband."

"Dr. Ru," said Hunter, "people need to know these stories. I don't think most people have a clue how many kids are suffering."

"I agree. Hunter, I know you don't want to think about this now, but scientists would love the chance to figure out why this has happened to you."

"Or use my ability for their own purposes," said Hunter. "I'd rather help kids than be used for someone else's benefit."

"I can certainly understand," said Ru. "Hunter, I need to tell you that I didn't want to use shock therapy on you. I thought we were making progress during our talks, but—"

"I understand." Hunter's eyes shot daggers at Joe. "I'm sure Dad preferred erasing everything in my head. I'll definitely talk to you again. Soon."

"Please give Detective Collins my number. We need to talk about what he's witnessed tonight. Goodbye, Hunter."

Hunter disconnected and continued to stare at his father. "If I had died, you would've moved in with Stanley and not had to worry about your son discovering your secret, which wouldn't have been that big a deal for Frankie and me had you made any attempt to talk to us. But what puzzles me is why you continued to stay away from Stanley and hate me more for keeping you from him? Why the stories about me raping Mom? Why did you have to feed that story to everyone?"

"Because," said Jazz, "he didn't want anyone to blame him for your mother's death. He did not want to be blamed for his wife's incest. In his story, Hunter, you were the cause of all the problems, and he was the dutiful father trying his best to help his psychotic son."

The fire scene with Anthony jumped into Hunter's mind. The boy's father had blamed his son. That's why Hunter had seen that memory, not because of the sex between the parents, which never took place. The truth was there, but he wasn't ready at the time to understand it.

Stanley shook his head slowly at Joe then turned to Hunter. "You mentioned two girls in a cage? We need to find them."

"Yes," said Hunter. "All I know is that they're in a house somewhere near the Nenana River south of here," said Hunter, "but I'm not sure I can find it on my own. I need to persuade a friend to help me."

"You can't rescue them yourself. I can help you, Hunter." He held up his phone so Hunter could type in his number. "Please call me when you have more information, and please don't try to do this alone."

Hunter entered the number into his contacts list. "Thanks. Maybe I'll know something more tomorrow. And here's Dr. Ru's number." He showed Stanley. Hunter opened a cabinet and pulled out two large garbage bags. "Jazz, help me get the rest of my clothes."

"Sure."

They walked back to his room and began stuffing the bags with items from his closet and dresser. After a few minutes they heard a car drive away. When they came back to the kitchen, they found Joe looking out a window.

"No matter what you want to blame on me," he said bitterly, "you were the one who killed your brother."

Hunter felt his stomach twist and bile rise into his throat. "It was my fault he chased the ball to the road. At the time I was angry with him for telling you about Mom and me. I was a jealous, confused 13-year-old, which is no excuse for what happened to Frankie. I'll have to live with his death forever. But you knew that something bad was going on between Mom and me, and you did nothing about it. You could've admitted your feelings for Stanley to her. You could've taken her to a doctor. You could've gotten me real help instead of torturing me with your lies. But you didn't. You chose to protect yourself instead, and where has that left you? Stanley's gone, and I'm leaving. Enjoy the rest of your life, Dad."

Hunter and Jazz stuffed the bags in the back seat of her truck and drove off.

"Are you ever going back?" asked Jazz.

"Not to him." He looked at her. "I guess I should've asked you first. Sorry."

"You don't need to ask." She cocked her eyebrows. "I'm not letting you go anywhere, Hunter."

He smiled. "I guess you want to get rid of all your cutting memories first, huh?"

"Yes. I certainly want you to do that."

"And after?"

"Make new memories with you, ones I never want to forget." She reached over to him with her right hand. He grabbed it. "Am I your girlfriend, or was that label convenient for the conversation?"

Despite all the anguish he had experienced during the last hour, her touch filled him with warmth and hope. "I'd like you to be."

Jazz bit her lip as she and Hunter stared at each other until she let her truck fade onto the rumble strips. "Woops." She pulled the truck back into her lane. "You're very distracting, Hunter."

"Sorry. So will you?"

"Will I what?" she asked coyly. "You have to ask again, please."

"Jeez. You gonna turn girly on me?"

"You don't like girly?"

"No, I like the Jazz who carries a gun in her pack and uses it when necessary. Who'll fight Eric or my father to protect me. Who won't freak when she finds me naked on the floor screaming and crying about things she can't see. Who has the softest, most luscious lips and the warmest body in the world."

"You can't know that," she giggled. "In the world?"

"In the freakin' world! Can you prove me wrong, Ms. Scientist?"

"No, and I wouldn't want to. And to answer your question, yes, I want to be your girlfriend . . . and lover when the time is right. And I know it's not right . . . yet."

"Not yet." He saw his mother staggering down the hall in her robe, then later opening it and begging his father to look at her. And all he did was tell her to kill herself. He tried to shake the image from his mind then scoffed at himself. Now that he had regained the memory, he didn't want to see it.

But without it, he could not know himself, who he was, how he came to be the young man sitting next to Jazz whom he would follow anywhere. He remembered his father saying "one of us had to know who we were." Until tonight, he hadn't known who he was, and he was still struggling to find out.

She glanced at him and smiled. "How's your head doing?"

"Like it just woke up. Like it's been wandering in a fog without knowing why."

"You need your memories to be fully conscious."

He raised his brows at her as she glanced over.

"You can't know who you are without context," said Jazz. "Being conscious depends on having memories. You can't think about what you've done or want to do in the future or why your life sucks or is wonderful if you can't remember your past. We're conscious beings who need to be grounded in context."

"So I wasn't fully conscious until tonight?"

"Not really."

He leaned his back against the door, facing her. "Then what was I? Unconscious?"

"Hunter, we can't even agree what consciousness is. Google it." She glanced at him. "There are a hundred definitions. No one knows what it is or how we got it." She turned her face back to the road. "But I think being conscious depends on our ability to connect to the other dimension, which holds our memories. When that connection is lost or broken, you can't function. You go into a coma or get dementia. Maybe autism is caused by broken connections."

"This is too complicated."

"Yeah. There are just too many things we don't understand about how our head works. And those who hypothesize about another dimension holding our memories are often ridiculed. How can science test that theory? Cutting up worms will not give us all the answers."

"I'm sure some scientist would like to get hold of me."

She shot him a sly smile. "Some scientist has already got hold of you and she won't let go any time soon."

She pulled her phone out of her pocket and gave it to Hunter. "Somebody texted."

Hunter read the message. "Your mother. Reminding you she needs to be picked up by 10:00."

"Text her back: *Will pick you up at 10.* And put the 'you' in caps."

"OK." He sent the message. "Why?"

"Because I think she wants to bring home the dude she got fired."

Hunter dropped her phone on the seat then pulled out his phone. "I need to call Eric." He punched in the numbers.

"Yeah," said Eric.

"Have you thought of a way to rescue those girls?"

Clearly frustrated, he said, "No."

"Have you tried?"

"Yeah, I've tried."

"I know a detective who's willing to help."

"What have you told him?"

Hunter heard the fear in his voice "Nothing about you. Just about the girls. I'm not sure about the directions. I'd need your help to find the place."

"Look, Hunter. No matter whether you send an army down there, he's got videos of me, so I get busted. I can't do that."

"Then what happens to the girls, Eric?"

Hunter could hear Eric breathing. "They stay there . . . until they're too old."

"Then what?"

"I don't know, but the last time I was there he made a comment about needing to get new girls."

"He won't let them go. You know that."

Eric paused, breathing into the phone. "No."

"Eric, we have to get them out. Wesley needs to be put away."

"Man, I don't know what to do."

"If we got them out, we could burn the house down and destroy all his hard drives or whatever he uses."

"Wouldn't matter. He uploads the stuff to the cloud. I'm not even sure he keeps any cards or flash drives at the house except for the ones he uses to record."

"OK. Then we destroy his computer and take the cards in the cameras. Wesley won't give the police access to his cloud files. How does he get internet?"

"Satellite dish."

"Can't we cut the wire going to the house to disable the feed to his phone?"

"Yeah, but not when he's there."

"Couldn't you pretend to want to visit the girls and get inside? Then we could surprise him with guns?"

"Who's 'we'?"

"Jazz and me."

"Are you kidding? You're going to get us all killed. He carries a gun all the time."

"I know. I saw it in his belt."

"Wesley will not hesitate to shoot any of us. Think of something else, Hunter."

"No! *You* think of something else. I'm calling the police tomorrow whether I hear from you or not. Maybe you don't care that he'll kill those girls, but I do." He disconnected.

"Sounds like we need a SWAT team," said Jazz as she turned into her driveway. "Home sweet home."

She parked the car, and they each gathered items to bring inside. Jazz took one bag of clothes to her room. "Where do you want to put these?"

Hunter followed with another bag. "Do you have any empty drawers or room in your closet?"

"Some. We'll make everything fit."

They dumped the bags on the floor.

"How awkward is it going to be with me in here and your mother on the other side of that wall?"

"It would serve her right to feel awkward after all the times I had to listen to her and the asshole of the month screaming at each other or banging the bed against the wall."

Hunter remembered the twelve-year-old Jazz listening to her mom and Micah outside their door.

"I guess we won't be so noisy," said Hunter. He reached out his arms for her. She ran to him and hugged. "Thank you for helping me. I'm sure my father never held me during all those years. I must've been a scared, confused kid who couldn't get the bloody nightmares out of his mind with nobody to hold him."

"You won't have to worry about that anymore." She pushed her fingers through his hair and wrinkled her nose. "You could use a shower. And a change of clothes."

"I know. I feel dirty. But I'm a little nervous about being by myself in bathrooms."

She played with his ears. "Take a shower, and I'll sit in there with you. We'll keep talking. You'll be fine."

"No peeking?"

"I won't promise anything. Besides, I've already seen you naked. As you have me."

"In very bad situations for both of us. Not very much fun."

"Grab your clothes. I'll get the water running."

She left the room, and Hunter soon heard the shower spray against the plastic curtain. He found a pair of boxers and a t-shirt then stripped off his clothes except for his underwear.

Jazz met him at the door with a towel folded across her arm. In a lousy British accent, she said, "I trust the temperature will be satisfactory, sir."

"I'll come to expect this level of service from now on."

"Cool. I'd be happy to oblige."

She hung the towel on the curtain bar then sat on the toilet. Hunter put his clothes on the rod just outside the tub. Standing in his underwear in front of her, he felt awkward.

"How do I get in?"

She giggled. "I'll close my eyes while you take off your underwear. Turn around and face the curtain. Butts aren't that sexy anyway. OK. My eyes are closed."

Hunter pulled down his pants then reached for the curtain.

"Hurry, Hunter. I'm not good at resisting temptation."

Hunter stepped into the shower and closed the curtain. "You can open them now."

"I already did, and forget what I said about butts. Yours is very cute."

He stuck his head out of the curtain. "You didn't!"

"You'll never know. If I did, it wouldn't be a bad memory, so you'd never see it." She waved her hand at him. "Get back to showering. Tell me if you need help with anything."

"Are you going to crack jokes the entire time I'm in here?"

"If it keeps your mind away from the past, then yes I will. So what are you washing now?"

"My chest."

"OK. How about now?"

"My stomach."

"Ooh! How about now?"

"Armpits."

"Why'd you change direction? Don't you have a pattern when you wash? People develop their cleaning habits when they're young and rarely change them."

"Really? By the way, you missed it."

"What? Oh, damn!"

"Where'd you come up with this pattern theory?"

"I read it. What you wash first says a lot about you."

"And your first part is?"

"My hair, of course. Why wash your body then let all the dirty stuff in your hair run down your skin?"

After a few more minutes, Hunter turned off the water. Jazz pulled the towel off the curtain bar.

"Jazz, I need my towel."

"I'm holding it open for you in front of my eyes. Just open the curtain and I'll wrap it around you. Trust me, Hunter."

"Why do I feel like Charlie Brown?" He stuck his head around the curtain to see the towel spread wide, hiding Jazz's face. He stepped out of the tub.

"By the way, my middle name is Lucille. Oops!" She dropped the towel. "Oh my, Hunter. You're entirely naked." She covered her eyes with her hand then opened her fingers, gawking at him. "I'm so embarrassed." She turned around, laughing.

Hunter picked up the towel and quickly dried himself. He pulled on his boxers.

"Is it really?" He put on his t-shirt.

"Is what really?"

"Is Lucille your middle name?"

She turned around. "Actually, yes. Jasmine Lucille Williams. And your middle name?"

"Charles."

She barked a laugh. "Really? No way!"

"Afraid so."

"Well, this factoid will influence many future interactions."

"OK. Your turn."

"For what?"

"To take a shower. I'll sit right there and behave. I promise."

She put her elbows on his shoulders and played with his wet hair. "My spidey senses tell me you're planning revenge."

He squinted his eyes and gave her a wry grin. "As you speak."

She kissed his forehead. "You are so amazing! I'll be back in a second."

CHAPTER THIRTY

The next morning Hunter drove his truck through the hills east of Nenana under turquoise blue skies and a bright sun that teased of days in midsummer. But the bare birch stands were still guarding snow patches around their bases. By this time of the year, everyone in the Interior ached for the lushness of summer. The fact that winter would linger on for another few weeks was a reason for depressive thoughts even when relief seemed so close.

Hunter had felt so comfortable sleeping with Jazz, snuggling against her chest after the joy of playing with each other in the bathroom. They'd dabbled on the edges of sex, keeping it light and silly, knowing Hunter's past was barely past, ready to slash him again. As proof, his dreams had been filled with worry about the girls in the cage, bloody images of his mother, and the lingering anger at his father for keeping the truth from him. The sound of his brother's death woke him three times during the night.

He knew Jazz's sleep was peaceful. Every time he'd jolted to awareness, she'd been snoring softly, almost smiling. He knew he would never sleep like that as long as the girls were trapped, waiting to be deleted like bad memories, only to be replaced by another preteen or two from Anchorage.

He needed to find a way to tell Claire her daughter no longer remembered Micah or the murder or the reason for abandoning Rosie. He didn't want her saying anything that would put those memories back into Jazz's mind.

They had drunk one shot each before sleeping last night. They'd both decided to stop using vodka, but knew that Jazz needed to ease off it. And they'd hidden the remaining bottles in the wall of Jazz's closet behind a loose piece of paneling, which they'd taped closed in the back corner.

Jazz expected her mother to have a bottle or two in her suitcase. They'd have to deal with that later.

After they drank their shots, they'd kissed each other's scars, softly, knowing the pain behind each one, knowing how things would've been different if they'd been together then like they were now. Hunter had told her everything he saw and heard and felt earlier that day. They'd drunk each other's tears and formed a bond of empathy no two teens should ever need.

Now, this morning, Jazz looked out the window as they drove. "I wish green-up would come early this year," said Jazz. "I keep searching for any sign of leaves. I can't wait for the first lupine to pop out of the ground. There's a place on the edge of my gravel driveway that I always see the first lupine. And the bluebells come in about a week later. And then the roses. I love the roses! What's your favorite color of primrose? I like the fuscia best."

"I've never seen them. I got here last July, and the roses were all gone by then. Just fireweed."

"Once the fireweed blooms, I worry about winter coming, especially when the bottom petals start falling off. Winter is too damn long. Spring and summer are longer at MawMaw's and PawPaw's."

"You still want to go back there?"

"Yes. I'd really like to move away from here. But only if you come with me."

"I wouldn't want to be anywhere else."

He pulled off the Mitchell Freeway onto South Cushman toward the rehab center.

"Over there," said Jazz.

He turned into the parking lot and headed toward the building.

"Shit! She's sitting over there with a man, just like I thought. I'm going to be a badass to him, so don't be shocked."

"You? Badass? Why would that shock me?"

She smiled at him then growled.

Hunter pulled against the curb near the bench where Claire and the man were sitting, both smoking cigarettes. The middle-aged man wore a beret and leather jacket and sported a ragged goatee. Claire looked like a thinner Jazz in bright blue leggings. Jazz leaped from the truck and confronted the guy.

"Are you the asshole who gave my mother booze?"

"Jazz, he just needs a ride," said Claire.

"He can find his own ride." Jazz jabbed her finger into the man's chest. "Pick up your pack, asshole, and walk away from here. Now!"

"Look, Jasmine, my name is—"

"I don't give a shit what your name is because I'll never need it. My mother came here to get off booze, not to have some slimy counselor give her booze for what, a blow-job? Is that the going rate for you? How many girls and women have you ruined in there before you were caught?"

The man picked up his pack and started backing away from a raging Jazz, who continued to scream at him.

Hunter picked up Claire's bag. "Hello, Claire. My name is Hunter. Your daughter is very special to me."

Claire tried to get the man's attention but gave up, threw down her cigarette, and stomped on it. "She can be the biggest bitch. You better hope she never gets angry at you."

"She's just trying to take care of you. Listen, I need to explain something to you real fast while Jazz is away." Hunter saw Claire's green eyes, slightly lighter than Jazz's, lock onto his. "Jazz doesn't remember anything about being raped by Micah or her killing him." Her eyes widened. "I took those memories away, so please don't say anything about him to her."

"What do you mean you took those memories?"

A scene flashed in Hunter's mind.

"Are you OK, Jazz?"

"Sure, Mom. I'm fine."

"Is Micah treating you OK?"

She'd heard noises last night coming from the other end of the mobile home. She'd gotten up to investigate, then decided she didn't need more trouble with Micah, so she went back to bed.

"You knew," said Hunter with utter shock. "You knew Micah was raping her."

Claire's brows scrunched together as her face reddened. "I didn't know. I swear."

"Let's get in the truck, Mom," said Jazz as she walked back toward them. "I want to get out of here before he comes outside." She laughed. "He ran inside the building saying he was going to call the police."

Hunter and Claire stared at each other wide-eyed, barely breathing.

"What's wrong with you two?" asked Jazz.

"Nothing," said Hunter. He picked up her bag and put it in the truck bed.

"Mom, this is Hunter—"

"He already introduced himself. He seems like a very fine young man." She continued to eye Hunter warily. "He says you're very special to him."

Jazz grabbed him from behind and kissed his cheek. "He's the best." She opened the passenger door for her mother. "You're in the back. We need to go to Fred's for some groceries."

Claire climbed into the truck, as did Hunter and Jazz.

As Hunter drove out of the parking lot, Claire said, "That man's name is Robert. He was a patient, not the counselor. He wanted a ride to his daughter's house."

Jazz turned toward the back seat. "Well, now he can call Uber or a cab." She turned back around. "You know, that felt good. I enjoyed that! What'd you think of my badass routine, Hunter?"

Hunter kept replaying the scene in his head, wondering why Claire hadn't pressed Jazz harder for answers.

"What's wrong?" Jazz touched his arm.

"I'm sorry. Just had a flashback. I'm OK." He turned his head and smiled at her. "You're a helluva badass. Remind me to stay on your good side."

"Anywhere close to me is my good side for you. Mom, Hunter moved in with me at our place."

"OK. Maybe you'd like to tell me a little more?"

On the short ride back to the Fred Meyer store on Airport Drive, Jazz told her mother about Hunter having no memories of his past until recently and what led up to him taking her memory of throwing Leon out of the house.

"You do realize how strange all this sounds, don't you?" asked Claire.

"Yeah, but I've seen and felt it happen many times. He took so many of my bad memories, Mom, and I feel incredibly better now. He can do the same for you."

Hunter looked in his rearview mirror and saw Claire's eyes fixed on him.

"Could you do that for me Hunter?"

"Do you have memories you'd like to forget?" asked Hunter, still watching her in the mirror, still wondering how she could have been so blind to what had happened to Jazz.

"I think you already know the answer." Claire averted her eyes outside.

The parking lot was crowded at Fred's, typical for a Saturday. This was the first store travelers encountered when driving to Fairbanks from the west. Besides groceries, the store carried clothes, as well as home, garden, and sporting goods. As a result, many shoppers came from out of town.

They entered the store, grabbed a basket, and followed Jazz's list she'd made on the drive up. For a few moments while Jazz looked for fresh meat, Claire and Hunter were alone.

"Was Micah Rosie's father?" asked Hunter. "I haven't been able to ask Jazz because she doesn't remember him."

"No. It was another asshole, as Jazz likes to call them. Micah didn't know I was pregnant when we hooked up. I had no money and no job, as usual. When he found out about the baby, he was pissed and threatened to leave. He had no desire to raise someone else's kid. I suspected he might be bothering her, but Jazz denied it. I . . . just didn't want to know bad enough. I'm a shitty mother, Hunter. You might as well know that up front."

"My mother seduced me when I was thirteen before she killed herself, pregnant with our . . . mistake. We all have regrets, Claire. You need to find a way to make it up to her. I'd probably be a mental case, trying to cut myself again without Jazz. Have you seen her scars?"

A look of horror flashed across her face. "Scars? From Micah?"

"Figuratively, I guess, but she made them herself. I have some, too, but not as many as she has."

Claire covered her mouth with her hand and reached out to hold Hunter's hand with the other. "You must hate me." Her eyes brimmed.

"No. We both need to support Jazz. There's already too much hate and abuse in the world. I don't want to add to it."

Claire hugged Hunter. "Thank you for being with her."

Jazz came back with packages of chicken and hamburger meat. She saw the hug and cocked her eyebrows. "Something I missed?" She smiled and dropped the packages into the cart.

"Something I've missed," said Claire, reaching around Jazz to include her in the hug. "Jazz, you're a good girl. I haven't told you that enough. I'm sorry."

Out of the corner of his eye, Hunter spotted a familiar form. His jaw dropped as he turned to see Wesley push his cart toward the bread section. His stomach swirling, he walked a few steps away in a daze, not believing what he was seeing.

"Hunter?" asked Jazz. "What's wrong?"

CHAPTER THIRTY-ONE

Everything else in the aisle disappeared in Hunter's eyes except for the saggy pants and ponytail of the rapist and pornographer stopping to grab a few loaves of bread. Hunter could've tackled him, even strangled him. His skin flushed with hatred as he fixed his gaze on evil, every muscle taut.

Wesley bent down to grab some hamburger buns, and Hunter saw the pistol shoved into his belt.

Then Hunter realized the girls were alone. They needed to get into the truck and leave. Now.

He turned around and found Jazz with their basket.

"What's going on?" she asked.

Hunter moved closer. "Behind me. That guy by the bread shelf is Wesley."

"Are you sure?"

"Positive. We need to leave and get to his house before he does."

Jazz nodded and pushed the basket up the pet food aisle toward the front of the store.

"Where's your mom?" asked Hunter in a panic. She had disappeared.

"Shampoo and conditioner," Jazz yelled back to him. "I'll get in line."

Hunter raced past the meat and frozen sections until he reached the clothes area and took a left. Claire was holding a bottle of shampoo reading the label. "We have to go." He grabbed her arm.

"What?"

"Now." He pulled her up the aisle toward the front. "Jazz is in line."

"Why?"

"Because two girls are going to die if we don't."

Hunter found long lines at every register and couldn't see Jazz. He moved back toward the produce section and found her waiting for a self-serve checkout station.

"I thought this would be quicker," Jazz said as she moved forward to claim a station. They both scanned items quickly until the voice from the scanner said to remove the last item. Then "Help is on the way."

Hunter looked around for a customer service agent and saw him helping a woman with children. Hunter walked over and tapped his shoulder. "When you're done, I need some help." The man nodded.

When Hunter turned around to return to their basket, he saw Wesley walking toward them from the produce section. "We need to leave."

"Why?" asked Jazz.

Hunter jerked his head toward Wesley. Jazz saw him and turned around. "Shit!"

Hunter's heart skipped as he watched Wesley turn his cart into the other self-checkout aisle and find a station directly across from them. The store employee walked to Hunter and scanned his card.

"There you go," he said.

"Thanks," said Hunter as he grabbed Jazz and Claire's arms and pushed them toward the exit.

"Hey!" yelled the employee. "What about your stuff?"

Hunter turned around. "Forgot my wallet." He saw Wesley look at him before he turned and pushed his friends out of the store.

"What's going on?" asked Claire.

"That man who was across from Hunter has two girls in a cage at his house," said Jazz. "We need to rescue them while he's in town."

Hunter started the truck. "Shit, I need gas," growled Hunter. He drove toward the pumps at the side of the store parking lot. "Jazz, keep an eye out for him coming out of the store."

"OK." Jazz got out of the truck and watched for Wesley.

After Hunter inserted the nozzle into his tank, he pulled out his phone and called Eric. The call went to voicemail. "Eric, this is Hunter. You need to call me. Wesley's in Fairbanks. We can get the girls." He disconnected and returned the gas nozzle to the pump.

Soon they were on the road heading back toward Jazz's house. Wesley's house was farther south, but Hunter didn't know the mile marker for the road leading toward the girls.

While Hunter drove, Jazz told Claire about Wesley and the girls. He tried calling Eric again, but all he got was voicemail.

Then he remembered Stanley. He checked his contacts and found the number. After a few rings, Stanley answered.

"Hello?"

"Stanley, this is Hunter. The man who has those girls is in town right now. I just saw him, so there's no one at his house. I'm heading there to get the girls. Can you help?"

"Where is his house located?"

"Somewhere near the Nenana River, probably close to the Coghill Bridge. I'm not sure of the mile marker yet, but I should know more in a while. I can call you back later. Can you send troopers to help?"

"What's the man's name?"

"Wesley. I don't know his last name."

"Let me check around, and I'll get back to you. And I will send help. Wait for us, Hunter. Please."

The truck was silent as Hunter sped through the curves in the hills. Hunter kept glancing in his mirror to see if anyone was behind him. He tried to recall what kind of vehicle was parked near Wesley's house during Eric's memory, but all he could see in his mind was the trampoline and platform.

Hunter's phone rang. He swiped to accept. "Yeah?"

"Hunter," said Eric. "Are you sure you saw Wesley?"

"Yes, silver tooth and all. He hadn't exited the store by the time we drove away. What's the mile marker for his exit?"

"Just south of 274. There's a red strip of cloth tied to a tree on the right side. Even if he's not there, he's going to see you at his gate. His phone will buzz when anyone pushes the gate button."

"So, what? We try different variations of 673 until the gate opens."

"I'm sure he can shut down the gate."

"The gate just crosses the road. We can walk around it through the trees and disable the satellite dish. Then he won't see us take the girls."

"The camera will see you anywhere on the road in front of the gate."

"What else can he do except yell at us through his phone while we get to the house? He's not there, Eric. I can bust through the gate with the truck. Look, I'm going in to get the girls. If you're concerned about what's on his computer or flash drives, then you need to be there to look for that stuff."

"What are you going to do with the girls?"

"Take them to Jazz's house and do what I did for you!"

"He'll hunt you down."

"Who's going to tell him where they are, Eric? You? Besides, he'll be in jail by then. I'm leaving Nenana now, so I should be there in thirty minutes. Are you coming or not?"

"Shit! OK, I'll be there. I should get there before you."

"Bring a gun." Hunter disconnected. "Jazz, you do have your pistol, don't you?"

"Always." She held up her pack.

"Are you going to drop me off first?" asked Claire. "This sounds dangerous."

"We don't have time, Mom."

Hunter punched in Stanley's number. "Hello?" answered Stanley.

"The mile marker is 274. There's a strip of red cloth around a tree where the road leaves the highway. We're about thirty minutes away."

"OK. There's a trooper coming from McKinley Park. She left ten minutes ago, so she should arrive just after you do. I'm in a helicopter. We're about ten minutes out of Fairbanks. We're almost there. Wait for us, Hunter."

"I'm in a blue truck with a suitcase in the back. I have no idea what Wesley's driving."

"Call me when you get close to his house."

They disconnected. Hunter pressed the accelerator.

After another twenty-five minutes, Hunter crossed the Coghill Bridge over the Nenana River then slowed and pulled onto the shoulder.

"Look for a red strip around a tree," he said.

"There's Eric's truck," said Jazz.

Hunter pulled up next to him and rolled down Jazz's window. Eric had attached a Boss snowplow to the front of his rig.

"Did you put that on just now?"

"No, I've been clearing snow from driveways. It was already on. Wesley's gate is heavy. I think it would ruin your truck if you tried to knock it down."

"What's the plan?" yelled Hunter.

"You'll follow me until we get to the last curve before his gate. I'll move ahead and punch the button. If he answers, I'll tell him I want a session with the girls and try to persuade him to let me in. I can find out how far away he is from the house. If he doesn't let me in, I'll ram through the gate and call you to follow me."

"Lead the way," said Hunter.

Eric moved ahead with Hunter close behind. After five minutes, Eric stopped, stuck his arm out the window and signaled for them to stay there. Eric moved on. After a few more minutes, they all heard the sound of ripping metal and knew that Eric had plowed through the gate.

Eric called. "He's about twenty minutes behind, so we need to hurry!"

Hunter moved forward as he called Stanley. "We're going through the gate. Wesley is ten minutes behind us. When can you get here?"

"The trooper got delayed because of a wreck on the highway. I'm probably ten minutes away. Wait for us!"

"I can't! If he gets here before you do, he'll kill the girls."

Hunter disconnected and drove through the broken gate. Eric drove around the house and knocked over the satellite dish then backed up and turned the truck facing the road out. Hunter looped around the trampoline and parked next to Eric, ready to drive out. Both kept their trucks running.

"He's pissing mad!" yelled Eric.

"Do you have a gun?" asked Hunter.

"No. Do you?"

"Jazz has a pistol. Eric, do the girls have any clothes?"

Eric shook his head. "He keeps them naked all the time. He thinks they'll be less likely to bolt if they have the chance."

Hunter grabbed Claire's suitcase out of his truck bed as Claire and Jazz exited the truck. "Claire, the girls are thin and have no clothes. Find something in your suitcase for them."

He carried the bag to the porch and set it down. Claire knelt and unzipped the bag. Eric opened the door, and they walked in.

"Destiny?" Eric yelled. "Danielle? We're getting you out of here."

Jazz went to the cage door while Eric searched for the key. The girls held each other and backed away warily.

"My name is Jazz. I'm your age. We want to take you to my house where you'll be safe. My mom's outside getting you some clothes. We have to hurry because Wesley will be here in a few minutes."

Danielle walked to the cage door. She was taller than the last time Hunter had seen her. Her ribs and hipbones pushed hard from beneath her skin. Destiny stood behind, her stomach caving into her backbone.

Eric stared. "He stopped feeding them. They weren't this skinny two weeks ago." He unlocked the door.

"We need to hurry," said Hunter.

Claire came in with an armful of clothes. She saw the girls and stopped in her tracks. "Jesus God." After a couple of seconds, she moved toward the girls. "Eric, you and Hunter get outside. They don't need any more guys gawking at them." The boys moved toward the door.

"Help me, Jazz," said Claire.

After they closed the front door, Eric said, "I swear, Hunter, they weren't that skinny when I was here."

"They don't look like kids anymore. He's starving them. No bullet holes or cuts to show they were killed." Hunter looked at Eric who stared at the ground. "Did you know that's how he'd do it?"

"You wouldn't believe me if I said no."

"No, I wouldn't."

Eric looked up the road leading to the house. "Shit! He's coming! There's a dust cloud over there." He ran to the door. "Now! Get in the trucks!"

They both heard a helicopter.

"That's Stanley," yelled Hunter, his heart racing.

The girls ran outside in baggy leggings and loose stretch tops.

"Hurry!" yelled Eric. He opened the back door of his truck. "Put them in here."

Jazz and Claire ran to the other truck. Hunter hopped into the driver's seat and switched the gear into Drive. Eric took off in front of him, then braked suddenly. Hunter hit his brake hard but still slid into Eric's back bumper.

They all heard the shotgun blast. Claire screamed.

Hunter tried to back up and ran into the trampoline.

Wesley walked in front of Hunter's truck pointing a shotgun at him. "Get out of the truck! Hands up! Now!"

Every nerve tingled as Hunter opened his door. "Jazz, take your pack."

"Got it. C'mon, Mom. Get out." Jazz opened her door and raised her hands.

Claire opened her door and stepped out to the ground, shuddering in fear.

Wesley shot at Eric's door. They all jumped at the sound. "Girls, get back in the cage!"

Hunter saw Eric's bloody face and the shattered windshield in front of him. The far passenger door of Eric's truck opened, and the girls ran into the house.

Wesley moved closer to Hunter. "You were the boy in the store. I knew there was something fishy about you. Just too desperate to leave."

The sound of the helicopter grew louder then circled above the house.

"Put down your weapon and lie down on the ground," came from above.

"Fuck you!" Wesley aimed at the helicopter and fired. The helicopter rose higher then circled.

"Get inside the house!" Wesley barked. "Now! Move! Move!"

Hunter and Claire ran over to Jazz, keeping their hands high.

"Be ready with your gun, Jazzy," whispered Claire through her teeth.

"Mom?" She stopped and looked at Claire.

"Don't stop, Jazz. Turn around. You'll know what to do."

Claire hung slightly behind them as Hunter and Jazz walked up the steps to the porch. Hunter saw Jazz unzip her pack and reach inside.

Claire stumbled on the last step. "Shit! My ankle!"

Wesley came up behind and shoved her in the back with the side of the gun. "Move it, lady!"

Claire dived from the porch into Wesley, knocking him backward. "Now, Jazzy!"

Claire and Wesley both grunted when they hit the ground.

Jazz pulled out her gun and leaped down the steps.

Using one arm to try to push Claire off him, Wesley lifted his shotgun with the other arm to fire at Jazz.

"No!" Claire dived on his arm as he pulled the trigger, sending the pellets under the house.

Jazz held her pistol in front of Wesley's face and fired. His body jerked and blood poured from his mouth.

Panting, Jazz glared at Wesley and cocked the gun again. "Mom, you OK?"

"Yeah. Just some bruises. Is he dead?"

Jazz pushed his head with her boot. "Yeah."

Danielle and Destiny screamed as they launched themselves from the porch onto Wesley's body. They kicked him, jumped onto his chest and stomach, all the time screeching and wailing. Their faces twisted into animal snarls, baring their teeth, as they pummeled his chest and stomach.

Claire put her arm around each girl and moved them away from the house. "Girls. He's dead." She pulled them closer to her. "You'll never have to see him again." They collapsed against her chest crying. Claire rubbed their backs and looked back at Jazz and nodded.

"Thanks, Mom," said Jazz. She knelt by Wesley's arm and pried his fingers from the trigger of the shotgun.

Hunter ran down the steps and pushed Wesley's body over, removing the pistol from his belt. He raced to Eric's truck and opened the front passenger door to find Eric slumped toward Hunter with several holes in his neck.

Hunter wiped tears from his face. Eric came because he felt sorry for what he'd done but only because Hunter had goaded him. He expected to be exposed and put in jail. Maybe he worried this might happen as well. Hunter pulled out his phone to call Stanley. "Wesley's dead. So is my friend. The rest of us are OK."

Hunter saw the chopper return.

"We've got no place to land," said Stanley. "I've called an ambulance, and a trooper is almost here. Can you move the truck blocking the gate?"

Hunter took a few steps toward Wesley's truck and heard the engine running. "Yeah."

Hunter climbed into Wesley's truck and drove it toward the house. He found Jazz, Claire, and the girls on the porch, hugging each other.

Hunter tried to steady his nerves. "The trooper is on his way. Stanley's meeting us at the intersection."

Danielle raised her teary face and looked at Hunter. "Where are we going?"

"To a new home," said Hunter.

"To my house, girls," said Claire. "Jazz and I will take good care of you."

"Jazz," said Hunter, "let's check his fridge for food and water."

They walked inside the house. "Your mother saved our necks." He opened the refrigerator and pulled out food and juice. "Think I know where you got your badass gene."

"I know. That was brave as hell. She said she owed me. Do you want to tell me what for?"

"I don't think for anything specific. Just all the time she brought assholes home." Hunter stood up and put the items in a box, avoiding her eyes.

"You won't tell me, will you?"

"Nope."

"Are she and I even yet?"

"She'll never be even with you, but she's doing her best, so give her credit."

"Eric's dead?"

"Yeah. He was trying to get even, too."

"Do you think he did?"

"Whether he did or didn't, he wanted to try. Maybe he was afraid of people knowing what he did to the girls, but he was more afraid of living with the truth that he'd done nothing to save them. He knew Wesley would starve the girls to death then drop their bodies somewhere."

"I'm glad I shot Wesley. I don't feel any remorse at all."

Hunter remembered watching the twelve-year-old Jazz crying as her mother left the burning trailer and a dead Micah behind. But not the pain or the guilt or the shame. Those followed her, attacking her arms and shoulders and legs.

"Good," said Hunter. He closed the refrigerator. "Maybe we can leave this place with no scars as souvenirs. Let's get the girls home."

They left the house and handed the girls water and juice. They opened the bottles quickly and drank. "Go slow, girls."

A trooper vehicle passed through the gate. A woman emerged and walked toward them. "Are you Hunter?"

"Yes, Ma'am."

"Detective Collins filled me in. You all were very brave. How are the girls?" She walked over to Danielle and Destiny who clutched Claire in between them.

"Better than they were," said Claire.

"My name is Helen. Some medics will meet us by the bridge to make sure you're both OK." The girls buried their faces into Claire's chest. "Do you know them?" she asked Claire.

"We just met. I want to take care of them. They've got no one else."

Helen smiled. "They seem to like you." Helen walked a few steps to look at Wesley's body.

"There's his shotgun," Hunter said, pointing to where he had leaned it against the porch. "And this is the pistol he carried in his belt." He handed her the gun.

"Who shot him?" asked Helen.

"I did," said Jazz. "I carry a gun in my pack. He was moving us into the house. We were going to be hostages trapped in the girls' cage. My mother jumped on him and knocked him down. He reached for his shotgun and fired it. Then I shot him."

"I know," said Helen. "Detective Collins watched it happen from the copter. How'd you know the girls were here?"

"Eric told me," said Hunter. "He wanted us to help them escape. We were about to leave when Wesley shot him through his windshield."

Stanley's voice came through her radio. "The ambulance is here. Send them up."

"Yes, sir," answered Helen. "You go on up to the bridge. I need to check everything here." She tipped her hat. "Thanks for saving the girls."

They nodded then moved toward the truck. Jazz sat in front. Claire sat in the middle of the back seat, the girls still clinging to her. Jazz passed two hard-boiled eggs and apples back to the girls.

"Eat them slowly, girls," said Claire.

After scarfing her egg and drinking some water, Danielle looked at Hunter through the rearview mirror. "What's your name?"

"Hunter."

"Jazz told us you were the one who wanted to save us. Why?"

"Because I know what abuse feels like, and I wish someone had saved me and Jazz, and even Eric. But you two have suffered more than all of us combined. I couldn't live with myself knowing you were still in a cage."

She moved her hand over the seat. "Thank you, Hunter."

He held her fingers. "When's the last time anyone held your hand?"

Her face clouded, and she bit her lip. "I can't remember."

"That changes today. We're going to give you and Destiny only good memories from now on."

Claire hugged them to her chest. "We'll take care of you."

As he drove, Hunter finally calmed down. The screams and shots and crying replayed like distant memories in his mind. And then he felt pride— in himself and Jazz. They had been broken by others, but they had healed themselves enough to save others. God, that felt good.

As he emerged from the bushes, he saw Stanley waiting with the helicopter in a rest area near the bridge. An ambulance was parked nearby.

He drove to them and stopped. They all exited Hunter's truck.

"The medics need to check the girls," said Stanley.

Danielle and Destiny still clung to Claire. "I want to stay with them."

"That's fine," said Stanley.

Claire and the girls entered the ambulance.

Hunter started to tell Stanley what had happened, but Stanley said he'd watched most of it.

"Supposedly," said Hunter, "Wesley had cameras everywhere, so you should find videos of everything. We want to take them to Claire's house in Clear Creek, if that's OK. Feed them, let them clean up. Wesley's computer and files are in the house, so maybe you won't need to debrief them too much. They lived naked in a cage for four years, and they haven't eaten for a while. If there's nothing seriously wrong, can we take them home then bring them to Fairbanks in a couple of days?"

"Sorry, Hunter. I'll have to take them into town."

Hunter's jaw tightened. "And stay where? In another cell? Or locked in a room?"

"I'm sorry."

After a few more minutes, the medics released the girls who still held Claire. Stanley and Hunter walked over to them.

Claire kissed the girls' foreheads. "Jazz has some clothes at the house which will fit you. And I have a nice soft bed for both of you."

"Ma'am," said Stanley.

"My name's Claire."

"Claire, I need to bring them with me back to the station."

Claire clutched the girls. "Why?"

"Because . . . it's procedure. I'm sorry."

"Are you going to question them today? Where will they sleep? Who'll be with them?"

"I'm sorry, but I have to take them." He reached out his hand to Danielle.

"No!" both girls screamed.

Hunter moved between Stanley and Claire. "Are you going to force them into your car, screaming and crying? We saved them. They want to stay with us. Send a trooper later today and tomorrow to check on them. We'll bring them up on Monday. What's wrong with that?"

The girls cried into Claire's chest as they squeezed her.

"They haven't had a mother for years, Stanley," said Claire. "They need one now. Let us take them home."

"They've already gone through enough," said Hunter. "Why make them scream and cry more. They've already felt more pain than you have in your lifetime."

Stanley nodded. "OK. I'll send Helen out to your house later today."

Jazz and Claire took the girls back to Hunter's truck.

"Thanks, Stanley," said Hunter.

He nodded. "I called your father and told him what you'd done. He started crying and said to tell you he was sorry. Maybe you can call him sometime."

"Maybe. Thanks for showing up, Stanley."

"Those girls owe you their lives. Thank you for saving them."

"I shouldn't have had to." Despite his efforts to hold his feelings in check, Hunter's face flushed and his throat ached. "Where were you four years ago for me and for Jazz and Eric and Tatiana? This has got to stop." He turned to walk away then stopped. "I'm sorry, Stanley. This is not your fault. I'm just tired of seeing everyone's worst memories."

"When you stop seeing them, you'll know they're still out there, but you won't be able to do anything about them."

"Not true. I can still care. Still help. All they need is for me to put their happiness above my own. Anyone can do that."

They shook hands, and Hunter walked back to his truck. "Let's go home." He pulled onto the highway and headed north.

CHAPTER THIRTY-TWO

Jazz watched her mother smiling in the mirror, holding both girls as they slept, one on each shoulder, and felt proud. Her mother had stood up for Jazz and herself today. When had Jazz ever seen that? When had she ever felt proud of her mother? "They haven't had a mother in years, maybe not even then. Do you want to take care of them, Mom?"

"Yes. Would that bother you?"

"Not at all. I think it would be great."

"I never held you enough. I'm sorry."

"I'm sure we'll make it up from now on, Mom. Besides, I have Hunter to hold me. Where will they sleep?"

"In my room. I can sleep on the floor."

"They might do better next to you."

Claire hugged them closer. "I feel so sorry for them. All anyone has done is use them. How could they survive all those years?"

How had Jazz? Or Hunter? Or Eric and Tatiana?

Jazz couldn't understand why some like Hunter's mother gave up and died, while others clung to life. Hunter would've killed himself years ago if not for the timely arrival of the police after Joe found him bleeding on the floor. Now with the full knowledge of his past, he wouldn't consider suicide. Why? Because he had seen the suffering of others and wanted to stop it.

Did Jazz feel better because Hunter had deleted her bad memories, or because she'd found peace and purpose through helping Hunter and now the girls?

Her mother had lived a miserable life, wallowing in the selfishness of men she hoped would love her, drowning in alcohol, beating herself up for losing Rosie. Now she was strong and happy. When had Jazz ever seen the look of peace on her mother's face as she did now, holding Danielle and Destiny? The reason for the change—saving the girls.

They all could have died at Wesley's. They'd been willing to give everything to help the girls. When had anyone elevated the girls' happiness above their own?

Destiny and Danielle would know forever they were saved by those willing to die for them. That knowledge had to help them heal even as it saved the rest of them.

After they arrived at the house, the girls helped Jazz look through her old clothes to find things they could wear. They acted as if they were given exclusive access to an entire department store, giggling and squealing as they tried on different outfits. Claire made a good dinner for all of them. Jazz had forgotten that her mother was a decent cook when she wanted to be.

Then the girls took showers, which they hadn't had for years. The sounds of their laughter and groans of delight filled the house and brought smiles to everyone. How could a simple shower bring such happiness?

Danielle and Destiny showed no interest in answering questions about their past. They wanted only to enjoy the present, relish the now, and explore an entire house without a metal bar anywhere.

After they fell asleep in her bed, Claire knocked on Jazz's door.

"Come in," said Jazz who lay next to Hunter on top of her bed, both in boxers and t-shirts.

"You sleep together?" asked Claire, her eyes bulging and mouth wide open.

"Yes," said Jazz, sitting up, "but we don't have sex. We just hold each other."

Claire's eyes widened, and she walked toward them. "Your scars." She reached out to touch Jazz's shoulder then put her hand over her mouth. "When?"

"Over the years, but I'm better now."

"And Hunter?" Claire touched his arm.

"We're good, Claire. They're from the past. Eventually they'll fade. Are the girls asleep?"

She sat down in Jazz's desk chair. "Yes. I love them," she said through her tears. "I know I've been a shitty mother to you, Jazz, and I'll try so hard to make amends. But these girls have had no one to care for them. And I helped save them. They're giving me a second chance to be a mother. Can they stay?"

"Where else would they go?" asked Jazz.

"Child services will want to place them with someone else," said Claire.

Jazz frowned. "Why?"

"Because I got kicked out of rehab, because we have no money or job. Because you killed Wesley."

"I'll talk to Stanley," said Hunter. "Maybe he can help us."

"You should call your father," said Claire.

"I will tomorrow. He made mistakes because he was too focused on himself. He needs to try something different."

"Jazz, do you have alcohol in the house?" asked Claire.

Jazz felt her stomach drop. Just when she thought her mother was acting more responsibly, more like a real mom, she slapped that thought away.

"A little," sighed Jazz.

"You need to get rid of it. I don't want those girls to be exposed to drinking."

Jazz felt her eyes bulge. "I thought—"

"I know what you thought, but I was sober for six weeks then had a couple of shots. I don't want any more, not as long as we have the girls. Are you still drinking?"

Jazz swallowed and grabbed Hunter's hand. "Hunter and I decided to drink one shot a piece each night for a week at bedtime to see how my body reacts to cutting back."

Claire frowned. "Do you drink, Hunter?"

"Just started three days ago. I don't need it, but I wanted to help Jazz get off of it. I don't think she should go cold turkey."

"OK. One shot at night for a week, then no more. If you have to detox at a hospital, then you will. Jazz, how would you have paid for food today?"

"Because MawMaw and PawPaw send me prepaid cards. They've been doing that since we left."

Claire's eyes teared up as she looked at her daughter. "Have you talked to them?"

"Sometimes. I want to see them . . . and Rosie."

Claire wiped the tears off her face. "Would they let us?"

"Maybe. If we're sober. If we explain what's happened."

"They wouldn't want Danielle and Destiny," said Claire.

"How do we know that? Let's give it a week, see how the girls do, and then talk to them."

"OK." Claire went to Jazz. She reached out her arms toward her daughter who stood and grabbed her mother. "I love you, Jazzy. I hope you can love me, too."

"I never stopped loving you, Mom. Despite everything, I love you."

Claire reached her hand out to Hunter. He stood and joined the hug.

"I know you've seen me at my worst, Hunter, but I hope we can start over."

"We already have. I need a mom who cares about me, so if you can possibly—"

Claire let go of Jazz and pulled Hunter into her. "I'll try so hard, Hunter. For you and Jazz and the girls."

She let go and wiped her eyes. "When I was sixteen, I loved a boy named Daniel, and he loved me. We gave ourselves to each other. Our love-making was the first for both of us. Then his family had to move, and every boy I screwed after that was not the same. It was just sex, like getting drunk just to feel good for a while. It didn't mean anything. And that's all those girls have experienced. But I think you two can feel something different with each other. You two are something special. You'd give your lives for each other."

"Like you would have today for us," said Jazz.

Claire nodded. "Like we all would have for those girls."

Jazz kissed her mother's cheek. "Good-night, Mom."

Hunter kissed Claire's other cheek. "Good-night, Mom."

"I love you both," said Claire, wiping her eyes then left the room.

Jazz climbed onto the bed and reached for Alessandro's poster. "Make sure I don't fall."

Hunter held her calves as she ripped the picture down.

She hopped off the bed and gathered the pieces in her arms. "I'll be back after I stuff him in the trash." Hunter opened the door for her.

When she returned, Hunter stood naked in the darkened room by the bed. After her eyes widened, she smiled, and held her hands over her eyes.

"Can I peek?"

"No more games, Jasmine Lucille Williams." He moved toward her and kissed her lips as he curled his fingers around the bottom of her shirt and lifted it.

Jazz pulled her lips away slightly. "Can I help?" He nodded, and she lifted the shirt off, then undid her bra. He helped her slide down her pants and underwear. They gently pulled each other closer.

"God, you feel good, Jazz."

"In case you're wondering, I've been on the pill for years."

He moved his hands down her ribs then across her hips to her bottom while she played with his earlobes. He kissed her neck. "I think tonight I'll kiss you in other places besides your scars."

"You'll have to search hard for empty skin."

He bent down and kissed her breasts. "Found some. Actually, a lot."

"Mmmm."

"I love you, Jazz. More than anything. More than myself."

"Despite everything?"

"Because of everything."

EPILOGUE

During their love making, Hunter saw only Jazz, felt only her skin, and heard only her moans of pleasure. She was his present and future, pushing his past to a time and place as remote as the planet Marian.

Claire slept with the girls every night, not because they had nightmares, but because they wanted a mother to love them.

Claire taught them how to cook and worked with them on reading and math. Jazz found some old art and craft supplies, and they all painted and glued creations, stringing them around the house. But what the girls liked the most were Jazz's science demonstrations and nature walks.

By the time the girls went to a clinic, they had gained some weight. The doctor gave them medicine for various minor maladies, but otherwise no one would have suspected what they'd endured for years. Trips to Pioneer Park to ride bikes and the train and to see movies at Regal Cinema with extra butter on the popcorn were pushing bad memories aside for good. Happiness and love led to a rapid recovery.

Danielle and Destiny refused to answer questions at the police station. They wanted no part of talking about the past. Stanley said they had enough evidence without their testimony. Wesley's videos identified many clients, including Leon, who were arrested and charged. He also said their entire encounter with Wesley was recorded on surveillance cameras, so there would be no charges or complications for any of them.

Hunter asked Stanley if they had to stay in the state for any reason.

"I didn't hear that question, Hunter. What did you say?"

Hunter smiled. "Nothing. Wasn't important anyway."

Hunter talked to his father and told him their plans to move to Oregon. "When I offered to take your memories away, I intended to take your pain and your guilt. I meant it. So I hope you understand that at some point."

"Thanks, Hunter. I know that now."

"Maybe you'll find someone you'd be willing to do that for."

"Stanley's giving me another chance, so maybe . . ."

"Good luck, Dad."

Hunter had not seen any more memories of his past since that night at Joe's, nor had he tried to take memories from Claire or Jazz. Everyone was too busy reveling in the girls' newfound freedom to look backward.

But Hunter's mind saw glimpses of the girls' pain when they drove by kids playing on a trampoline or saw a bearded man in a store. Danielle and Destiny quickly turned away and talked or laughed while the images faded. When the day came they wouldn't fade, he would add their memories to the hundreds in his mind, protected by Jazz's love and his desire to save others.

Had he seen all of his past? No. The years of doctors' visits and self-mutilation before they moved to Alaska were still unknown. But Hunter was in no hurry to relive that time. He had too much to do with his life going forward. Besides needing to help the girls and Claire and Jazz, he knew there were many others he could help if given the chance.

Joe, along with Claire's parents, split the cost of plane tickets for the five to fly to Portland where they would be met by MawMaw, PawPaw, and Rosie.

Before they left, Hunter compiled all his stories, including those about his mother and Frankie, changing the names of people and places, and sent them to Dr. Ru.

Along with this note. "Deleting bad memories doesn't cure anything. People start to heal when someone cares enough to accept their suffering. They finish healing when they kiss someone else's scars. But first they have to feel the pain of others. Use these memories, Dr. Ru. Help people see the scars."

THE END

ACKNOWLEDGMENTS

I have known too many teens and adults who have endured similar events described in this book, many who gritted their teeth and lifted themselves up again, and many who never found the strength or support from others to mend their bodies and minds. They are all a testament to the façades that most of us live behind.

Though I published this book myself, I received much help and guidance from others. Many beta readers and editors contributed, including Marni Macrae, Corrine Sosa, Sarah Abiz-Strugala, and especially Elisann Grant, who understands what I write better than I do. Jerrica McDowell was the first to read the beginning chapters, after which she ordered me to write more and finish. The story was too compelling in her mind to give her a taste then wait months before another bite. Every writer needs such an enthusiastic supporter.

And a special thanks to Barbara Kuzic, who refused to be swayed by "shocked" or "tired" or lots of other modifiers that meant nothing to her without specific physical and emotional responses. She has made me a better writer—no, can't use "better." She forced me to live every moment through each character's eyes and gut and share the details.

This story challenges the limits of the YA genre and the reader's ability to endure. I was very worried how my first reviewers would respond and considered the possibility that Hunter and Jazz's story might never be told. But Jamie Michele, K.C. Finn, and Jack Magnus from Readers' Favorite allayed my fears and gave me the confidence that my message was worthwhile and should be shared.

Cherie Chapman is an awesome cover designer. Every option she gave me was original and beautiful and true to the story. The best is always hard to choose from her creations because all are the best.

And to my two favorite characters—Hunter and Jazz. How often does a writer get to create a gun-toting, vodka-drinking, science genius female with the biggest heart in Alaska? And a boy who sees the amazing gem she is "despite everything"? Though both were nearly destroyed as young teens, they found resilience in sacrifice for others. More is in store for these two.

ABOUT THE AUTHOR

Brooke Skipstone lives in Alaska, where she watches the mountains change colors with the seasons from her balcony. Where she feels the constant rush toward winter as the sunlight wanes for six months of the year, seven minutes each day, bringing crushing cold that lingers even as the sun climbs again. Where the burst of life during summer is urgent under twenty-four-hour daylight, lush and decadent. Where fish swim hundreds of miles up rivers past bear claws and nets and wheels and lines of rubber-clad combat fishers, arriving humped and ragged, dying as they spawn. Where danger from the land and its animals exhilarates the senses, forcing her to appreciate the difference between life and death. Where the edge between is sometimes too alluring.